Beware a seductive stranger. . . .

"I'll take you someplace very far away." Ronan's voice was subdued, and it came out as a rasp. "Far from your father. From the people who don't understand you."

He'd touched a nerve . . . and it made some delicious, dangerous sensation shiver inside me.

He toyed with the hair at the nape of my neck, and again I felt that buzz of electricity shimmer across my skin. He gave me a little half smile. "But will you have the courage?"

"Yes," I heard myself whisper. "I will."

As I opened my eyes, he pulled away from me, and cold clarity prickled my brain like blood returning to a numbed limb.

I watched Ronan as he studied his fisted hands. His muscles were tensed and his eyes looked fierce, making me suddenly uneasy. . . .

"Where are we going?"

He stared blindly out the window, resting his hands on the steering wheel. "Far away. Life as you know it will change utterly."

ISLE

of

NIGHT

the watchers

VERONICA WOLFF

NEW AMERICAN LIBRARY

New American Library
Published by New American Library, a division of
Penguin Group (USA) Inc., 375 Hudson Street,
New York, New York 10014, USA
Penguin Group (Canada), 90 Eglinton Avenue East, Suite 700, Toronto,
Ontario M4P 2Y3, Canada (a division of Pearson Penguin Canada Inc.)
Penguin Books Ltd., 80 Strand, London WC2R 0RL, England
Penguin Ireland, 25 St. Stephen's Green, Dublin 2,
Ireland (a division of Penguin Books Ltd.)
Penguin Group (Australia), 250 Camberwell Road, Camberwell, Victoria 3124,
Australia (a division of Pearson Australia Group Pty. Ltd.)
Penguin Books India Pvt. Ltd., 11 Community Centre, Panchsheel Park,
New Delhi - 110 017, India
Penguin Group (NZ), 67 Apollo Drive, Rosedale, Auckland 0632,
New Zealand (a division of Pearson New Zealand Ltd.)
Penguin Books (South Africa) (Pty.) Ltd., 24 Sturdee Avenue,
Rosebank, Johannesburg 2196, South Africa

Penguin Books Ltd., Registered Offices:
80 Strand, London WC2R 0RL, England

First published by New American Library,
a division of Penguin Group (USA) Inc.

First Printing, September 2011
10 9 8 7 6 5 4 3 2 1

REGISTERED TRADEMARK—MARCA REGISTRADA

LIBRARY OF CONGRESS CATALOGING-IN-PUBLICATION DATA:

Wolff, Veronica.
Isle of night: the watchers/Veronica Wolff.
p. cm.
ISBN 978-0-451-23462-9
1. Vampires—Fiction.   I. Title.
PS3623.O575175 2011
813'.6—dc22   2011014571

Set in Bembo
Designed by Ginger Legato

For Monica, because "Monica said. . . ."

Isle

of

Night

CHAPTER ONE

I looked around my room for the last time. I was leaving.
Finally.

For good.

There was only one way I'd ever return to the town of
Christmas, Florida, and it involved my dead body. Which
meant I needed to make sure I had everything. I fished my iPod
out of the front pocket of my old duffel and hit Play. Putting in
my earbuds, I did a quick inventory of my stuff.

I had my clothes, of course. Not too many of those. Working
the evening shift at Fuddruckers didn't exactly buy someone a
passport to fashion. What I did own was mostly cheap and
mostly black, though I had managed to collect a few prized
possessions. A vintage Pretenders T-shirt. Fingerless gloves in
an awesome plummy black color. An ancient pair of Converse
sneakers, broken in just right.

My bag was heavy with books, too. I was a little worried the zipper would pop from the strain, but there was no way I'd leave without them.

My French-English dictionary was especially gigantic. It was unabridged, and had cost several days of hard-won wait-ressing tips. But it held such promise, like I might be jetting off to Paris any day, where I'd sit around in bistros, grappling with issues and nibbling madeleines.

And then there was my biggest treasure of all: a framed picture of my mother. I patted the top of the duffel, feeling for its hard profile, checking for the umpteenth time that I'd packed it.

She'd died when I was only four. For some reason everyone took great pains to assure me there was no way I could possibly remember her. I'd look at the photo in secret, though, and I could still hear her voice and smell her crisp, lemony scent. With her blond hair and wide eyes, she reminded me of Uma Thur-man, and I liked to imagine her wearing a tight yellow pantsuit, kicking my dad's ass, *Kill Bill*–style.

Dad. Ah, the sound of shouting and the stench of warm Coors. Now, those were some personal gems I wouldn't stow away in the old duffel, even if I could.

"Bye-bye, Daddy Dearest. I am so out of here. Not that you'll notice." I pulled my iPod back out of my pocket and zipped through the playlist to my favorite Radiohead song. Standing up to check my drawers one last time, I bellowed out the lyrics. *"I don't belong here. . . ."*

"Annelise Drew!" Somebody banged on the door. "Shut the hell up!"

I scowled. It was my stepmother, the Yatch.

So I turned up the volume and sang even louder. *"But I'm a creep. . . ."*

"I'm trying to get some rest," she screamed from the other side of the door.

"Oh yeah." I tore out the earbuds. "Because it's eleven in the morning and you've been working since dawn?"

"You think you're so special," she shouted. "Genius? You're a *freak*. And now you graduate early from high school, and we're supposed to think you're *so special*."

I smirked at how her words echoed the lyrics, and opened the door to the sight of her pale, haggard face. The Yatch. It was my pet name for her, the progression having gone a little something like *Beatrice . . . Bee-yatch . . . Yatch.*

"What are *you* laughing at?" The faint bruise on the side of her cheek had paled to a sickly yellow.

Imagine that. She'd fallen in the shower. Again.

Just ask Daddy.

I shook my head. It was a two-bedroom apartment—there was nothing to hide. I'd "fallen in the shower" before, too.

"Don't give me that holier-than-thou look, young lady." She shouldered her way in, peering around the room as though I'd been caught trying to steal the family silver. "Have I heard a thank-you for all I've done for you, all these years?"

"No," I said, after a moment of elaborate contemplation. "I don't imagine you have."

Her eyes skittered nervously from me. She never had been good at standing up for herself. I imagined it was why Daddy kept her around.

She scanned what remained of my belongings, her gaze

lingering on the threadbare bedspread I'd had since I was eight, when I'd liked all things lavender. Believe me—nine years is a long time in which to learn to despise a color. "You're welcome to keep that," I assured her.

"You better clean this crap up," she said instead, her voice shrill with disbelief. You'd have thought I'd left her a steaming turd right there in the middle of the tan shag rug. Her eyes came back to me. "Or were you going to sneak out like a thief?"

A little something like that, yeah. I remained silent.

"Where the hell have *you* got to go, anyway? It's not like you've got any friends."

Friends.

I thought of the crowd at Dale R. Fielding High School. A bunch of half-wits who spent their time going to the mall or making out, or doing whatever it is kids my age did to fill their time.

As if.

No, *I* was going to college, thankyouverymuch. Not that I'd ever tell them that. They'd just suspect me of embezzling tuition money from Dad's vast stores of wealth. Which was a laugh. If there was any money, it came from a disability check he'd probably drank away long ago.

No, I was going to college *tuition free.* It was one of the bennies of having a genius IQ and crazy-high GPA. My preference was to get the hell out of Florida, and though my guidance counselor said I could get a scholarship wherever I wanted, fancy private schools didn't take Needs Cases (gag) like me midyear. Graduating from high school one semester early was the best I could wrangle, and so it was state school for me.

"I suppose you think you're taking that car you've been driving." The Yatch crossed her arms, believing she'd gotten one over on me. "But who do you think has been paying for your insurance?"

"*I've* been paying for my insurance, just like *I* paid for the car." I glared, challenging her to just try to argue.

"Bea!" Daddy Dearest crowed from the other room.

My stepmother and I continued our silent stare-off. Finally she snarled, "You think just because you're smarter than the rest of us—"

"Bea! Get in here!"

God forbid the man got up from the Barcalounger to grab his own freshie from the refrigerator. He had no idea I was leaving, and wouldn't care if he did. I gave her my best saccharine-sweet smile. "I think Daddy needs another tall boy."

The Yatch shot me a final scowl and bustled into the living room.

Out. Of. Here. I heaved my duffel onto my shoulder, giving a farewell glance to the Einstein poster on my wall. He was sticking his tongue out at me, and I stuck out mine right back. "Ciao for now, Al."

I snuck out the front door and was on my way.

CHAPTER TWO

———⦿⦿⦿———

Florida is famous for a variety of things:

1. Disney World
2. Serial killers
3. Bizarre alligator accidents
4. Bizarre lightning accidents
5. Ginormous universities

A fan of neither princesses nor pain, it was number five for me. *Gator Nation*, God help me. But hey, say what you will—the University of Florida in Gainesville wasn't exactly Paris, but it was a start.

I drove my Honda carefully, winding through campus, goggling at all the crazy architecture as I went. I was hot and sweaty after three hours of driving with a broken AC and the sun broiling overhead, but still, nervous excitement surged through me.

So what if the stately brick buildings were surrounded by spindly palm trees instead of ivy? This was *college*.

I popped a chocolate madeleine for courage.

UF had more than fifty thousand students. Surely there'd be some other misfits like me. Surely there was at least one other girl on campus not sporting a French pedicure (do girls *really* think we're fooled by the little white lines painted across their toenails?), who had some black in her wardrobe, and actually thought about things. You know, someone who knew the word *French* could imply more than just a way to kiss.

Surely I'd make a friend. Right?

I downshifted my little Civic, pulling into the parking lot off Museum Road. I didn't need to look at the campus map for directions—I'd already memorized the thing. In fact, the moment the school catalog arrived in the mail, I'd studied every single aspect, inside and out, up to and including the bedbug advisory.

Walking into the registrar's office, the blast of air-conditioning made my skin crawl. That was another thing that really freaked me out about this state: Cooling a room was one thing, but the compulsive need to superchill every indoor space to a brisk sixty-three degrees confounded me. It was January, for crissakes.

I shoved my favorite hat farther down on my head. It was a beige raffia fedora with a narrow brim, sort of like something you'd see on an old Cuban man. Mostly I wore it to tone down my conspicuously blond hair. But it wasn't without its practical applications—I was feeling a little less chilly already.

Once my eyes adjusted, I spotted the bouffy-haired receptionist. She sat in a little glass-fronted kiosk that made her look like one of those old-fashioned carnival fortune-tellers. She was greeting each new student with a forced, coral-lipsticked smile.

If you resent teenagers so much, don't work at a college, lady. She caught my eye, and I returned her stiff smile.

But it froze the moment I saw *him*.

Tall, dark, and *hot* leaned against a pillar, watching me as I took my place in line. Tousled dark hair went every which way on his head. His eyes were slitted and intense, like he might need to have sex at any moment. Maybe even with me.

I had to look down, I was so flustered. I felt like *I'd* been the one caught staring.

But just as my eyes flitted away, I caught a glimpse of the tattoo peeking out from under his T-shirt sleeve. It was a quote.

Something niggled in the back of my mind and I looked back, feeling my cheeks blaze red with the fear that he was still watching me.

The first half of the quote was obscured, but the end bit was clear: *c'est le paradis perdu.*

My breath caught. Goose bumps rippled across my skin in a way that had nothing to do with the excessive air-conditioning. I knew the line well. *Le seul paradis c'est le paradis perdu.*

The only paradise is paradise lost.

Wow. My first college boy, and he liked *Proust.* I'd found home at last.

Holding my breath, I forced myself to raise my eyes to his. His hair was dark but his eyes were . . . lighter. Green. They locked with mine, and the rest of the world fell away.

The receptionist called my turn and I stepped forward, a ventriloquist dummy's grin pasted on my face. I tried not to trip. God, I was such an idiot.

"Hi," I said to the lady, thrilled that I'd managed to get a word out despite the college boy's laser-sex stare. "I'm here to . . . I'm here. I need to register."

Such an idiot.

"Name," she croaked, bringing me back to the matter at hand.

I gave her my facts, wondering if the college boy was still watching me. Clenching my hands, I forced myself to stop fidgeting.

He was the kind of guy I dreamt about. At least he seemed like my ideal. Smart and worldly. He'd drink espresso with a twist, and do the Sunday crossword, and recite lines of intense and passionate poetry from memory. He'd appreciate a bright and quick-witted companion. He'd see *me* as a bright and quick-witted companion—not a weirdo with a freaky-high IQ. Just a girl who was really good at *Jeopardy!* and some of the more obscure Germanic languages.

I'd even do the whole French-manicure thing if it meant attracting a guy like him. Did sophisticated college guys think that was sexy? I stole a look at my chipped, stubby nails.

I was supposed to have a mom around who could give me advice. I'd always felt like the other girls had been issued some sort of Girl Handbook that I just wasn't privy to. How had my mother worn *her* nails? Long press-ons the color of berries, or short like mine?

". . . I'm sorry," the woman was saying. The smile on her face was almost real, and it alarmed me.

"Sorry?" My fake grin was back up like a photon shield. "Wait. What did you say?"

"I said, you can't matriculate until you've been issued a diploma."

Did they need to see a piece of paper or something? I racked my brain, trying to remember whether I'd been given an official document among all the other reams of paper I'd received. "What are you talking about?"

"You need to finish high school before you start college."

"But I did finish high school. I *graduated*."

"Not yet, you didn't." She gave me a condescending smile.

It made me want to smash her little windowpane. I gripped the counter. "I did. In December. I'm registered for the spring semester."

Tap, tap, tap. Those fuchsia nails flew over the keyboard. "I'm afraid the best I can do is defer your enrollment to the fall semester."

"Wait." I leaned my forehead against her window. "Are you sure you have the right person? *Annelise Drew?* Dale R. Fielding High School."

"Yes." Behind the glass, her eyes narrowed, making her look like a pinched, angry Muppet in some *Office of the Registrar* puppet show. "They haven't issued your diploma. We can't accept you without a full transcript. Officially, you're still in high school."

"No." Not possible. *Not effing possible.* I could *not* still be in high school. I thought I might vomit. "That's impossible."

She tapped some more on her computer. Her fake smile crackled into a frosty glare. "You need to pass your swim test."

"Swim test?" I practically shrieked the words, distantly aware that I was no longer conscious of the cute college guy. My dignity was shot, anyhow, if I wasn't even going to be recognized as a *high school graduate*. "Is this a joke? There's no swim test at Fielding."

"I don't joke, young lady." Mrs. Registrar was getting snippy.

Tap, tap, tap. "Dale R. Fielding High School. New procedure." *Tap, tap.* "A swim test will be administered at the end of each academic year." *Tap tap tap tap tap.* "There was an endowment requiring all students to pass a swim test in order to graduate."

"I'm still in high school," I mumbled like a zombie. My head buzzed, and my fingers felt icy and thick as I shoved my paperwork back into my messenger bag. *Still a high schooler.*

"You need to go back to high school, take the test, and return in the fall."

I could only stare blankly. I'd rather die than go back to Christmas.

Trying to give me the hint, she looked to the person behind me in line. "Just pass the test, Miss Drew."

Thanks, Sherlock. "But I can't swim."

Shock and pity dropped across the woman's face like a veil. Everyone in Florida could swim. They practically handed out droppers of Swim-Ear to newborns in the hospital. Everyone had a damned pool, every kid was on swim team, every Caucasian face was tanned, every body smelled of chlorine and snack-bar ketchup.

"I'm afraid you need to sort this out with your school. Perhaps we'll see you in September." Her gaze went to the line forming behind me, her forced smile already back in place. *"Next."*

I mumbled something—who knows what?—and stumbled out of the registrar's office. At least the hot college boy was no longer standing there. Maybe he didn't witness my shame. I emerged from the refrigeration and somehow made it back to the car.

But there he was in the parking lot. The sight of Mr. Tall/Dark/Tousled leaning against a very shiny, very expensive-looking sports car made my eyes burn with tears. As God was my witness, I would *not* be the *high schooler* who cried in front of the good-looking college guy.

I snuck another glance his way. Such an *adult* car. In a green so dark it looked black. Only someone as gorgeous as him could pull it off without irony.

Clumsily unlocking the door to my Civic, I dropped into the bucket seat, its cracked vinyl squeaking with my weight. I slumped close to the steering wheel.

I would get out of there with a modicum of dignity.

I would *not* cry.

Nor would I hit any person or thing on the way out of the lot.

Buckling my seat belt, I turned the key. There was a click and then nothing.

"No," I whispered. *No, no, no.* I slapped my hands on the dashboard. "Wake up."

It'd taken me *years* to save up for this hunk of junk. I'd endured hours of tutoring meathead boys who thought casting lingering stares at my almost nonexistent bosom would make me wilt with desire. I'd sold term papers on eBay. And of course there was Fuddruckers, which, BTW, falls in the same constellation of life experience as setting one's hair on fire or enduring an *America's Next Top Model* marathon.

My car would *not* die on me now, in the parking lot, in front of this guy whose half-lidded stare was boring a hole into the side of my head. Witnessing me, at the pinnacle of my loserdom. I beat my hands against the steering wheel for good measure.

Again I turned the key. Again, *click-click-click*, then nothing. I couldn't even swear up a storm; my tongue felt paralyzed with *him* watching me. *Crap.*

Was it the ignition? How much did it cost to fix something like that? Hundreds? More than that, even?

Fan-freaking-tastic. What was I supposed to do now? I was way the hell in the middle of *Gainesville*. I couldn't call home. I had a big picture of how *that* would go. The Yatch would go ballistic, and Dad would just scowl, belch, and then demand the remote. Or would he smack me instead for spending all that money on gas when he could've spent it on beer? I swallowed the ache in my throat.

I couldn't go back to that. I *wouldn't* go back.

No college, no place to live, no car, not enough money to fix the car . . . Tears of frustration stung my eyes and rolled hot down my cheeks. *Why this? Why me? Why now? Could the universe just please cut me one break, for once in my life?*

There was movement in my peripheral vision. He was walking over.

Oh, crap. I scrubbed my face, certain I was leaving inky trails of eyeliner all over what were surely splotchy, puffy cheeks.

He came right up to my driver's-side window. His eyes were looking *really* intense now, like he was the Terminator and he needed to scan my body for radioactivity. His key ring was looped on his finger, and he was flipping it deftly around and around. Tall, dark, hot, *and smooth*.

My mouth went dry. He gave me a slow, predatory smile. But I was still just a *high schooler*, with an awkwardly high IQ and a broken-down '92 Civic.

This was not happening.

CHAPTER THREE

———❦———

"Trouble?" He smiled, and up close I saw he had slightly crooked teeth, but somehow it only made him hotter. Like he'd been too masculine to suffer through something as trivial as braces for something as inconsequential as vanity. "Lift the bonnet for me, aye?"

Oh, God . . . He had an accent. I knew custom required a response, but I could only gape.

He smiled again. His snaggle-toothed accent gave the impression that a young Gerard Butler had stepped off a movie screen and stood before me, live and in 3-D.

"I said, pop the bonnet, love." He spoke slowly this time, as if I'd fallen too hard off the short bus that morning.

Must respond. Bonnet. *WTF is a bonnet?*

He just stood there waiting. I clamped my slack jaw shut. High schooler, maybe, but I would not be mistaken for a mouth-breather. I followed the line of his eyes. "Ohh, the hood. Yeah, got it."

Pop the hood. Check. I got out of the car just as he leaned over to peer at my engine.

As I mentioned before, I'm no dummy. I took the opportunity to assess a tight butt and a pair of muscular legs. I love a guy who wears just straight-up jeans. No fancy metrosexual nonsense, just an old, worn pair of Levi's. I wondered whether they were button fly.

He straightened, and I managed to tear my eyes from his nether parts before he caught me staring. "I think it's your carb," he said, clapping the grease from his hands.

"The only carb I know is the bagel I had for breakfast." My face froze in place, shocked at the idiocy of my own joke. *Moron! I am such a moron.*

He just stared. Of course he did, since I'd just said the Dumbest Thing Ever. I used to wish I were average, but I took it all back. I wanted to be sparkling and witty and magnetic.

"Kidding," I mumbled. "I know you meant carburetor. Internal combustion, et cetera."

He strolled around the car, eyeing it with the indifference one might give a bit of rubbish in a bin. "Shall I arrange a tow?"

Not unless there's a nearby bank I can rob. "No, thank you," I told him instead.

He came full circle to lean against the side. He crossed his arms, and I had to pull my gaze from the thickness of his biceps and from the quote tattooed there. "Is there someone I can ring for you?"

"No." I cleared my throat, inexplicably sad that our little encounter was quickly drawing to a close. *Paradis perdu.* I had the feeling he'd forever be *my* lost paradise. "I'll make it on my own."

"Oh, dear." He shook his head, and I thought my heart might pound out of my chest. A man of such gigantic hotness saying *"Oh, dear"* was just too unbearably sexy. "A fine woman like you, all alone . . ."

Did he just call me a *woman*? I bit my lip, trying not to blush like a child. I tried to act flip, but my laugh in response sounded more like a weak puff of air.

What could he mean, *like you*? If I had a type, I'd be qualified as Surly Valedictorian. Definitely never have I ever been placed in a category even close to Fine Woman.

His eyes roved up and down my body, and I gave a quick tug on my shirt, even though I knew all my bits—modest though they were—languished safely in their appropriate places.

"A nasty predator could come and snatch you up." He gave me a wicked smile, his accent making what was probably just a playful comment sound dangerous. And then he *winked*.

Jeez, I thought my heart would explode on the spot. The last time a guy *winked* at me was years ago, and that'd been a creepy mall Santa.

"I'll be fine," I managed. "I'll just go back into the registrar's office and . . ." *And what?*

He eyed me speculatively. "Aren't you a bit young for university? What of your parents?"

Okay, that stung. So much for me looking all fine and womanly. I fought the urge to tug on the brim of my hat.

Really, did he have to ask about my parents? I normally liked to give a conversation ten minutes before hashing out the Painful Life Story. He's lucky something—I swear—softened around his eyes, because that's the only reason I answered. "Early graduation. I moved out."

"You can't be much older than sixteen," he mused. "You must be very bright."

I bristled. People see a petite blonde and assume you're some impressionable schoolgirl. "Eighteen on my next birthday."

He gave me a wicked smile. The guy was *toying* with me. So which was it: *a bit young* or *fine woman*? I wished I were gutsy enough to ask.

"But you're not going home?" He pinned me with a steady stare, and suddenly the prospect of discussing Ye Olde Home Life wasn't such a bummer.

"To Christmas?" Taking his raised brows for confusion, I added, "Yeah, some loser named a town Christmas, if you can believe it. And no, I don't think I'll be going home. It's just Coors—that's my dad—and the Yatch." I could tell he wasn't following, so I spelled it out. "You know, as in *bee-yatch*."

No smile, no response. Then he said, "Is the insipid slang intended to make you sound tough?"

Floored, I gaped at him. I was pretty damned tough already, thanks for asking. Or at least that's what I wanted to say to him. But his voice had been low and quiet, as though he'd identified some truth about me.

"Never mind that. Come, Annelise." He stepped toward me, reaching out his hand. "I'll drive you."

It took a moment for my brain to register the words, as my hormones sent a million other thoughts *(He's even taller up close! We'll sit all cooped up together in that fancy car! We'll talk about Proust and share chocolate madeleines!)* running roughshod over logic and reason.

Finally, a single nugget of good sense hit me: *When did I tell him my name?*

I eyed him. He didn't seem like a serial killer. But, then again, what did serial killers seem like? Would a cold-blooded killer have been so obviously hanging out at the registrar's for all to see?

Why *not* hitch a ride somewhere? What could happen? The car windows were clear glass, and I imagined the doors were fully operational. Plus, the trunk was way too tiny to hide a body.

More important, where else was I supposed to go?

"I don't even know your name," I said, wanting to trust him.

His arm was outstretched, and it was gallant, not so much *Let's shake* as it was an exhilarating *Take my hand*. He locked his eyes with mine, and I felt as if I might spin into their green depths. Goose bumps shimmered across my flesh.

I couldn't help it. I let my hand slide into his, and he gave it a gentle squeeze. His grip was strong and smooth and warm. "Ronan," he said simply.

At his touch, all my concerns dropped away. My skin warmed, the surface of it buzzing, as if electricity were arcing between us.

He led me to the passenger's door. As my hand slid from his, my mind seemed to clear. I watched as he walked around to tuck my duffel in the trunk.

I knew a flicker of doubt, then recalled the feel of his fingers grazing across mine. I decided he seemed nice enough, just a kindly stranger. What would be the harm in catching a ride to some spring break town?

I made my decision. Opened the door. *Here goes nothing.* I folded myself into the tiny cockpit, smoothing my hands over the buttery black leather and pristine cherrywood dash.

Ronan got in, and the scent of male wrapped around me like a musky and intoxicating incense.

"Where are you from?" I asked a little dreamily, wondering what the hell *this* guy's major could be. "You can't really be a UF student. Can you?"

He pinned me with those intense eyes and inhaled deeply. It felt like he was breathing me in. Did he feel my presence as intensely as I felt his? A shiver rippled across my skin.

"Oh, God," I heard myself murmur.

He gave a husky laugh, and a sensation so overpowering thrummed through me, I was grateful to be sitting down. "*God*, is it? Do you believe in God, Annelise?"

"*Somebody* had enough irony to pack a hundred eighty-five IQ points into a blond head."

Startlingly, Ronan laughed outright. Deep and loud, like he was at the pub and his team had just scored on the telly.

Honestly, it rocked my world. Usually I felt like I was cracking jokes in a language nobody else understood. Or sometimes *I* was the punch line—and believe me, it was a *really* awkward one. He got the joke, though, and the camaraderie of his laughter silenced me.

He held my gaze, finally asking, "Where to?"

"I don't know." Where was I supposed to go? I had to find a place to crash ASAP, and then there was my car to deal with, too. I could call a tow truck in Gainesville once I scraped together enough money, so I needed to find a job, like, yesterday. Preferably someplace where employees got free food, which meant back to waitressing for me. I knew the average Florida beach town had a crappy chain restaurant on every corner—maybe that was the answer.

I was riding the buzz of his laughter, elated by the sensation that somebody *got* me. I let the feeling shine through in the nonchalant tone of my response. "How about the coast?"

"The coast," he repeated simply, and the power of it was heady. I was sitting in a car that cost more than anything *I'd* ever seen, with a guy drop-dead gorgeous enough to be a movie star, who'd not even blinked when the lady mentioned that perhaps she might have a yen for the coast.

Ronan turned onto the interstate, headed south. It was your standard-issue hideous stretch of highway. If you've ever wondered why Florida produced so many serial killers, take a drive along one of the state roads that cut through its very middle. You could practically see the menace wafting off the tarmac like those heat waves you got on long and desolate road trips.

Finally, he broached our destination. "What awaits you on the coast?"

Probably a homeless shelter, followed by a frantic search for a waitressing gig. But I chose not to say those bits. Let him think me a casual, come-what-may sort of girl.

Instead, I told him, "It's what *doesn't* await me." Namely, a drunk dad, an evil stepmother, and another semester of being a social outcast at my high school.

My shoulders slumped the way they did every time I thought of Christmas, and deliberately I pulled them back, lifting my chin for good measure. "You try living in the boonies outside Orlando. It sucks. It's hot. The rest of the state has all kinds of water and waves, and what do we get?"

He merely raised a brow.

"Gators, that's what."

"A hunter like any other." He shrugged, not seeming very

impressed. He slipped the car into fifth, and it hummed like a tenor warming up at the Met. "This is what has you so out-raged?"

I considered the nature of my outrage, and defaulted to my dear, sweet hometown.

"Come on. The place is called *Christmas*." If I'd had sleeves, I'd have rolled them up—I could do my Florida rant in my sleep. "Check out some Christmas fun facts. We're known for two things. We get lots of mail for Santa—I mean, duh. And we've got the largest alligator in the world. Name's Swampy, he's two hundred feet long, and there's a gift shop in his belly where you can buy crap like alligator meat. I tell you," I said, in my best fly-girl voice, "Santa ain't been home to Christmas since God knows when."

He chuckled, and the sound made my belly vibrate in a crazy way. "Indeed?"

Who said *indeed* anymore? "Yeah, indeed."

"Annelise?"

"People call me Drew."

"So I gathered." He cut me a look over the tops of his designer shades. "Annelise?"

The way his accent rolled out my given name brought the phrase *death knell* to mind. My chest was practically sore from all the heart thumping going on. "Yes?"

"You don't need to adopt that . . . attitude. It's unimagina-tive, and it's below you. You're capable of more."

His candor threw me. "Not easily impressed, I take it?"

"You impress me. Just not the act."

The act. He was right, actually. Call it my act; call it my armor. I called it coping. The only trouble was, I didn't know anymore if I could let my real self shine through. What would I even sound like? Who would I be?

I watched as he downshifted. The car whined in low gear. He quickly raked his dark hair from his brow and then popped the car back into third. His arm flexed with the movement, and each glimpse of his tattoo transfixed me.

I hadn't known guys like this even existed.

"Wait." I noticed he'd turned off onto a weird one-lane road. Alarm instantly cleared the dreamy thoughts from my head. Just my luck—the guy really was a serial killer. "Where are you taking me?"

"I'm thinking perhaps you'd rather travel to the coast by plane."

CHAPTER FOUR

⎯⎯⎯ ◦⊶⊷◦ ⎯⎯⎯

"A plane?" My voice was shrill with disbelief. Ronan had driven us to a private airport, where he'd parked in front of an *airplane*. A sleek, shiny, private jet–looking thing. I craned my neck, looking out the window at a dingy, grayish brown airstrip. Small puddles spoke of a recent Florida downpour, and moisture blackened fissures along the pavement, making it look like crackle pottery.

The concerns that'd nagged me earlier slammed full force to the front of my mind. Hopping in a sports car with a mysterious fellow student was one thing, but private jets were a whole other reality. Uncertainty brought back my sarcasm full force. "Who are you, John Travolta?"

"John Travolta?" He pulled off his sunglasses to study me. There were flecks of gold in his green eyes.

"You know, the movie star. He's got all those planes. I just mean . . . who are you to own a jet like *that*?" *And what makes you think I'm getting in it?*

"It's not *my* jet, precisely." He crooked his mouth into a half smile.

I had to look away, back to the plane. I refused to let him distract me. The feel of this strong, attractive, huskily accented guy sitting so close was a lot to bear, but not so much that I'd *get on a plane* with him. Surviving my father had honed my instincts. It didn't take a sage to know that smart girls don't fly off with strange men.

"Well, okay," I said warily. "Then who are you to have *access* to a jet like that?"

"The question is: Are you brave enough to find out?" The challenge in his voice brought my head swinging back to face him. He was staring at me with those smoldering eyes that made my breath catch. He reached over and placed his hand on my shoulder, leaning closer. "The question is," he repeated, "are you ready to embrace a whole new life?"

A new life. No way something like that was even possible. Was it?

I looked back at the plane, holding my arms stiffly in my lap, desperate not to fidget. Because I knew the answer was *no*, good things were *not* possible. I'd had *that* lesson backhanded into me from a young age.

The real question was: How was I supposed to get myself out of this situation? We were alone, in the middle of nowhere. Where was I supposed to go and how was I supposed to get there?

A shadow flickered in the cockpit and then was gone. So, okay, check that—we weren't *entirely* alone. There was a pilot

in there, readying for takeoff. Almost as though he'd been waiting for us.

And I'd discovered a new problem. The longer Ronan's
hand rested warmly on my skin, the less intense my concerns
became. I shifted away from him, at least as much as I could in
that tiny sports car. His touch was muddling my mind, almost
as if he had some hypnotic power over me.

Because I was starting to ask myself some crazy questions.
Like, what if I *did* climb into that plane? It'd be an irreversible
thing, a path from which there'd be no return. But was it a
dangerous path, or might I find a pot of gold at the end?

But how was it that some guy from the registrar's office spotted me and decided *I* was the one for his jet-fueled getaway? I
leaned away from him, into the car door, and tried my best glare.
"Why me?"

He shifted so that his hand still rested lightly on me. It was
a casual gesture, and yet I felt the heat of his touch like a brand.
"Why not you, Annelise?"

Why not indeed?

I gave my head a shake. *Because normal people—safe, sane
people—don't whisk seventeen-year-old girls they don't know off in
private jets.*

I flinched my leg away from his hand, and as I broke contact,
doubts swamped me. Was he part of some high-tech slavery ring
with a penchant for younger girls with high IQs and lame senses
of humor? "But we just met."

"You're special," he said in that husky voice, shifting his
hand to my shoulder.

Special. The word echoed in my head, and for once in my

life, it didn't sound like a curse. I wanted to wrap myself in the feel of it even as I struggled to get a grip. I tried to concentrate on my skepticism, but that touch was burning through the fabric of my shirt. I felt myself slipping.

"Don't you wish to go?" he pressed. "With me?"

Ronan was waiting for my answer. His expression was tight, and it exaggerated the cleft in his chin. The shadow of a muscle flickered along his jaw. He was fierce and masculine in a way I'd never before encountered. What girl didn't wish for such a man and on such a jet?

But this was feeling too unreal, too much like the genie in the bottle had come for me. I struggled to think rationally. "Where would we go, exactly?"

"You wanted the coast. But tell me, Annelise: Will any coast do?" He gave me a squeeze, then removed his hand, and my shoulder felt chilled from the loss. But then he swept the hair from my neck and I tingled—no, I *burned*—where his fingers brushed my bare skin.

Any coast, I had the urge to answer him, *as long as it's with you.*

I chafed my arms from the shiver rippling across them. I needed to get a hold of myself. I wanted to flee Florida, flee my family and my life, but was I ready for the point of no return? "Why not drive? Florida's big, but not *that* big."

"Are you saying you don't want to leave Florida? The Gulfstream IV can travel more than four thousand nautical miles."

"Oh, well, that's a relief, then. Particularly as I generally calculate things in terms of nautical miles."

His answering silence was loud.

What was he thinking about? I spared a glance for him,

unable to stop myself. He was watching me with that *I expect more* face I now recognized.

I took a deep breath. Though I felt raw and exposed, I mustered some honesty. "I mean, yes. Of course. I *long* to leave Florida. My life here . . . It's been hard. I've always dreamt of leaving."

I'd spoken the truth, but it had come out so quietly. Did my voice always go all hesitant and soft when speaking truly?

All this honesty. And with a total stranger. It was too intense. I felt too defenseless. It was too much.

He was too much. He made me feel so strange. Like, for the first time in my life, I knew what hope was.

I looked back at the plane, wondering just who this guy was. I strained my eyes, trying to make sense of the shadowy cockpit.

Ronan touched my chin, and it was a shock. His finger was warm and gentle, and I wanted to shut my eyes. I wanted to lean my cheek into his hand and stop time.

What was happening? Maybe there was such a thing as knights in shining armor, and mine had a black T-shirt and a tattoo, and liked to hang out at the registrar's.

He turned my face to his. Not that it took any great feat of strength. I'd been longing to clamp an uninterrupted stare on him since I first spotted him.

"I'll take you someplace very far away." Ronan's voice was subdued, and it came out as a rasp. "Far from your father. From the people who don't understand you."

He'd touched a nerve. I considered pulling away, but didn't have the heart. Instead, I let my eyes fall into his, and they were so very green, the color of a deep, dark, haunted forest, and it made some delicious, dangerous sensation shiver across my skin.

He toyed with the hair at the nape of my neck, and again I felt that buzz of electricity shimmer across my skin. He gave me a little half smile. "But will you have the courage?"

I squinted my eyes shut tight, trying to clear my head. Something wasn't right. He was just a guy, and I never had this sort of reaction to guys. Yet every time he touched me, I went all limp and easy. With one brush of his hand, the guy could probably sell me a bridge, much less sweet-talk me onto some swanky private jet.

"Will you or won't you, Annelise?" Heat fanned from his fingers, penetrating deep into my brain, confusing me, making me putty to his touch.

"Yes," I heard myself whisper. "I will."

As I opened my eyes, he pulled away from me, and cold clarity prickled my brain like blood returning to a numbed limb.

I watched Ronan as he studied his fisted hands. His muscles were tensed and his eyes looked fierce, making me suddenly uneasy. I was itching inside my skin, longing to feel his reassuring touch once more. Eager to break the silence, I asked, "Where are we going?"

He gazed blindly out the window, resting his hands on the steering wheel. "Far away. Life as you know it will change utterly."

I stared hard at his profile, wondering if I'd seen uncertainty shadow his face. Did he regret asking me? Had I heard hesitation in his voice, or was it just my imagination?

He'd pulled his eyes from mine, and that earlier sense of unreality was creeping back in, clinging in the back of my mind like shadows in corners. His silence unnerved me, and I wanted to normalize the situation. "Far away?" I asked. "Are we going west?"

"No. We're leaving the country. For an island."

My brows rose at the word *island.* "Like the Caribbean?"

He faced me, his eyes grown hard. "Not that kind of island. It's far away. Far north. North of Scotland. North of the Shetlands. It's a dark place. A cold place."

Why was his voice so flat? Renewed doubt was making me queasy.

"Is that where you're from?" I asked, desperate to experience that warmth again, for this to be all right. Images of maps flitted through my head—a photographic memory was good for something. "Is it the Faroe Islands? Iceland?"

"Near there. It's not a place you've heard of." He looked back at me, and I tried to summon the ease he'd made me feel before. "And, aye. It's where I'm from."

He was taking me to see his home? I found it hard to believe we were even having this conversation. My thoughts were so jumbled, as though not my own. "How will I get back if . . . if I don't like it?"

"You won't want to leave."

I mulled what he could mean by that, but he seemed to sense my anxiety, and the shadows cleared from his eyes. He stroked a finger down my cheek. "I'm taking you to a place where there are other girls like you. Girls with . . . *gifts.*"

This took me aback. It was looking like this . . . *thing* with Ronan was less run-away-together than it was some sort of recruiting exercise. Oddly, the prospect reassured me, explaining his presence at a university and why he'd want someone like me.

The fog cleared a bit from my mind. "Like a special school?"

"Aye. Like a special school. To train girls."

"Train them to what?"

"To become women."

My breath hitched. Oh, God, this was a sex-slave thing. He could give me all the mesmerizing looks and lingering touches in the world, and *never* would I vibe with anything like that.

He rolled his eyes, reading my thoughts. "Not like that. Successful women, with skills and depth."

He traced his finger down my arm, resting his hand on my thigh. Heat plumed up my leg, coursing through my body. I let out a sigh I hadn't realized I was holding. *Not a girl . . . a woman.* With skills and depth. Did that mean I'd finally found a place where I could really learn? Where I'd meet other girls who liked to learn, too?

Suddenly all things seemed possible. Could I really get on this plane? Could I finally, for once in my life, begin to realize my true self?

Visions cascaded into my head . . . me goofing on campus with the other girls. We'd wear white anoraks with fur hoods and have snowball fights. We'd discuss things like medieval Latin and rap music of the Asian Diaspora. I'd meet Ronan for coffee after class. I wouldn't be so different. I wouldn't have to hold back.

Never again would I have to hold back.

I should've been scared, but not many things frightened me anymore. My father's opened hand careening toward my face no longer scared me. The dead-eyed stares of the other high school kids had stopped scaring me long ago. But being stuck in the same small town for the rest of my life? *That* scared me.

Could I be a real woman? Someone self-determined, who hopped onto private jets headed for islands far, far from home. I wanted to be.

"Okay." I opened the car door. I stepped onto that tarmac, onto the path of no return. I turned to look at him. Those haunted-forest eyes were intense on me, and I hoped I was making the right choice, because standing alone on the runway, I felt suddenly isolated and alone. I forced a lightness into my voice that I didn't feel. "So, what's this island called?"

"Those who speak the old tongue call it *Eyja næturinnar*," he uttered, and a peculiar melancholy sounded in his voice. "The Isle of Night."

CHAPTER FIVE

I stood at the rear of his car, watching as he strode to the
plane. "Wait," I called, knocking on the trunk. "My bag?"

"You won't need it where you're going."

When we were cozy in his car, with his hands and eyes wrapping warm reassurance around me, I was champing at the bit to
go. But now, standing in the glare of the Florida sun, uncertainty
crept in.

"But . . . my stuff." My mom's picture. My ginormous dictionary. My Converse and my iPod. I needed to keep some
reminder of who my mother was. Of who I was.

"You'll be issued new *stuff*," he said dryly.

I knew a sharp pang of loss. There were likely dictionaries
where I was headed. And Converse wouldn't do well in snow.
But that picture was all I had left of my mom.

And music? Music had become my survival. It's what got

me through. No Led Zeppelin, no cheesy French pop, no Death Cab for Cutie. *Not happening.* "But my iPod—"

"Isn't allowed on the island," he finished for me.

"But—" My gaze shifted from Ronan to the plane. I shaded my eyes against the glare of sunlight on smooth metal. The jet door opened, and though the interior was dim, I caught a glimpse of a catwalk-worthy attendant floating past, bearing a tray of drinks.

I'd never stood this close to such luxury. I stepped closer, and a stuffed leather seat came into view. I craned my chin up for a better look. The interior looked cool and plush, all beige carpet and tan leather. Luxurious, and a bit daunting.

My eyes went back to Ronan. His gaze was waiting for me, and that same warmth rippled along my skin. My response to him was immediate, like he'd imprinted me, my body primed for him, and I knew I'd follow him wherever he led.

I tore my eyes away, back to the trunk. I wasn't leaving without the picture of my mom. And as long as I was going to smuggle a photo on board, why not my iPod, too? If they discovered it, what was the worst they could do to me? I'd endured my *father* for seventeen years.

"Just a sec," I called, dashing back to the car. I met his suspicious look with a shrug and poised my hand expectantly over the trunk. I tried to look as casual as possible. "My hoodie. I hate air-conditioning."

His eyes hardened and I felt a shot of panic, but then Ronan popped the trunk using the remote on his key chain. It made a little vacuum-suck sound and the lid slowly elevated. Though he remained standing at the front of the car, my heart was pounding in my chest.

Forcing myself to look neither too relieved nor too guilty, I dug through my duffel, snagging my iPod and the picture. I hastily shoved the photo out through the back of its cheap cardboard frame, cracking the glass in the process. Hands shaking, I grabbed my tan velour hoodie and crammed everything in the pocket. The photo would get rumpled, but the iPod was awkward enough—I couldn't risk smuggling a cheapo Wal-Mart picture frame, too.

I shut the trunk, slamming it a little harder than necessary in my nervousness. *Success.* And what Ronan didn't know wouldn't hurt him.

I jogged to the plane, joining him on the sleek metal stairs. He took my hand to steady me. For a guy in jeans, he was quite dashing, quite gallant.

Cool air washed down to us from the open hatch. I felt on the brink of a grand, worldly adventure. It was the first step toward reinventing myself.

It would be exciting, this starting over. I'd discover a true me lingering down deep. Maybe there really would be a fox-fur anorak waiting for me on this island. I'd be like Nicole Kidman in that crazy snow-bear movie, where she glided around wearing ivory gloves and a fur stole. I'd be like porcelain. I'd be a *woman.*

The kind of woman worthy of a mysterious man. Worthy of Ronan. I'd quote all the Proust he wanted. In the original French. He'd want me.

Following him up, I couldn't resist stealing a glimpse of his posterior. Dark blue denim, not too clingy, not too loose, and tight muscle flexing beneath. A strange feeling shimmered in my belly.

I stepped through the door. Through the portal to my fabulous new world. I let my eyes adjust.

And then my heart fell.

Two other girls were already on board. Two *gorgeous* girls.

I forced myself to breathe. And I forced myself not to look at Ronan, even though I felt that green-eyed stare boring through me.

I scanned down the aisle—quickly assessing the girls, the cabin, the situation—without seeming to stare. There were eight seats total, and they were all the same mushy, tan leather, like really pricey versions of my father's Barcalounger. They were arranged into two sets of four, with pairs of seats facing each other.

The girls sat side by side at the rear of the cabin. Was I expected to join them? To sit facing them, brushing knees, like we might giggle and gossip the trip away?

I tried to have an open mind. After all, Ronan had said the girls were like me. I assumed he meant they were geniuses. I swallowed hard. Why'd they have to be such *hot* geniuses?

I took a hesitant step forward, pretending bored disinterest in my seat selection, as if I rode around on private jets every day. But really, it just gave me an opportunity to weigh these teenage interloper hotties.

One looked like a Playboy Bunny in training, with a tight, low-cut designer shirt that made the most of her sizable assets. My seventeenth birthday had come and gone, and I was *still* waiting for *my* assets to make themselves known.

Bunny Girl had large, round, flawlessly made-up eyes to go with her other large, rounded goods. Her hair fell in long, perfect waves the color of maple syrup. She was glaring at me with the same look the Yatch liked to use. My stomach clenched into a knot.

I flicked my eyes to the other girl, hoping a friendly face might greet me. Hope fled, and the knot in my belly became a nauseating rock of ice.

Girl Number Two was perhaps the most beautiful creature I'd ever seen, with skin the color of milky coffee and black hair falling in tight spirals to just above her shoulders. Two tiny teardrops were tattooed beneath one eerily light, almond-shaped eye.

"*You're* what we've been waiting for?" Almond Eyes spoke in a lush, husky accent. Her vowels were thick and rounded. *Cuban,* I thought.

I considered fleeing—nodding a quick and apologetic *never mind* to Ronan and backing out of there. I *needed* to flee. Ronan had mesmerized me with those eyes and that touch, but these girls shattered whatever magic it was that'd seduced me on board.

I took a step backward. "I'm sorry. I think I need—"

The door sealed shut with an elegant *shush*. Sealed me in.

"Hey, Charity Case." The other girl's voice was sharply feminine—like a cheerleader who'd lost all patience. "Move it, so we can get out of here."

I gave her a blank look, parsing her words. *Charity Case?*

Raising a sculpted brow, she scowled at my top.

Oh. The shirt. It wasn't exactly used, *per se*. It was real vintage. A Velvet Underground concert tee, to be precise. It had little cap sleeves, and I liked to think it was something Kristen Stewart might wear. I fought the urge to tug at it. "Sure thing . . . Bunny," I muttered, thinking as long as we were using nicknames.

"Just here," Ronan said, coming to my rescue. His presence comforted me, but not enough, not like before. Because now mingled with that reassurance was the nagging sense of betrayal.

He motioned to the front bank of seats, and I followed him like a robot, sitting with my back to the shark tank in the rear of the plane. I wedged my hoodie under my leg. It was a Juicy knockoff, and I braced for the scorn I was sure *that* would elicit.

I ran my finger along the hard edge of the iPod hidden in the pocket. I'd need to figure out how to stash the thing more securely without it slipping out and clattering to the floor. In my jeans, maybe.

Ronan claimed the seat next to mine, and I wasn't sure if my jangly feeling was relief or anger. The girls' disdain radiated at my back. I felt duped. And, well, jealous.

"I have no money, you know." I spoke to him in a low hiss. I would *not* let those girls overhear our conversation. "Like, to pay? Whatever this special school is you're taking me to, I can't afford tuition."

The gorgeous, uniformed attendant buckled herself into her jump seat. She gave him a mysterious nod. It felt like a stab in the back, and my cheeks blazed with irrational embarrassment.

He buckled his seat belt. Defiant, I didn't touch mine. I contemplated hopping up and escaping through the emergency exit.

Ronan reached across and buckled me in. The hot sweep of his fingers on my thighs made my breath catch. Kept me glued to my seat.

"We know you have no money," he said simply.

"We?" I asked, my voice cracking.

The overhead lights flicked off, then on, then off again as the plane hummed to life.

I fought not to panic. What had I expected, getting into a zillion-dollar private jet with a stranger? "Who's the *we*?" I repeated.

The plane eased forward. I looked out the window, watching the tarmac begin to roll beneath us.

He answered only, "Think of it as a scholarship."

We picked up speed, and I had to flick my eyes to follow the horizon whooshing by in the distance. Horror bloomed, a sickening pit in my belly. There was no going back.

I stared at Ronan's profile. I shouldn't have let him convince me to come on board. Why had I listened? I wasn't naive, not by a long shot. Nor was I a girly girl, falling for whichever cute guy looked my way. What was it about him? What had I been thinking?

I studied him. He was a guy's guy, with a rugged, dimpled chin. A faint haze of dark stubble dusted his jaw. He'd convinced me with those stares, those touches. I willed him to look at me, to make me feel better again.

Doubts seized me. On the surface, he was out of my league. What would he want with me? I was smart, but lots of people were. I skimmed my eyes down, taking in my chipped purple nails and faded jeans. I knew guys went for blond hair, but there had to be more to it than that.

I clenched my hands, forcing myself to think. "Had you tracked me down *before* we met at the registrar's?" I'd fantasized he'd simply seen me and swooned. But this scenario—this special school, this *scholarship*, how he knew my name before I told him—implied otherwise. "So it's not that you saw me in the registrar's office and, I don't know, just . . . knew?"

He shook his head. Mutely. Maybe even regretfully. "Your name appeared in our system."

Their system? How had my name gotten into a *system*?

I thought of all the Florida universities that'd offered me full rides and got a clue. "Did you get my name from Bright Futures?" Our state scholarship program had always sounded to me more like a Scientology pamphlet than a grant.

"Aye, your name did pop up." There was something colder in his voice. His eyes no longer glimmered with suggestion. Why wasn't he giving me one of his looks? One of those brushes of his hand?

"Why me?" I gripped my armrests, not knowing if I wanted the answer. The leather was as soft as it looked. "I mean, I can't be the only kid who got a perfect score on her SATs."

"But you are the only student with perfect SATs and a father with a history of domestic assault."

Of course. Daddy Dearest. There'd be all sorts of information about him, me, us in the school system, with Social Services, in the Orlando Criminal Justice database.

I wrenched my shoulders back. I'd be more than what Daddy Dearest had made me. "So, how'd you find those two?" My voice came out sharp as I gave a sneer and a nod behind us. "Are they some of Florida's brightest lights, too?"

"No, Annelise. I said the other girls were *gifted*. You're the only genius." Something softened in his face as he delivered the news, like it was something for me to be proud of.

I gulped convulsively, thinking I might sick up all over the beige Gulfstream rug. Abruptly, I began to fumble around my seat, beneath it.

"What is it?" he asked. I thought I saw concern flicker in his eyes, but it was gone in an instant, making me doubt it'd ever been there.

And why would he need to show sympathy? Ronan had gotten me on the plane, and now I was on my own. Again.

How had he done it? How had he duped me? It wasn't drugs—he hadn't given me anything to drink. It was like he'd mesmerized me with that stupid accent. I felt like a total idiot. A cute guy paid me some attention, and I fell over myself, following him to God knew where. *Idiot.*

The blood drained from my face. I wondered if I looked as queasy as I felt.

I felt like more of a freak than ever. If I'd been chosen because I was smart, why were those other girls here? I was proficient in a few languages and had aced AP calc in ninth grade. Their gifts were probably Varsity Hotness and an uncanny ability to torment nerdbots like me.

The plane slowed, turned onto the runway for takeoff. There was a tugging in my gut as it lurched forward. The sight of tarmac skimming by made my head spin with vertigo.

I breathed through my clenched teeth, frantically running my hand along the gleaming wood panel at my elbow, searching for a hidden compartment. "Don't they have any of those airsick-bag things?"

I felt his hand on my arm, and froze. Despite his treachery, a tiny part of me willed his touch to warm me once more.

"Annelise," he said, and his husky accent was gentle. I felt that familiar warmth spread from his fingertips, and the tight coil squeezing my chest loosened. "Your gift isn't simply a high IQ. You are more than that."

"Right." I leaned back against the headrest and shut my eyes. *More than that?* Really? More than a weirdo? More than a hopeless social case?

I thought of the girls in the seats behind me. I had to swallow the sourness in my throat. *If I'm more than that, what are they?*

CHAPTER SIX

"Mimi? And Lilac von *what*?" I kept my voice down, but I couldn't do anything about my disdain. After withstanding five hours of my incessant prying, Ronan finally told me the other girls' names, though surely I must've misheard. "You're kidding, right?"

"Lilac von Straubing," he said under his breath. He avoided my eyes, and I wondered if I spied amusement on that stony face of his.

"Lilac von Straubing," I repeated to myself, marveling. *What fresh hell was this?* as my girl Dorothy Parker might've said. The only *von* anybody I'd ever heard of was that superrich Claus von Bülow, and he'd been suspected of murdering his wife. Was this Lilac of the idle superrich, too? She sure looked capable of murdering loved ones.

A bell dinged, and the cabin lights went up. It was a gentle tone, in stark contrast to the alarms ringing in the back of my head.

Ronan unclicked his seat belt and stood. His gaze locked with mine and lingered for an unsettling moment. I looked away, but regretted I did. I was furious with him but impulsively longed to feel that connection we'd had in his car. It made me even surlier.

He went to the front and whispered something to the attendant. I watched avidly as she unlocked a closet at the front of the plane.

He retrieved three large satchels, handing one to each of us. They were canvas kit bags in a drab olive color, like we were off to boot camp instead of this whatever-they-called-it school. Getting issued new stuff gave an air of finality to the whole thing. I rubbed my arms, suddenly chilled.

I was in deep now.

"What's the name of this place, anyway?" I settled the bag between my legs. Private jets offered more than a little legroom, and I was determined to rifle through *my* satchel as soon as I could. I was desperately curious about what might be inside.

"I told you already," he said as he sat back down. *"Eyja næturinnar."*

"That's it? But I thought you said that was the name of the island."

"There's naught much else on the isle *but* the school."

Hopefully they didn't go for any lame *Go, fight, WIN, Eyja Tigers!* nonsense. I bit my cheek to avoid succumbing to nervous tittering. "Either way, *Nætur . . . Eyjan* doesn't sound like any university I'd ever heard of."

"Eyja næturinnar." He looked thoughtful for a moment. "But you were close."

I shrugged. It was pretty simple once you parsed the roots

into recognizable bits. "I've got a thing for Germanic languages."

"Aye." Looking distracted, he stared past me out the window, even though the only view was a flat wall of black and two flickering red lights on the wing. "We knew that."

"We, we—who's this *we* you keep mentioning?"

He stayed as he was, looking into the blackness, a grave expression on his face. "You'll find out soon enough."

I was determined to drag some sort of information out of him before we landed. I tried a different tack. "But your accent sounds Scottish. If Icelandic is the *old tongue*, well, your old folks must be pretty old." It was an attempt at a joke, but he merely frowned.

Finally, he looked back at me. "Many of our . . . old ones . . . speak the language of the Vikings. We value their culture. And so our island still holds their traditions close."

Focusing on my questions was keeping me from freaking out, and so I kept probing, despite the intensity on his face that was gravitating from serious to scowling. "So are you from—"

"This?" A squeal from behind interrupted us. The shrill tone identified it as Lilac, aka Bunny von Slutling. "You're replacing my Murakami bag with *this*?"

"What*ever* with your origami bag," I muttered.

"Clearly they don't carry Louis Vuitton at the local Goodwill, do they, *Charity*?"

I cringed. Maybe preternatural hearing was Lilac's gift. I turned my attention to my own bag nestled between my knees, eager to see what had the girl in such a lather.

It was jammed full of clothing. On the top of the pile was a sturdy gray tunic and what looked like leggings.

"You've been issued a uniform, standard to all first-year recruits," Ronan explained to all of us.

Recruits? The peculiar word stuck in my mind. But I shoved it away, thankful that Lilac would no longer be able to lord the whole *Charity* thing over me. Uniforms—the great equalizer.

"Cool boots." I wrestled a pair of black, knee-high boots from the kit bag. They were lined with some sort of short fur and had laces running up the front. Kind of like a sexy version of Eskimo mukluks.

Ronan nodded. "You also have workout clothes and a set of oilskins."

"You're going to make us wear *animal skins?*"

Lilac's comment was so ridiculous, I had to turn in my seat to steal a glimpse of her. I smirked, wondering if anyone had ever broken it to Miss Thing that her leather ankle booties had once been, in fact, the skin of some unwitting creature.

Ronan furrowed his brow at her question, and then recognition dawned. "Ah. Your oilies aren't really skin. They're made of canvas. For inclement weather."

Lilac stared blankly.

"He's saying *oilskin* is another word for *raincoat*, Einstein."

Lilac curled her upper lip in a dead-eyed sneer, and it made my skin crawl. The girl looked like she might fillet me and have me for a snack later. She made the Dale R. Fielding High School Cheer Squad look like *Barney and Friends*, and I vowed to give her a wide berth.

"You're to change and leave all your old clothing on the plane," Ronan instructed us. I tuned back in, tensing, thinking of my smuggled goods. I couldn't do anything about it with

Ronan next to me, and it wasn't like I could tote this ginormous bag into the airplane lavatory.

The attendant knelt at Ronan's shoulder, and I startled. "Shall I administer refreshments?"

He gave her a brisk nod, and before I knew it, we all had crystal tumblers filled with a thick, dark red liquid.

"What *is* this stuff?" I sniffed. It managed to smell both cloying and sour, like a kid's sweaty palm after holding a fistful of pennies. My stomach lurched, and I wondered again at the location of the airsick bags.

"It's what you're being served," Ronan said sternly.

I contemplated the glass. "Can't I just have, I don't know, a Perrier or something?"

"You must drink it." He tossed his back in one gulp. "No questions."

I forced myself to follow suit. It was viscous, like syrup, the last of it dribbling down my throat slow and thick, like I'd just done a shooter of ice-cold Robitussin. I shuddered.

But then a strange thing happened. A buzzing began at the backs of my legs, crackling up my spine and out to my fingertips. Was it some sort of weird Viking alcohol? Whatever it was, it made me feel *alive*. Like I could breathe more deeply, and there were new scents all around.

From the hideous hurling sounds erupting from the rear of the plane—not to mention Lilac's shrieks—it seemed as though the drink wasn't having the same effect on Mimi.

Ronan stood, watching wordlessly as the attendant handed the girl a damp towel. Mimi must've shown some warning signs prior to throwing up, because she was already chin deep in a white airsick bag. So I guess they did have them hidden somewhere.

Ronan wasn't aware I watched him, he was so preoccupied with Mimi, scrutinizing her with a strange look in his eye. Almost like he was angry. But then he told her, "It's all right, love," in such a kindly tone of voice.

Mimi raised her head, wiping her chin with the towel. She spat one last time into the bag. "We don't drink *mierda* like this in Cuba." She wore an angry snarl and pronounced her country *Coo-ba*.

I began to mutter a sassy retort, but then I realized everyone was distracted. I'd never get a better chance to deal with my photo and iPod.

Besides, my limbs were really tingling now. I *had* to act. I was hot and alive with the sense that I was becoming aware of each individual cell in my body. That there was some epiphany within my reach, if only I'd just *move*. I felt empowered, capable, and it made me brave.

"I'd like to get changed and ready." I grabbed a stack of gray clothing and slipped by Ronan. I didn't look back to see if he'd protest.

Keeping my hoodie balled at my stomach, I snuck into the bathroom, hoping the pile of wool in my arms amounted to a complete outfit. Sliding the lock shut, I began to undress, taking off my hat, clothes, socks, everything. The prospect of being barefoot in the bathroom gave me pause for a moment—I'd left the uniform boots by my seat—but one look at the pristine lavatory floor changed my mind. It was cleaner than our bathroom at home had ever been.

Leaning against the wall, I hitched myself into the leggings as best I could in the small space. I ran my hands over my thighs, smoothing the material into place. It was dark gray and soft, but thick and supportive, too. Not quite natural, but not entirely synthetic, either.

I unfolded the tunic and made a little *hm* sound. It was a lighter gray than the leggings, and seemed to be some sort of wool. I slipped it over my head, working my arms in awkwardly, knocking my elbow against the wall more than once. But when I finally got it on, it fit perfectly. It was long, with a squared-off neck, and like an Indian *kameez*, it fell to just above my knees and was slit up each side to my hip.

I squatted and did a few high steps to test it all out. The outfit was warm but not too hot, and not itchy at all. Like something I could really move in. There weren't any identifying tags—of course—but the whole thing seemed high quality and tailored just for me.

Pulling my hoodie from where I'd balled it on the counter, I retrieved my iPod and photo. Ronan's voice echoed in my head. *Leave all your possessions.* The picture was an easily hidden thin slip of a thing, and a no-brainer. But the iPod? I studied the cold, glassy face of it. Was it worth the risk?

As though in answer, I felt a fresh tingling up the backs of my legs. *My music.* Music was my one solace. My one friend. I wouldn't give it up.

As it was, it was killing me to surrender my favorite hat. And that decided it. I would keep some semblance of myself, wherever this place was we were headed to.

I secured my smuggled goods in my panties, grateful that regulation underwear included big cotton briefs. I smirked. I guess no thongs for the old island fogies.

I smoothed myself back into place and looked at my reflection, canting up and down on my tiptoes to get a full view in the tiny lavatory mirror. I let myself smile full-on. The weird uniform kind of worked. I looked like Madeline from the kids' books, if she'd spent her days in juvie instead of a French boarding school.

My hair, though. I pursed my lips. A hat, some Florida sweat, and a dry plane flight were the recipe for some serious hat head. You'd think nothing could go wrong with long, straight-as-an-arrow hair, but mine always managed to find a way. I raked my fingers through, shaking it out as best I could. Light yellow blond, with a conspicuous crimp just where my fedora had been. I shrugged, hoping there was something for it in my kit bag.

"Now or never," I told myself, swinging the door open.

Lilac flinched back to avoid getting hit. She'd been looming outside, her own uniform in hand. It was a shock seeing her up close. My stomach clenched to see she was even prettier than I'd thought. And she was staring at me with hate in her eyes.

I took an inadvertent step back. Why had she taken such an instant dislike to me? Did she despise *everyone*? She'd acted amiable enough with Mimi.

I glanced her up and down, as though that might give some clue, and my eye caught on a chink in her gorgeous armor. The hint of a burn scar rippled Lilac's skin, peeking from beneath her neckline.

"What are *you* looking at?" she asked in that evil-cheerleader voice. She'd noticed me noticing her weird scar and didn't like it.

"Nothing," I said with a quick shrug.

Lilac's *Mean Girls* act was overkill, and it made me wonder what she might be hiding. I'd endured the broad cruelty of my father, and my well-honed survival instincts told me to steer clear.

She glared at my hair and then the crown of my head, taking in the staticky limpness of my hat head, and let out a short, sharp cackle.

I pinched my lips into a flat line. Steering clear was one thing, but I hated when people dissed my hair. Long, pale blond hair wasted on a nerd girl . . . *ha ha.*

"I have no words," she said.

"Well, *there's* a surprise," I snapped, the words escaping my mouth before I could stop them. In it now, I gave her my brightest smile. I'd sworn off sarcasm, but some things just couldn't be helped. Wit was my armor as much as Lilac's prettiness was hers.

And I needed some armor, because, honestly, the girl was starting to scare me. Her reaction to me was over the top, and it made her seem both bitchy *and* unstable. A charming combo if ever there was one.

She looked me up and down, scorn oozing from her pores. "I didn't know the uniform came in children's sizes. Did they give you a training bra, too?"

Great, here come the height jokes. Though I was a perfectly respectable five foot two, of course Lilac had to have several inches on me. I estimated she was a solid five-nine.

My smile grew broader. Sometimes the best defense was a good offense—I hoped that was true here. "Lucky for you, it comes in extra large."

My new pal narrowed her eyes. Then she shoved me aside, elbowing her way into the lavatory.

I stared at the slammed door, rubbing my arm where she'd pushed me. The game, I supposed, was on.

CHAPTER SEVEN

A Range Rover with black-tinted windows met us at the island's airstrip. That is, if you could call a snowy field bisected by a thin stripe a runway, and if the bleak rock we'd just landed on qualified as an actual island.

I unzipped the neck of my navy blue parka and gasped at how surprisingly temperate the climate was. "Wow. It's actually not that bad out."

"Aye, it's never so bad between weathers." Our driver smiled at me, revealing more than a few missing teeth. I wondered if he was one of the old ones Ronan had mentioned. His accent was slow and loping, but easy enough to understand. "Excepting the wind. When she's blowing, stand fast, or she'll lie you flat."

I thought of the view from the airplane. A small, treeless, and mostly uninhabited island in the middle of the Atlantic. I imagined the wind, when it came, would be violent.

I turned a slow circle, taking it all in. Long, flat shelves of rock stretched into the distance. The shallow dusting of snow was already beginning to evaporate, fading to a uniform gray a few shades darker than the colorless sky overhead.

Bleak. And yet somehow utterly breathtaking. "It's beautiful."

"Beautiful?" Lilac stepped from the plane, lithe as a cat and gorgeous as ever in her uniform. Apparently, navy and gray were just the things to bring out the highlights in maple-colored hair. I frowned, but she met it with a smile. "Whatever you say, *freak*."

That word again. I cringed. But then I caught Ronan's eyes. There was warmth in them, wrinkling just at the corners. His gaze flicked quickly away.

The old man sniffed the air. "The snow, she never lies long. My guess, we'll be up to seven degrees by noon."

"Seven?" Lilac jammed her fists in her parka, as though chilled by the mere thought.

I looked at her, unable to conceal my amazement. "Celsius." *Duh.* "That's"—I did the quick calculation—"mid-forties to you."

"God, you really are a mutant." She shouldered past us, dropping her bag unceremoniously at the rear of the car for someone else to deal with, and then climbed in.

As the driver loaded the trunk, Ronan took shotgun. That left the three of us to wage a mini standoff to see who'd get stuck in the back middle spot. As if it really mattered. But, apparently, Lilac deemed me too repugnant even to sit next to. Rather than upset me, the notion brought an amused smile to my face. She was one queen-bee alpha bitch, and must've positively ruled her high school.

Lilac's icy stare tilted the balance and Mimi lost, situating herself on the smooth, slightly elevated stretch that was the middle seat. I got in, cramming myself as close as possible to the door so as not to touch my thigh to Mimi's. I glued my forehead to the cool window to endure the drive in blessed silence.

The sea pressed in from all around. Even though I'd grown up in Central Florida, the state wasn't that wide, and despite my aversion to swimming, there was something familiar about beaches, about the ocean. But *this*, this churning sea, was completely foreign to me. It was furious, treacherous, slapping against the coast like it was out for revenge.

The landscape was rock and more rock. Tremendous, flat expanses like tabletops, jagged outcroppings, sheer cliffs. And just offshore there were towers of it, spearing up from the sea like chimney stacks or the skeletons of giants.

The Range Rover slowed, turned, stopped.

I came back to myself, sitting up, craning my head for a glimpse out the other side. A medieval-looking fortress loomed on a hill in the near distance. It was rough-hewn, constructed of beefy gray stone, and stood in contrast to what appeared to be well-manicured gardens hidden beneath a light blanket of snow. The snow was the dry, powdery sort that made everything seem fragile and frozen in time. A shiver crawled across my skin.

We'd parked at the edge of a courtyard, where a crowd was already gathered. Though it was hard to tell with all the people, the yard seemed to be circular, in a slight depression in the earth. A cluster of standing stones ringed the far edge of the circle in a half-moon, with a gigantic granite platform at the center that looked ready to receive human sacrifices.

Between the milling throngs and those Stonehenge-wannabe stones, the alarm that'd been tripped when I'd first spotted Lilac and Mimi shrilled back to life. I realized the buzz from my airplane "refreshment" had worn off, and I found myself craving another drink of it. The stuff was like liquid courage.

We got out and, at Ronan's urging, joined the crowd at its fringes. I guessed there weren't more than one hundred people there. Ignoring my misgivings, I stepped in. It was just enough to separate me from Lilac and Mimi, but not so much that I couldn't find Ronan if need be. I didn't know exactly what *need* there might *be*, but I did know that crowds like this put me on guard.

It was like being dropped into a buzzing hive of female chatter. Many of the accents were from the U.K., but I caught a few American voices in there, too, as well as the occasional foreign language.

I picked up on a distant conversation in French and shut my eyes, letting the familiar, sultry sound of it wash over me. Maybe this place wouldn't be so bad after all.

But then my eyes flew open, realizing. I scanned the crowd. Girls . . . *just girls*. A sea of them, all around. Some had their navy parkas slung over their arms. All wore the gray tunic and leggings. And they were, every last one of them, pretty.

I scowled. How could Ronan think I'd ever fit in with all these *Top Model* rejects? I couldn't resist the urge to compare myself to them. I definitely wasn't ugly, but I also knew for sure that I was far from classically pretty. My big eyes annoyed me— I thought they made me look like a bug. Between that and my wide mouth, I was fairly certain I resembled some sort of backward fairy-tale frog that had yet to turn into a princess.

And then there was my hair. Though long and blond sometimes felt too conspicuous, it'd actually helped me blend in. I'd discovered the need for Florida camouflage the hard way at the age of twelve, with the discovery that not all girls can pull off bald as pertly as Natalie Portman. Granted, I hadn't cropped it *all* off, but with my light blond hair, it'd looked close enough. I'd thought I looked Swedish. Not Daddy Dearest, though. He'd thought I looked like a lesbian, and commemorated the whole affair with the gift of a split lip.

Like that, I'd become the repellent fascination of all the coral-lipsticked mommies at my middle school. Attention was always the last thing I craved, so aside from evening out the layers, I hadn't cut it since.

The memory stung, and I sank into my shoulders, imagining myself disappearing into the crowd. Wandering deeper into the fray, I stared in horrified fascination. It was just like high school. Ronan had plucked me from obscurity and dumped me into a surreal high school from my nightmares. And it was a *girls' school*.

Cliques were already beginning to form, like finding like. Stoner girls with flat stares gravitated toward one another. There was a large contingent of gang girls circling one another warily. And a small group of slightly bedraggled, once-homeless waifs, looking like diamonds in the rough but for the raw fury in their eyes. Then there were the Lilacs of the crowd—just a very few of this rare breed—all reeking of drug-addled yacht parties with other bored socialites.

No weird, smart girl clique in sight. If I'd thought I'd finally make some friends, I'd need to think again.

I heard the strains of French again. My whole life, I'd dreamt of traveling to Paris. My accent was flawless. I adored madeleines, and Vanessa Paradis, and the films of François Truffaut. I was practically a native. If I belonged anywhere, their group was it. Lifting my chin, I strode toward the sound of their lilting voices.

I found the pair of them at once and stood for a second, listening to what sounded like a eulogy to their confiscated cigarettes. If their language hadn't given them away, their looks would have. They were both pale and model thin. One had the supershort, blunt-cut bangs that only French girls and maybe Katy Perry could pull off. The other had pixie-short black hair that made her look wistful and bohemian.

"*Bonjour,*" I greeted them, trying to walk the line between friendly and cool. "*Quel bordel, n'est-ce pas?*" I thought it a clever yet insouciant version of *Some mess, huh?*

They froze, staring at each other in wide-eyed shock. Pixie didn't even deign to look at me. But Bangs turned her head slowly and in a thick accent informed me, "You will not speak to us."

And like that, they resumed their chatter as though I weren't even there.

Suddenly, I felt ill. More than that, I wanted to disappear. Apparently, not even sharing an effed-up, life-altering experience like *this* was enough to make me friend material. Not even a crazy island in the middle of nowhere counted as enough in common where Weird Smart Girl was concerned.

Snow began to drift down. The temperature seemed to have done a nosedive, much like my outlook.

I zipped my parka back up. Mid-forties, my ass. So much for our driver's charming local wisdom.

"It's like that scene in the Santa movie." An American voice cut into my thoughts. Could I *please, for once*, get away from the Christmas references? I stole a look, spying a matched pair of brunettes with vaguely New York accents.

"You mean the one where all the kids get off the train—"

"Except *he* doesn't look like Santa," Brunette Thing One interrupted.

I followed her line of sight. The most beautiful man I'd ever seen was stepping onto the massive platform I'd spotted in the shadow of the standing stones. The throngs of girls had obstructed my view, with only the sight of his shoulders and chest rising above the crowd to tell us any sort of stage was even there.

"Hel-lo," Thing Two purred. "He can stuff my stocking anytime."

"Ick," I heard myself grunt.

They spun on me, and the shorter of the two snarled, "Shut it."

I held her stare for a moment, then turned to face the stage full-on. It appeared that many of these girls' so-called *gifts* were bitchiness and spite.

Though I did have to hand it to them—this was one pretty extraordinarily perfect guy. Chin squared off just right, a naughty glint in his eyes, and a head of tousled hair featuring about a hundred shades of gold, he reminded me of a pale California dude. Early twenties, I guessed.

I found myself smiling at him. I imagined I wasn't the only one. I stepped closer.

He beamed back at the crowd, and the sensation was of a gentle heat radiating over us. "Hello, lovelies."

My hand flew to my belly. His voice seared me through, sexy and deep, with the hint of a barely there French accent.

And I wasn't the only one affected, either. An awed hiss swept over the crowd. He chuckled, obviously used to this sort of adoration.

"My name is Claude Fournier"—his accent grew thick when pronouncing his name, and I just about swooned—"but you shall call me Headmaster Fournier."

Headmaster? He was the youngest headmaster *I'd* ever seen. Or I guessed he would be, if I'd ever seen a headmaster before.

He began to stroll the few steps back and forth along the length of the platform. "We use many formal terms of address, and you will soon learn all of them. Tradition, you see, is the cornerstone on our isle, and though many of you might find our manners . . . passé"—he gave a little flourish with his hand—"if you embrace the old ways, you will soon find yourself a much-improved young lady."

Young lady? Something was wrong here. My smile faltered, and by the hum of murmured comments around me, I imagined I wasn't the only one chafing at Mister Old-Fashioned. I wondered how such a hot guy came to be so stodgy. Maybe it was an affectation to distract people from the fact that he was the youngest headmaster on the planet.

"Our old ways, you see, are quite old." He gave us a wicked, pouting smile that made my instincts jangle in warning. "We live by a code. Only those who abide by our principles succeed. Our standards are high; our expectations, higher. But a few will exceed expectations. They are the girls who shall flourish."

What sort of bizarro finishing school was this? I forced myself to focus on his words, not his looks. All this talk of manners and traditions—something was amiss.

Oh, crap. Was this some sort of wacked-out reform school my stepmother had masterminded? I'd heard nightmare stories of boot camps for bad kids. I studied the girls to my left and right. They all had that same hard edge that I'd seen in Mimi and Lilac. Something cold and defensive in their eyes.

I shivered. Did *I* have that flat-eyed stare? Did *I* look like a bad girl?

"You see"—he paused dramatically, and the ambient whispering stopped as all eyes returned to him—"we are *Vampire*."

You could've heard a pin drop.

I looked around, searching for a camera crew. I'd known the guy was too hot to be normal. Headmaster, my ass. He was an *actor*. Ashton Kutcher was going to pop out any minute, letting us know we'd been punk'd.

And yet, some primal instinct in the back of my mind warned me to be very, very careful. I held still, expectantly, and I watched.

The chatter exploded again, but this time a broad laugh pealed above the din. I stood on my tiptoes to see. It was Mimi.

Headmaster Fournier grew still as stone and just as cold. His eyes swept the crowd—dancing over me for one chilling moment—and then rested on Mimi. "Do I amuse you?"

"Yeah," she said in that tone of bored outrage that bad girls have perfected through the ages.

"Then please"—he stretched his hand out, beckoning—"come join me. . . ." He raised his eyebrows, waiting for her name.

"Mimi." She'd thrust her jaw out, holding her mouth open on the word as though too annoyed even to shut it.

"Girls, make way for your fellow student." He spoke in an indulgent tone of voice that scared me more than the word *vampire* had. It was the sound of an adult ready to give someone a good lesson.

Everyone had enough sense to clear a path for her, and almost comically fast. Mimi, though, wasn't so bright. Her hackles were up like a pit bull on the offensive, looking ready to tell this guy a thing or two. Sneering, she strode to the platform. It was smooth and level, like a gigantic granite tabletop.

Distantly, I wondered if Mimi wasn't justified in her reaction. Maybe I should be doing something other than just standing there. I mean, the guy just told us they were vampires.

The in-flight refreshment. I frowned, remembering the buzz it'd made me feel. Mimi had thrown it all up, but had the rest of us been drugged into obedience? Was I still drugged now? Should I be outraged, too?

I thought of Ronan. Did this mean *he* thought he was a vampire? I recalled his features. He hadn't seemed particularly pale, and I definitely would've noticed fangs.

If I could've smirked without attracting attention, I would have. What sort of Goth freak world had I landed in? I peered at Fournier, trying to sneak a peek at his teeth, wondering if these guys actually went so far as to file them into points.

But then a dreadful sort of uncertainty niggled at the back of my mind as I remembered the very real feeling I got when Ronan looked at me, when he touched me. It was like he'd hypnotized me, and though I didn't believe in magic, he sure did seem to have some sort of crazy hypno-hoodoo up his sleeves.

Mimi reached the stone, and Fournier took her hand, guiding her up the last steps and onto the stage. When he spoke again, it was gently and only to her. It felt like we were spying on an intimate moment. "As I was saying, we are Vampire."

She pulled her hand from his and scanned the crowd,

shaking her head in disgust. "I seen some effed-up shit in Miami, *pero esta casa de putas?* Count me *out*, man."

The next part happened so fast, at first my brain didn't register what my eyes were seeing. And even when I got what I saw, it took me a few heartbeats to *get it* get it. I stared, frozen from the inside out.

Mimi hung limply in the headmaster's arms. Because he'd just shredded her belly up the middle.

He grinned at us with bloody lips, and I spotted one inhumanly long, razor-sharp tooth as it caught on the corner of his mouth.

A few heartbeats of silence, and then the girls began to scream.

Not me, though. I'd weathered casual cruelty before. It was random and merciless, and I knew not to court it. I forced my breath to draw in, then out. I imagined myself being as inconspicuous as possible.

Eyja næturinnar. It *was* an island of darkness. And Ronan was right. I *would* fit in here.

Because if I didn't, I'd die.

CHAPTER EIGHT

S o, okayyy. Vampires.

I stomped my boots, urging the blood to flow in my feet. The temperature had continued to drop, and just standing there outside wasn't helping matters.

Were there other vampires hiding in the crowd? I looked around, feeling in equal parts the absurdity and the horror. Never would I ever have thought I'd be considering their existence. I mean, really—*vampires?*

But if the scene with Mimi had been any indication, it seemed there was a good chance that exist they did. I supposed in a universe that fostered everything from black holes to hostile, mutating bacteria, vampires actually seemed like a pretty pedestrian phenomenon.

I wondered how many of the myths were true. Could vampires be killed? Were they *undead?* Could something really live forever?

I remembered the strain of 250-million-year-old bacteria that was found in a cavern in New Mexico. And then I thought of the extinct things—the *dead* things—that have simply been coaxed back to life, thanks to DNA technology.

Vampires, on the face of it, seemed eminently possible. I just needed to wrap my mind around it. Not that I needed to think so hard. The proof was right in front of me.

As though on cue, Headmaster Fournier dropped Mimi's broken body onto the stone. "Whose is this?" His eyes danced over us, stopping just over my shoulder.

I couldn't help but turn.

His gaze had locked on Ronan. I hadn't realized he'd been standing just behind me. "Ronan," he snapped.

Was Ronan in trouble? Would he be next on the menu? I bit my cheek so hard, I tasted blood. *Please, not Ronan. Anyone but Ronan.* It wasn't like I trusted him—if anything, I was furious with him for getting me into this—but after the headmaster's demonstration, Ronan definitely seemed the lesser of two evils.

Plus, he was human. At least partly. Or I hoped he was.

Ronan stepped forward and the crowd parted, avoiding him like the plague. "Yes, Headmaster?"

"Is this yours?" Using his foot, Headmaster Fournier nudged Mimi onto her back. Her eyes were still open, staring blindly, the vivid blue irises so light against that milky coffee complexion bearing the outlines of two teardrops forever stenciled on her cheek.

Her parka slid open to reveal her mutilated belly. Gasps washed over the crowd.

Ronan lowered his head. "Yes, Headmaster."

"I told you, no facial tattoos." Tilting his head, the vampire coolly assessed Mimi's face. "They are so . . . *déclassé*." His eyes snapped back to Ronan. "Clear it away. Make certain it gets put to use."

Horror stole the breath from my lungs, wondering what *that* had meant.

"At once, Headmaster."

Two guys who seemed to be Ronan's peers joined him on the stage. They whisked away the body and swabbed the blood from the platform in a matter of moments.

Like that, Mimi was gone.

All eyes went back to the headmaster, none of us brave enough to utter a sound. He gave us a paternal smile, and it made my skin crawl. "Where was I before our little . . . *object lesson*?"

Paternal indeed. Just how old was Claude Fournier?

He scanned the crowd, lingering on some girls longer than others. "Such lovelies this year," he exclaimed. "And I see I have your attention now. You are a very special group, you know. Very privileged. You, among all others, have been chosen. You, among all others, have the chance to join us."

I chafed my hands along my arms. *Is he going to make us vampires?*

"No, no, sweets." He chuckled, and at first I panicked, thinking he'd read my mind. But then I saw the wide-eyed terror writ clear on the other girls' faces and realized that everyone had jumped to the same conclusion.

"*You* will not be vampires," he assured us. "Never that. To be Vampire is a *man's* destiny. But we cannot survive without *you*, my fair ones. You see, only you have the opportunity to be a part of an elite group. A group that ensures the survival of the coven. This group is known as the Watchers. And to be Watcher is a *woman's* fortune."

He said that last bit as though it was the greatest honor girls like us could ever attain. My thoughts turned grim. It was once considered an honor to be a sacrificial lamb, too.

"Despite our powers, those of a vampiric nature cannot travel everywhere. We cannot *be* everything. And so we create Watchers. To represent. To defend. And sometimes to kill. The Watcher is the agent of our will. She is an extension of our power."

I dredged every girls' face in that crowd from my memory. I wondered what kind of gifts they had that'd been spectacular enough to catch a vampire's eye.

Why had *I* been chosen? I was quite smart, yes, but so were lots of other people in the world. Though Ronan had mentioned I was one of the few geniuses who came with an abusive father. So was I here because my father had beaten me up? My specialty was that I knew how to take a punch? It appeared that spending my formative years getting smacked around by my dad may have earned me the privilege of getting smacked around by a bunch of vampires. The thought sent cold dread twining through my belly.

And just how many vampires were there? Ronan had mentioned the *old ones*, plural. *Old.* Well, *duh.* I steeled myself, thinking of the verbal flogging I'd give *him* next time we met. Him and that stupid Proust tattoo.

"But not all of you will ascend." The headmaster's voice dripped with mock regret, and I tuned back in, and fast, imagining that the girls who failed weren't exactly put on a Carnival Cruise back home.

"Look around you," he commanded.

I felt the crowd around me shift. And I felt eyes on me, even as I stared right back. These girls had backbone. They looked defiant, angry even. Where in the world had they found this many girls resilient enough to withstand such a place?

The girls were tough. And the other unifying characteristic? Every last one of them was as lovely as the headmaster had said.

But why? Why was everyone so attractive? They were selecting and making what? Secret Agent Barbies?

Why not? I thought. If you lived for all eternity, better to be served by an army of teenage hotties.

And I was the odd one out, yet again. Because I had a brain. The only Skipper in a sea of Barbies.

"Look at your peers," he pressed. "Only fifty of you will rise to the next level of training. Then but twenty-five the following year. You will eventually be whittled down to an elite group of five."

I wasn't ready to consider what happened to the remaining, oh, several dozen other girls.

"Your training will be intense. You will work hard. You will learn strength and fortitude. You will learn to toil and to do without. Through the years, you will cultivate yourselves, learning elegance, embracing lives of intellect and sophistication.

"The *crème* among you shall be chosen to be our representatives in the world. But it is a *dangerous* world, as many of you have experienced." It seemed like his eyes lit on me, and I told myself it was my imagination. "And so your training must also be dangerous."

He chuckled, and I felt that warmth flood me again, despite

myself. "But you are my hothouse lovelies, and if you let me, I shall teach you to gavotte as expertly as you garrote."

I shoved the warmth away, focusing on his words, on his gruesome little pun that likened dancing to strangling.

But then, in the darkest recesses of my mind, I went there, just for a moment. I'd felt the urge to throttle someone before— Daddy Dearest came to mind—but never could I bring myself to actually kill someone. *Right?*

"For the next year, you will be known as the Acari. That is from the Greek. It means '*mite*.' Like . . . a tick. A parasite. And, like parasites, you shall feed off of our knowledge."

This time he really did look at me, like I was his student and he wanted to explain some fascinating linguistic bit just to me. I made my face like stone, even though I thought my heart might explode from my chest. Being noticed was the last thing I wanted. His lips peeled into a smile as he turned his attention back to the rest of the crowd. "Indeed, you will gain strength by feeding off our very lifeblood. You already have."

I gulped back bile. He meant blood. Like, real blood. As in, our little in-flight cocktail.

"Our lifeblood will aid you. Fortify you." He waved his hand impatiently. "But I touch on topics that are for others to broach. You will reside in the Acari dormitory, where you've each been assigned a roommate. Every floor has a Proctor. The Proctor is ahead of you in your training—she has ascended to what we call Initiate. Your Proctors and teachers will inform you of any details I've withheld."

He narrowed his eyes. I couldn't tell where he was looking, and the effect was that he looked at all of us simultaneously.

"And remember. You will show your dormitory Proctors and all Initiates respect. Never forget, you are merely Acari."

The snow drifted down, and it cast its own shroud of silence over the crowd.

The headmaster's voice pierced the calm with one final proclamation. "Stand warned, lovelies. Initiates are encouraged to teach you cruelty. And you should thank them for it. For to understand cruelty is to know strength."

And then Headmaster Claude Fournier simply disappeared.

CHAPTER NINE

The crowd was dispersing, splitting into smaller groups and piling into a fleet of monstrous SUVs. I gave a last backward glance to the fortress on the hill. What *was* that place? Was it where all the vampires lived? Did it house stuff like dungeons and underground catacombs and imperiled virgins?

Either way, I was relieved it wasn't going to be my new dorm. The thing looked haunted. And those standing stones had given me the creeps, too. Archaeologists may not have known what megalithic stones had been used for, but it sure seemed to me that I'd just seen my first human sacrifice.

I should've listened to my doubts and not joined him on that damned plane, but Ronan had made me feel safe, with those stupid green eyes and that stupid husky voice.

I caught up with him. "Don't tell me *you're* a vampire, too."

I felt that heavy, green-eyed gaze on me. "Do I look like a vampire?"

"How the hell should I know?" Bracing myself, I forced my eyes to him. "I don't understand why I'm here. Why would you bring people to this place? I *knew* I should've trusted my instincts, but no. All you had to do was look at me, and—" I froze, understanding coming like the flash of a bulb in my head. I glared accusingly. "You used some sort of vampire mojo to get me on that airplane."

He opened his mouth to speak, but snapped it shut.

Aha. I was onto something. But before I could press him, he grabbed my arm, leading us toward a super-oversized version of a Ford Excursion. It reminded me of those ghastly stretch Hummers that kids rented for dances.

I stopped in my tracks. By this time I was panicked and scared and freaked and angry, feeling capable of either sarcasm or hysteria. I chose the former. "Wow, now *that's* a real date getter. It's like vampire prom night."

"Annelise." Ronan stopped walking. "You must never mistake human for Vampire, nor should you even joke about it."

"In the same way you're not supposed to joke in line for airport security?" I felt his exasperation and stared him down. "Well, how should I know, Ronan? I'd never seen a vampire before today, so I'm not exactly an expert. So, what, did you fail your vamp final exam? Is that why you're not one . . . *ov zee undead?*"

I'd used my best Hollywood Dracula voice, but Ronan did *not* seem amused.

Leaning close, he gave my arm a little shake. "I told you, *no jokes.* I'm what's called a Tracer. We find, track, and retrieve *girls like you.*" He'd said that last bit as though it left a foul taste in his mouth. I tried to pull my arm away, but he held firm. "I am not, nor have I ever wished to be, Vampire." He gave me a squeeze before letting go. "Heed me, Annelise. There is no *failing* where vampires are concerned. Only dying."

His tone of voice chilled me. I rubbed my arm, still throbbing where he'd gripped me, and wondered about the Tracer thing. How elaborate did this whole scene get? "What did you get me into?"

"What did *I* get you into?"

"Yes." I was sure he'd used some sort of persuasive powers to get me on that plane. But still, I hadn't been entirely helpless; I'd *known* Ronan wasn't exactly swooping me away for a hot weekend getaway. But neither had I thought I was going to be a candidate for evisceration. "You'd said *special school*, but I didn't realize *I* might be the one up for dissection. And what's with all the hotties? Training in elegance and sophistication? What is this—some sort of geisha camp?"

Standing there, withstanding my rant, Ronan suddenly seemed tired. "I tried to warn you. In my way." He saw my furious look and amended, "As much as I could."

"Because you told me it was serious, all the while using your hypnotic googly eyes?" I brushed by him as he opened the car door for me. I kicked the snow from my boots before I got in. I had to admit, they *were* cool boots. "Hmph."

I clambered in. It truly was a beast of a vehicle—*ghastly* wasn't an understatement. It had seating for eleven, and I crawled straight back to the far rear corner.

Ronan followed, sitting beside me. Despite my anger, the tug of his weight on the seat gave me a momentary jolt. Until I saw one of Ronan's peers take the driver's seat and his hot strawberry blonde charge claim shotgun.

"You had no place else to go," he reminded me in a hushed voice.

"I *had* a place to go until they said I couldn't start college. Wait. . . ." I inched away so I could face him full on. "Did *you* set up that whole swim-test thing at the registrar's office?"

He shrugged.

Busted. The bastard. "You did, didn't you? How'd you even know I couldn't swim?"

"I know many things."

"What, you've got, like, a Goth mind probe in addition to powers of persuasion?"

He gave me a blank look, and I barreled ahead, sensing I'd hit a nerve. "That's right, don't think I couldn't tell. You used some sort of weird hypnotism or touch, or something, to convince me to come."

"Believe me, you're not that easy." His tone implied I was *all-around* difficult.

"So *that's* how"—I looked to the open car door, lowering my voice—"that's how you Tracers do it? You have persuasive powers?"

"In varying degrees." Ronan glanced at his colleague in the driver's seat. The guy was immersed in a chat with Strawberry Blonde, oblivious to the conversation in the back-back. "Most girls respond when I use my eyes alone. You're more difficult."

"Don't tell me. That's why you kept touching me?" My heart fell, seeing the answer on his face. The way he'd taken my hand, all those touches to my arm, my shoulder—the purpose had been to enthrall me, to convince me to get in his car, onto his plane.

I scowled. I'd *known* guys like him weren't interested in girls like me, and yet stupid me had gone there in my mind for just a moment. "You *tricked* me."

He went on the defensive. "You'd hit rock bottom, Annelise."

"And *this* is better? In what universe is avoiding a drunk father and subsisting on waitressing tips more rock bottom than *this*?" I slumped against the door, the window cool on my forehead. "Silly me. Being totally alone on an island of bloodthirsty monsters is a real step up."

"Believe me, you only arrive here if it's your last stop."

"Harsh." I stared blindly out the window, wondering if he was right. Had I sunk that low? All I knew was that I wasn't ready to give up yet. I had to find a way out. "I'm not *that* pathetic."

Movement caught my eye. Lilac was approaching. She already had a mini posse following her. A bunch of mindless electrons buzzing around her radioactive core.

But then I realized. If this was my last chance, it was *their* last chance, too. Lilac and her ilk were just as desperate as me. And that meant Lilac had secrets. She and I had *something* in common; I just couldn't imagine what.

She climbed in—gracefully, I might add—and glowered at me. Gaze shifting to Ronan, she held up her parka. "Could you toss this in the back for me?" Her tone was saccharine sweet.

At his nod, she whipped it right at my face. The metal nub at the end of the hood string snapped me in the eyes.

"Oops!" Smiling, she gave an innocent shrug.

That was it. I *would* find a way out of this place. When he'd talked me onto the plane, I'd thought I'd be in for some cool schooling, but this was brainwashed-cult crap, and I was *not* down with it.

It was only a matter of time before I annoyed someone as

badly as Mimi had, and I refused to have my guts spilled in front of an audience of Barbies. My last stop would *not* be on some vampire's dinner plate.

Once everyone settled, I leaned close to Ronan's ear. "How do I get out?"

"Shush," he hissed. "You can't get out."

As the other girls loaded in, I considered my situation. I was more helpless and alone than I'd ever been in Florida, only now I was surrounded by things that wanted to eat me. The driver put the truck in gear and drove. I felt as desolate as the bleak, gray world outside my window.

I called my mom's picture to mind, taking strength from the memory of her yellow hair, that bright yellow pantsuit. It seemed that, yet again, I'd be forced to make my own way, in a world bled dry of color.

Ronan was wrong—I *would* get out. I'd survived the most difficult and loveless of childhoods, and I'd survive this, too. I leaned close again, and felt him bristle. "So Watchers aren't allowed to leave the island? Ever?"

"Of course," he said, his voice tight with tension, "Watchers are allowed to leave."

"Then how do I become a Watcher?"

He cleared his throat to speak in a hoarse whisper, and I had to strain to hear him over the chatting and posturing of the girls. "First, you stay alive. And then you must prove yourself better than all the others."

We pulled onto a rough, cobbled drive, and the truck jostled Ronan's body into mine. I inhaled sharply. I trusted this guy about as far as I could throw him. I would *not* be affected by the warm press of his thigh on mine. I *would* focus.

I'd focus and excel and stay alive. Long enough to escape.

"You're here." Ronan nodded to a forbidding structure that made me nostalgic for the fortress we'd just left. It was a rambling old mansion of pale reddish stone. Each window was a narrow Gothic archway rising to a fine point. A colonnade of lanky towers, chimneys, columns, and turrets gave the impression of a spindly, ethereal thing, reaching skyward.

"*That's* my dorm?" As I got out, my eyes went to the clusters of bad girls spilling from the other SUVs, cursing their fates. "It's like Hogwarts in Gangland."

"This is the edge of the quad." Ronan pointed to the tops of some other buildings just beyond the dorm. "There's the Acari dorm, Initiate housing, academic buildings, and a chapel."

"Chapel?" I was dying to walk alongside the building for a better view, but something told me that'd be frowned upon. "You're shitting me."

He rolled his eyes. "Annelise, your language leaves something to be desired. And, no, I'm not exaggerating. There is a chapel, though it hasn't seen a priest in my lifetime."

A tall black girl emerged from the building. Spotting Ronan, she approached us, a warm smile on her face.

"Here comes one of the Proctors now." He pointed her out, but he needn't have.

She'd stood out the moment she glided from the dorm. Dramatically so. She was gorgeous—what else?—but in a fierce, self-possessed way. Though she looked only about nineteen or twenty, something about her seemed much older. She wore a sort of catsuit in an austere navy color, instead of the gray Acari tunic. I knew without asking that I was looking at the uniform of an Initiate.

"Amanda." The warmth in Ronan's voice made me do a double take. A spurt of irrational jealousy made my belly lurch, and I swallowed it down.

"Ronan," she replied with humor in her voice. She turned her attention to me, studying me with a speculative tilt to her head. "This one of yours, then?" She spoke in a thick Cockney accent.

I couldn't take my eyes off her. Dreadlocks twined to her shoulders, but not in a Rasta way. It was more at tastefully bohemian, like a latter-day Lauryn Hill.

"Aye, one of mine," Ronan said. "There are just two this time. I . . . lost one. During the Induction."

"Let me guess. This would be Annelise. Though you prefer Drew, don't you?"

I could only nod lamely, totally awed. Above and beyond her clothes and her hair, there was something in Amanda's bearing that set her apart. Like she'd been tested and proven worthy. I saw it in her stature, in the steel of her dark eyes, and in the taut lines of her body visible beneath her clothing.

Lilac appeared from nowhere, shouldering past me. "Hope you survive the night, Charity."

Her pack knocked me and I stumbled. I heard her trilling laugh, feeling my cheeks burn deep crimson.

Amanda chuckled, a rich, throaty sound. "Don't mind her, dolly. There's a slag like that in every batch."

A laugh escaped me, like an awkward, relieved puff of air. Was this Proctor someone I could trust? I forced myself to remember I could trust no one. Least of all one of the Initiates the headmaster warned us about.

But Ronan seemed to like her. And, not too long ago, she'd

have been just like me—a clueless girl in one of those SUVs. I remained on guard, but let myself be cautiously optimistic.

We watched Lilac prowl around the other girls like a lioness hunting for fresh meat.

"Who's she?" Amanda asked.

"Lilac." I rolled my eyes to show how ridiculous I'd thought *that* name sounded.

"Von Straubing?" The Proctor's face was suddenly veiled. Even though this woman was a veritable stranger, I knew enough about body language to tell something was up.

"What?" I demanded. I could tell she was wary of telling me something. "What is it?"

"Sorry, dolly. I'm afraid Lilac's your roommate."

CHAPTER TEN

———

Cracking the door, I braced myself. It wasn't every day a girl got to bunk with her archenemy. If I hadn't already decided to get the hell out at the first opportunity, the privilege of rooming with Lilac for the next year would've been enough to drive me to *swim* to the mainland. And that from a girl who didn't know how.

I pushed it open a bit more and shut my eyes in horror at the hideous creaking sound it made. *Note to self: There'll be no sneaking in and out of this room.* On a sharp exhale, I shoved it open all the way.

All my caution was for naught. Lilac hadn't even been there yet.

I stepped in and looked around at what I imagined resembled your average military-school dorm room—if you were in the Bavarian army. While regular kids in regular schools had things like Target bedspreads and *Twilight* posters, we'd been issued a bed on a simple, unpainted iron frame, a dresser that looked like it belonged in a monk's cell, and a desk that I'd wager had been haphazardly hewn from a giant oak by someone short on time. A pile of blue-gray woolen blankets were folded atop white sheets. I didn't need to feel either to know how coarse they were.

I shrugged. At least we didn't have to suffer bunk beds.

I needed to hide my iPod and photo—how I longed to take a quick peek at my mother's smiling face—but where on earth could I stash them without Lilac finding out? I wouldn't put it past her to rifle through my stuff, and I had the dreaded feeling that I'd be wearing my iPod and picture in my panties for the rest of the semester.

I eyed the desks. Each had a stack of books on them, and I made a beeline to each one in turn, immediately deducing which was mine. The elementary German grammar workbook had Lilac's name all over it. I chuckled to myself. *Good luck with that, von Slutling.* She also got a book on Norse culture and one of those English-lit tomes that contained every story ever written, printed on paper thinner than onion skin.

My pile left a lot to be desired, though. I fought not to be too disappointed. I mean, what'd I expect? A first-edition Byron or something?

Yeah, I realized. I kinda had. I mean, if these vampires were old—and I assumed they were—wouldn't they have some really old, really cool books?

All I'd been issued was something on Norse mythology and a Spanish-English dictionary. The Norse stuff was cool, yes, but not enough to occupy me for a week, much less a semester. What was I going to be studying, anyway?

Going to the dresser, I automatically opened and shut the drawers out of habit, and was surprised to find something tucked away in the bottom drawer. A lovely handcrafted box, painted red, with a crane etched in black on the lid. I thought it looked Japanese.

I carefully pulled off the lid—someone had gone to a lot of trouble to make the top and bottom fit together perfectly—and I gasped. Four throwing stars sat nestled atop a swath of black velvet. I could tell it was old. Not that the fabric was threadbare; it just *looked* ancient.

I traced my finger over the stars. They were a dull, steely color, with six razor-sharp points. I tested a tip with my thumb and then smudged the flat of the blades. My touch didn't leave so much as a fingerprint. A shiver ran up my spine.

The door swung open, and I slammed the box and the drawer shut.

Lilac looked at me with suspicion, her gaze jumping from me to my hand on the dresser, then back again. "It's not like I'm thrilled about this, either, Chari—"

"Would you stop calling me that?" Standing straight, I pulled my hand back and fisted it at my side.

She sauntered in. Dumping her kit bag on the floor, she went to her desk, grunting when she rifled through her pile of books. Wandering to her dresser, she opened the drawers just as I had. When she reached the bottom drawer, she paused, chuckling to herself, and then slammed it shut again.

Did she get throwing stars, too?

"Why are you staring at me?" She kept her back to me as she spoke. "You're not some kind of dyke, are you?"

I couldn't deal with this right now. I had to get out of there before I said something I regretted. Curfew was eight p.m., but I didn't think that meant we weren't allowed to leave the room. Snagging my Norse mythology book, I left.

I figured I had at least a few hours to burn until Lilac went to bed, and so I took myself on a tour of the dorm. Clutching my book to my side, I walked purposefully, being careful not to make eye contact with any of the other girls who appeared in the halls.

The building had four floors. Each was exactly alike, with sixteen rooms per floor, except for the ground level, which had only fourteen rooms and a large foyer. Each floor shared four bathrooms, two on either side of the hallway. A kitchenette and common area with couches and a fireplace were at the far end of each hall.

From what I spied through an open doorway, two rooms on the end of each hall were actually suites with their own bathrooms. I assumed each was occupied by a Proctor. That meant two Proctors per floor, for eight Proctors total.

I did the math. One hundred girls. Fifty rooms occupied, plus eight Proctor suites. That left four empty.

Maybe I could land myself a single room.

Yeah, right. Somehow I got the feeling that Lilac or I had to die in order for either of us to be granted a single. The thought gave me a chill. I hoped my roomie wouldn't come to the same conclusion and murder me in my sleep.

I went back up to the second floor, but our light was still on. Even though it was late and I was beat, I decided to give it a bit longer until Lilac was asleep. Putting on my jammies and tucking into bed in front of her was something I was going to need to work up to. Instead I plopped down on a couch in the common area.

The dorm felt empty, like everyone was in for the night. It was peaceful, and the couch uncharacteristically cozy, covered in wide-wale corduroy colored a deep burgundy. The iPod jammed into my belly as I settled in and I pulled it out, deciding it was safe to risk it. I smoothed my mother's photo over its hard surface, getting strength from that wide-eyed stare. She'd have rocked a navy blue catsuit—I could tell.

With a sigh, I toggled to The National and played them extra low, careful to keep the earbuds hidden in my hair. Then I opened my book and read. And read.

Two attempted forays back to the room were enough to tell me that Lilac and I were playing some sort of passive-aggressive game of chicken. She wouldn't turn out the lights until I went to bed, and I wouldn't go to bed until she was passed out asleep.

Needless to say, I was becoming *very* well acquainted with the pantheon of Norse gods and goddesses.

The hall clock had just chimed three o'clock when I heard the footsteps. At 3:01, I heard the shrieks.

I ripped the buds from my ears and shoved my iPod in the belly of my regulation granny panties. Slinking to the hallway, I watched as seven Initiates went from door to door, pulling Acari from their beds. Girls stumbled from their rooms, dressed in full winter gear, fully packed kit bags slung on their backs. The uncooperative ones were dragged out by their hair.

I panicked. Was I supposed to be in bed? Had there been a lights-out curfew I didn't know about? Should I hide? Would I get in trouble already?

"You," a voice called behind me.

I spun, startled. I had enough sense to look down submissively, but not before getting a full glimpse of the creature standing before me. Black hair in a severe bob; hard-edged features. She wore the midnight blue catsuit of an Initiate.

I thought of the headmaster's speech. A black bullwhip unfurled from her hand, and I remembered. She was here to teach me pain.

CHAPTER ELEVEN

"Y es . . ." I answered warily, fumbling for how to address her. *Yes, Master? Yes, Ma'am? Yes, Ms. Bizarro Dungeon Queen?*

"I am Guidon Masha." I detected the faint strains of a Russian accent, just the barest hint in her elongated vowels. "And you are late for the party."

I forced my gaze to meet hers. I knew I needed to be agreeable, but something told me it'd be dangerous to let anyone scent fear. "Yes, Guidon."

A frightening smile curved one corner of her mouth. I'd gotten the term of address correct. I guessed Guidon was a more advanced level of Initiate. I recognized it as a military word, though its exact meaning escaped me.

This was an ordered world I found myself in, one of hierarchies and titles. But I was smart; I could learn. I felt my shoulders relax a bit.

The smile evaporated from her face. Apparently she'd sensed the relaxation in my posture and didn't much like it. "*Move*, Acari. You will go to your room and return in full uniform, carrying everything you own." She cracked her whip, snapping it against the couch. The couch, by the way, was at least seven feet away. "Now. Before I make you run."

I didn't need any more urging than that.

Great. I'd broken Annelise Drew Cardinal Rule Number One: blend. At all costs. And now my penalty was the attention of a girl with a *bullwhip*. Though, arguably, it beat catching the eye of someone with a lasso.

My brisk walk sped into a jog. I passed Lilac in the hallway, and the evil eye she gave me said she blamed *me* for her lack of sleep.

I zipped into our room and frantically gathered my stuff. It didn't take long, since, aside from a dry pair of socks and a little bag of toiletries, I hadn't unpacked in the first place.

Nerves slicked my skin with a fine sheen of sweat. I became aware of the metal and glass of my iPod, heavy and damp in my panties. I froze, crooking my thighs to stop it from slipping free.

I shot a glance at the door open behind me. Would anyone notice? Something told me I needed to take the risk. Jamming my hand down the front of my leggings, I retrieved both my iPod and the photo and shoved them deep into my kit bag.

I turned to bolt out the door, my heart pounding in my chest, but then paused, thinking of the throwing stars. She'd said *everything*. Dashing back in, I tugged off my pillowcase and wrapped it around the Japanese box, quickly nestling it in the center of my bag. I hoped it'd be safe.

Hoisting it all on my back, I ran out the door. The shoulder strap snagged on my parka and was dragging my sleeves up in an annoying way. I took a split second to adjust it.

"Acari Drew," Masha snapped, punctuating her words with a flick of her whip. "Get in the ranks."

I jerked my hands back to my sides. The other girls stood two by two, and I joined them, my heart thumping sharply in my chest. A scrappy, heart-faced girl and I merged together to bring up the end of the line. We didn't make eye contact.

"Acari," one of the Initiates ordered. "March."

It was the weirdest thing, but march we did. Without training, without direction, we fell into step as though marching were something hardwired into our reptilian brains.

"Halt," the same Initiate shouted when we reached the end of the hall.

A couple of the girls pitched into each other and were rewarded with a snap of Masha's whip on the backs of their thighs.

The Initiates had stopped us in front of the bathroom and now stood, whispering among themselves. My gaze twitched to them and then quickly back again. The last thing I wanted was accidental eye contact. In their catsuits, they seemed like a cadre of diabolical supermodels.

I tried to measure my breathing and slow my pounding heart.

Why were we standing there in front of the bathroom? What, were they going to let us use the *potty* before our night of hazing?

The group of Initiates split up to surround us. "Get in," a statuesque redhead ordered.

A girl at the front of the line looked dumbfounded, and

Masha cracked her whip onto the white tiled floor. "Yes, Acari. In there. Now."

Oh, God. They *were* taking us into the bathroom. Dread unfurled in my belly as my imagination ran with all the possible hazing that could happen in a *bathroom*. My brain was swamped with images of things cleaned with toothbrushes and heads submerged in toilets.

Of all my wildest imaginings, though, nothing came close to the reality.

"It's a *Hot Party*, girls." The redhead shooed us into the showers, an open space with six nozzles sprouting from antiseptic white tiles. "First one to fall loses."

Fisting my hands at my sides, I shuffled in behind the others. My palms were sweaty. Like everyone else, I'd donned my outdoor gear, including a pair of what I guessed were ski gloves.

Just don't slip. I found a spot at the edge and widened my feet to brace myself. I imagined myself anchored to the tiles. It'd be easy enough not to fall, right?

Wrong.

The Initiates turned on the showers. Full blast, and all the way to hot.

Masha leaned to whisper in my ear. "Happy Hot Party, Acari."

Despite the rising temperature, we all pulled our hoods up over our fleece hats. It was that or get scalded. My brain felt like it was boiling.

Some got it worse than others. I was grateful not to have a spot directly beneath the jets. Regardless of position, everyone shifted from foot to foot, withstanding in stoic silence. The parkas protected our skin, and our boots were sturdy, but there was a small stretch of lower thigh and knee that felt roasted pink.

I could tell by the shifty looks on the other girls' faces that everyone was waiting to see who would fall first. I'm sure I wasn't the only one who feared what the penalty might be.

I'd thought the scalding water was the punishment, but I soon discovered I was mistaken. It was the steam.

After a few minutes, the steam became uncomfortable. After five, it was suffocating. By ten, it was unbearable. It choked me. A white haze of vapor hung all around, pressing down on my chest. Burning my lungs. Making me woozy. I longed for a gulp of cold, fresh air.

I sensed rustling. Girls shifted. They were parting to let Lilac pass. She had me in her sights.

I could see it in her eyes. She wanted a single room as badly as I did.

The girl with the heart-shaped face stood just in front of me. A swatch of her auburn hair was soaked a burnt sienna color and plastered to her cheek. She looked disoriented.

Heart Face didn't step aside quickly enough, and Lilac shouldered past her. The girl started to tumble forward, and I instinctively caught her by the elbow to steady her. Our eyes met for a flicker of a second. She looked stunned and almost uneasy at my touch. I flinched my hand back.

Saving her had been instinctual. But, really, if I'd been thinking strategically, I could've let her fall. A tiny, shameful part of me wondered if maybe I should have.

"Sleepy?" Lilac's perky voice chimed in my ear, jerking me back to myself.

It took me a moment to register her point. My skin felt parboiled, and my brain muzzy and slow. I hadn't snagged the few hours' sleep that the other girls had managed. Nor had I slept on the flight out here. Which meant I'd gone for God knew how many hours without rest.

But Lilac was in the same boat.

"No, not *Sleepy*." I mustered a broad grin, pretending the air I breathed didn't feel like wet fire. I pulled my shoulders back, imagining brisk mountain breezes and a big chug of ice water. I'd have one the moment I got out. It would spread cool tendrils through my belly. The glass would be cold in my hand. I'd drink so much and so fast, it'd dribble down my chin. "I'm *Happy*, which must make you *Dopey*."

"You have *no* idea what you've started." Lilac spun away from me, hard. Her pack smacked me across the jaw.

I stumbled—a sideways *hop-hop* on my right foot. The tile was slick under the rubber tread of my boots. I slipped.

My arms clawed the air like slow-motion pinwheels. I heard the dead-weight *oof* of my body slamming to the floor, the sick slap of my head against the tile. The weight of the kit bag walloped the air from my lungs.

A whistle blew.

I'd lost.

I lay there trying to catch my breath. I heard eager stomps rushing out. Suddenly the air seemed more open. I was vaguely aware that the stinging spray of the shower had stopped.

Rough hands gripped under my arms, pulling me to standing. What was my punishment? I braced myself. Whatever it was couldn't be worse than the steam.

But then I heard Masha speak. "Need some fresh air, Acari?"

I forced myself to look at her. I knew I should nod, but wasn't sure if I managed more than a twitch of my head.

"Oh, poor little Acari," someone crooned. Initiates

surrounded me. "Let's get these hot clothes off you." Hands pulled off my kit bag, unzipped my parka, removed my hat, my gloves.

The hands grew rougher, tugging the wool sweater over my head. It caught on my chin, tore over my ears. "It's time for your cooldown."

CHAPTER TWELVE

"Outside?" I asked, suppressing a shiver. The Initiates had led me to the ground-floor foyer, where I stood, stripped to my underwear. I'd hurt my ribs in the fall, and my trembling intensified the pain.

Along the hallway, a few doors were cracked open, and I spied wary eyes witnessing my torture from the safety of the dorm rooms. Even though we'd all been issued the same ugly, regulation beige bra and granny panties, the shame of it burned my cheeks.

It was the only thing that burned, though. My teeth had begun to chatter and I was already nostalgic for all that heat. The front door was open, and I contemplated the black and gray swirl of starlit snow outside. Why had I found the Hot Party uncomfortable? The concept was unthinkable now.

"What's the punishment?" I huddled into myself, chafing my arms in vain. "Parading around half naked, or is it the pneumonia I'm contracting?"

"Neither." Someone shoved me, and I lurched forward, catching myself before I fell. "It's the running."

"And you just earned yourself an extra lap, smart-ass." I thought I recognized the redhead's voice.

The ache in my ribs turned to nausea. *Running.* That explained the white Nikes they'd let me put on, dug out from the bottom of my pack.

"*Four* laps around the quad," Masha said. "Take every corner."

I nodded, wriggling my toes in the running shoes. The soles were soaked and squeaky from the showers, but despite it, I was pathetically grateful. I wouldn't put it past these girls to make me run *barefoot* in the snow.

"Every corner—*no matter how dark*," another Initiate ordered. I felt another push.

Masha leaned close, purring in my ear. "We're watching."

A survival instinct clicked to life in the recesses of my brain. I bounded forward, springing out the door, determined not to feel the final shove I knew would come.

The night air seared my lungs. I told myself it couldn't be *that* cold—the snowfall had actually brought the temperature up to what I estimated was mid-forties. If I just kept moving and got this over with, the weather wouldn't kill me.

Those girls, *they* could kill me. This wouldn't.

But I wasn't athletic. I'd never run a mile in my life, and I raced too quickly down the path. I wasn't even halfway to my first corner and already my throat ached with each breath. A cramp seized the side of my belly, a claw with icy talons.

I forced myself to slow my pace, but the cold made my gait awkward, and my legs thudded along like frozen stumps. I was chilled to the core, my flesh puckered into tight goose bumps.

As I pumped my legs, my arms, I became aware of strange things—the cold slab of flesh that was my butt, the way the skin of my legs felt so cold, it burned.

I approached the first curve and made sure to stick to the far outer edge, even though a giant, gnarled hedge reached over the path like it might curl down and swallow me. The Initiates had scared me with thoughts of bogeymen hiding in the dark.

Not bogeymen. Vampires, I corrected myself. It was *vampires* who hid in the night, waiting to grab me. I was still getting used to the thought.

But the Initiates had made a mistake by inadvertently warning me. I'd been straining to see amid the eerie silhouettes of branches, expecting a monster, and so wasn't surprised when I saw him.

At first I thought it was a statue. Standing still as death, with a lifeless gray complexion to match. Ambient moonlight shimmered on his face, making it gleam.

He might have been carved from stone but for the glow of his eyes. They weren't red, like in the movies. Just a shimmering, steely glint. A predator waiting, watching in the night.

It wasn't the headmaster, either. This one had black hair and black clothing that merged with the shadows. In his pallid skin, I saw that he wasn't truly alive. But his eyes told me neither was he truly dead.

Those undead eyes tracked me. They seemed to glimmer into a grin as I neared. I told myself it was my imagination.

My heart exploded into high gear, but I forced myself to keep my pace. Forced my arms and legs to pump neither faster nor slower.

He hid in the shadows, but something told me he wouldn't

do anything. Something told me *these* vampires craved an audience. I assured myself of this as I ran toward him, into the blackness of the hedgerow.

A whisper echoed in the leaves. The sound didn't originate in a single spot; rather, it cloaked me from all around, a hiss that felt as ancient as the land. "Run."

Adrenaline dumped into my veins. I tasted it, sour on my tongue. But with it came fury. Torture and hazing and monsters lurking in the dark. I'd hoped for some sort of special college for geniuses, but this macabre mockery of a school? *This* was definitely not what I'd signed up for.

I relished my anger. Let it bloom into determination.

Time compressed.

I didn't see or hear the vampire again. My thoughts distilled to two single, bright lights. *Vengeance. Freedom.* I'd make Lilac suffer, and then I'd get out.

Ronan had said the only way to get off the island was to succeed. I'd wanted to stay under the radar. I'd thought I could quietly do well and then find a way to escape. But Lilac had screwed that up for me. Now all the catsuits knew who I was. I was no longer anonymous—I was the girl who'd fallen in the shower.

By my third lap, my feet had cut an irregular band of black footprints through the melting snow. The rhythmic *thump-thump* of my pace mesmerized me. The path was slushy and muddy and squished with each stride. All I knew were these sounds. All I perceived was the up-and-down pounding of my breasts. The up-and-down of my frozen cheeks as each step threatened to jostle the flesh free from my skull. The air still stung my lungs, but I forced my focus instead on the white cloud of each exhale.

Thump-thump. Vengeance. Thump-thump. Freedom.

I knew three things: I was cold. This was Lilac's fault. Lilac would pay.

When I reached the dorm at the end of my final lap, my Proctor Amanda was standing outside, waiting. She was a vision, standing still and tall in a fitted coat. She'd donned her hood, and it haloed her face with a cloud of fur. Her dark skin was luminous in the watery moonlight.

I was watching her, not my step, and I slipped, catching myself with a hand to the ground before I toppled all the way.

"Careful." She chuckled. "The snow's a bit dodgy."

"Yeah." I stood and dusted myself off. My hands ached to the bones with cold—I felt they might shatter from it. "I got that."

"Care for a pointer, dolly, before you head back in?"

The moment I stopped running, I'd started to tremble. My face was a frozen mask, too cold to speak, so I just nodded jerkily, my curiosity piqued.

"Them's wolves, not girls. You let this stand, and *boo*, Lilac's the boss of your little pack."

Lilac had to pay—Amanda didn't need to tell *me* twice. But how?

By now, I was shivering violently, my brain was addled, and I could only stare dumbly in reply.

"And he tells me *you're* the clever one? Listen," she said simply, as though she had to explain something to a particularly dim child. "Lilac wins this round, you're as good as snuffed. Maybe not today, maybe not tomorrow. But our girls are wolves, and Acari who smell weak don't last long." She kicked at the snow, fighting a smile. "Now, then . . . Your roommate's like a babe asleep in her bed. And have you felt how *cold* the snow is?"

I looked at her like she was insane. I was practically hypothermic, and she was asking me if I knew how cold the snow was. "N-no, I'm finding it quite balmy, actually."

"Drew," she scolded sharply.

I cursed myself. She may be my Proctor, but she was still an Initiate.

"Drew," she said again, more kindly. "I promised Ronan I'd help you, but I can't paint you a picture."

She told Ronan she'd help me? Had he asked her to look out for me? If he and Amanda were that close, were they, like, *that* close?

I forced myself to focus on the matter at hand. "A picture," I repeated.

"You might . . . say . . . bring our Lilac a memento." She looked meaningfully at the snow. "Let her know you was thinking of her." Her *thinking* sounded like *finkin'*.

Finally I got her gist.

"Whatever you do, make it fast," she said. "You need to get inside before you catch your death."

"B-beats evisceration," I muttered. My cheeks were so frozen, I could barely form the words.

She swung on me. "For fook's sake!" she whispered in an angry hiss, sweeping her eyes left and right. "Don't you ever let anyone hear you say that, or you'll wake belly-up under the stones."

I gaped.

"That's more like it. Now, keep your trap shut and start acting as clever as they say you are." She began to walk away. "Cheers, dolly. Go get some sleep."

But I didn't. Not right away. Even though my body was

quaking uncontrollably, even though I'd lost feeling in my fingers, I bent to gather snow. I scooped it into a huge mound, carrying it in my arms. It seized my aching joints with a burning cold. But the thought of Lilac asleep in her warm bed numbed the pain.

My legs thudding clumsily under me, I staggered back into the dorm. The blast of heat sent relieved tears streaming down my cheeks. I made it up to our room. Though soaked and shivering, I bypassed my bed. I didn't grab my blanket, my towel, my coat.

I went straight for Lilac.

She was sleeping soundly, her lips parted, hands pressed, palms together, under her cheek as though in prayer. Her shining hair swept behind her on the pillow, gleaming and perfect, even in sleep.

She was vulnerable, and I stood for a moment, savoring the power of it. I felt creepy, like an intruder, hovering there, staring.

But then I smiled. And I dumped the mound of snow in the crook between those peacefully bent arms and that long, pale neck.

Lilac's shriek was piercing enough to shatter glass.

"What the—?" She sprang from her bed, hopping free from her tangle of blankets. "Fucking snow! This *fucking* place." Panting and screaming, she frantically brushed snow and ice from her body. "What the fuck? Who the—?"

She spun on me. "You! I'm gonna kill you." She jabbed her finger toward me, her eyes looking as if they might bug from her head. She was like a madwoman, the front of her hair soaked and hanging in limp strands around her face. The neck of her flannel nightgown was plastered to her. "I'll get you for this, Charity. Oh, I will get you. It's *on*."

But I found it hard to care about her threats when I was about to freeze to death. My body was wracked with tremors now, bones locked and muscles spasming from the cold. I'd despised the showers earlier, had sworn never to stand under hot water again. Now I couldn't get there fast enough.

I turned and stumbled to the washroom. Lilac's shrieks followed me down the hallway.

A few girls peeked from their doors, questions in their sleepy eyes. "What happened to *her*?" one asked me.

I shrugged. "I must've tracked in some snow."

I BOLTED UP IN BED, heart pounding. I clutched my blanket to my neck, expecting to find last night's vampire looming over me. His silver eyes had glinted through the night, watching me from my dreams.

But the only monster in the room was Lilac. She sat on the edge of her bed, brushing her hair methodically, *staring* at me. She looked all dead-eyed, like some sort of maniacal doll you might find in a horror movie. It gave me the creeps.

I turned away and didn't glance back, managing to get dressed and ready without looking at her again. I was aware of her, though. Of her movements, her breathing, her location and distance from me. I'd need to watch my back every moment from now on.

Despite functioning on only a couple hours' sleep—and those fraught with nightmares—I felt remarkably clearheaded. I had a plan. Survive, excel, escape.

I was lacing up my boots when I heard a rustling outside our room. Lilac and I both froze. Two envelopes slid under the door, each bearing a name in elaborate script.

My roomie sprang up first and, with a look of disgust, tossed me my envelope.

She opened hers right away, but I sat on the edge of the bed, contemplating mine. The paper was yellowed, like parchment.

"Aren't you going to open it?" she taunted.

Not with you watching. "Later."

She was using hers as a fan. "Are you *afraid*, Charity?"

Frankly, I was. That we'd both gotten one made me wary. Did someone find out about my stunt with the snow? Was I in trouble?

"It's just your class schedule. Freak." She flounced out the door, slamming it behind her.

I jumped from the bed, shoving the envelope in my pocket. I'd been desperate for a moment alone so I could hide my iPod and photo in a safer place. I had no choice—the Initiates had made it clear that I could be disrobed and hazed at any moment.

I'd emptied most of my kit bag in the wee hours. Though many of my clothes were still strewn about the room to dry, I'd tucked the Japanese box safely in the bottom drawer of my dresser.

I retrieved it, taking a moment to touch a reverent finger to the metal throwing stars. I wondered what they could possibly expect me to do with them, but still, they were the coolest things I'd ever seen. I took them out, then carefully pried out the tiny brass tacks that secured the velvet lining to the box. I plucked out a corner of the fabric and slid my treasures underneath before putting it all back together.

The iPod was flat and smooth, and the box made the perfect

camouflage. I just hoped the odd weight wouldn't betray my hiding place, should my roommate get curious.

A gong rang. It was a beautiful sound, heavy and clear, like something you'd hear in a Tibetan monastery. It resonated in my belly, and for a flicker of a moment, I felt I was a part of some bigger thing. The call to breakfast, I realized.

Which meant I was running late.

I swooped out the door. The morning was clear, and the snow melting fast. Only scattered patches remained, whitish gray in the center of the quad.

Jogging down the path, I felt unburdened, empowered. It was like I knew a secret. I'd braved this path in the darkness. I'd seen one of its monsters.

I bounded up the steps to the dining hall and pulled open the heavy oak door, anticipating the delicious blast of heat. I stepped inside, and the low hum of chatter enveloped me. I smelled fried foods and coffee.

And then I gasped. All thoughts of Lilac, last night, and that envelope were replaced by one much more pressing development.

There were *boys* here.

CHAPTER THIRTEEN

———◆———

"There are *boys* here?" Plopping down next to Amanda, I set my tray on the table a little too hard, and black coffee sloshed over the lip of my mug.

"As you see." She smiled coyly, concentrating on stirring her yogurt. Proctors dined with their Acari, and I was determined to get as much information out of mine as I could.

Unfortunately, the arrangement meant I also had to sit near Lilac. The heart-faced girl was there, too, staring into a bowl of oatmeal, as was a posse of girls I wouldn't want to meet in a dark alley.

Amanda eyed the boys' table, taking a spoonful of yogurt. "I was just explaining to the other girls. They're Trainees."

"I thought only girls could be Watchers."

"Not Watchers. Vamps in training, like."

"In *training*?" I stole another look. I'd thought the girls were attractive, but right there, at the far table, scarfing down plates of scrambled eggs and sausage, was like a retreat for wayward soccer stars. Some of them looked a little dim, posturing like jocks before the big game, but I knew not to underestimate anybody who managed to end up here.

If all vampires had to do was find a guy, train him, and *boom*, instant undead, just how many were there? The possibilities were chilling. "I thought vampires were ancient. But they can just . . . *make* new ones?"

"Many *are* ancient. But otherwise, yeah, they're creating new vampires all the time. It takes years, though, and few Trainees survive." She took another bite. Her tone of voice was casual, like she was talking about training a new batch of Wal-Mart employees. "And you dollies best learn the ground rules. You'll have some classes with the boys. You can sit together for meals. But there's no seeing each other after curfew."

"Where do they sleep?" the heart-faced girl asked. The sound of her voice startled me. With her quiet manner, wide eyes, and faint dusting of pale brown freckles across the bridge of her nose, she seemed unassuming—wholesome, even. I wondered what her deal was.

"The boys stay in the castle on the hill." Amanda scraped the last of her yogurt from the bottom. "Which, by the way, is strictly off-limits for you dollies."

That was fine with me—that place had given me the creeps. But sharing classes and meals? I looked from the boys' table back to the girls around me. Already everyone was puffing and preening like a bunch of peacocks during mating season.

Teen hormones plus a few hot guys equals Barbie bloodbath.

In other words, high school. *All over again.*

I stabbed a bit of egg with my fork. My food had gone cold while we were talking. I'd lost my appetite, anyway.

"So, we can eat with the guys?" Lilac clutched the edge of the table, looking eager to spring up then and there to join them at breakfast.

"Aye, luvvie, you can."

Lilac pushed from the table, her chair scraping against the timber-plank floor.

Biting back a smile, Amanda glanced across the room. The boys looked as interested in us as we'd been in them. "Seems like you'd be welcome."

Lilac was already sauntering over to meet them. Not to be left behind, a handful of Acari were hot on her heels. The heart-faced girl watched from the end of the table, and I watched her staring silently, weighing everyone. I'd figure out a way to pry about her, too. But it was Lilac who was at the top of my list.

The exodus had left Amanda and me basically alone. I dove in at once. "*Where* did Ronan find that girl?"

"Von Straubing?"

I nodded.

Amanda opened her mouth, hesitated, shut it, and then opened it again. "Jail. Fort Lauderdale. Ran away from some . . . special school in Connecticut and got nabbed for public indecency."

I wondered what *special school* might be code for. The way she'd said it implied anything from the wealthiest of boarding schools to juvie.

She turned to me with a smile. "But that's more than I should've told you." She added under her breath, "I heard her last night, by the way. Howling to wake the dead."

I kept my face unreadable, but inside I cheered. "Yeah, turns out when I came in from my run, I accidentally tracked in *a lot* of snow."

"Oh, dear." Sipping her tea, Amanda suppressed a smile. "I don't suppose it ended up in her bed?"

I nodded. I'd kept the door open when I got home, just in case. I had to make sure the whole floor would hear Lilac's shrieking. I didn't understand the inner workings of mean girls, but it seemed she had a posse already.

"You're bang on for now, Acari Drew. Nicely done." She pushed back her chair, ready to leave.

"Wait. Can I ask a question?"

"Yeah . . . ?" She scooted back in, leaning her elbows on the table. "I'm surprised you haven't asked more."

I looked at the boys' table. They were all good-looking, occupying that long-limbed nether land between boy and man. Would their bodies change? Would they grow long fangs and get pale? "You know all the myths about vampires? Are they true?" My head swam with them. Sleeping during the day. Coffins and stakes. Absent reflections in mirrors. Aversions to garlic, wolfsbane, crosses. I remembered the headmaster—he'd given his speech in daylight. "Like, I thought they could be out only at night."

"You said it yourself. *Myths*." She shrugged. "Look, dolly, much of it is nonsense that's mushroomed through the years. Celebrity gossip, like. They don't sleep in coffins. Don't sleep at all, in fact." She paused for a moment, considering. "Though they do like to laze a bit after feeding." She saw my question forming and answered it. "Yes, they drink blood. As we drink theirs."

"Is that what we had on the plane?" I shuddered.

"It makes you stronger." Her tone was flat, like she wouldn't tolerate any teenage hand-wringing on the topic. "If you want to survive, you'll drink and not question."

I tried to work it all out in my head. I thought back to the plane—the stuff *had* made me feel stronger, braver, more alive.

Sighing, she pushed her plate away and stretched back in her chair. "But, as with gossip, some of it bears a bit of truth, or near to it. Like, they can't see well in bright light." She looked to a bank of windows along the far wall and to the slate gray day beyond. "It's why we live on *this* sodding isle," she grumbled. "You'll see. We've got two times of day: dim and dark."

"Are they immortal? Can they"—I lowered my voice to a whisper—"can they be killed?"

"A stake through the heart does 'em in—that bit's true enough." She took another sip of tea, scowling at how it'd gone cold. "But otherwise, yeah, they live on and on. Don't know about you, but that's the bit that'd drive *me* batty."

"When will I see other vampires?" I thought of the monster in the moonlight. He'd seemed otherworldly, and I could believe he was a creature immune to death. Were they all like that? It was hard to imagine the boys at the far table ever transforming into such still and ethereal beings. "How will I know someone's Vampire? Can you just . . . tell?"

"Oho." She chuckled. "You can bloody well tell. And you'll see other vamps soon enough." She looked to the front door and gave a nod. "But the interrogation's over. It's time for your first day of school."

I followed her line of sight, and my chest tightened. *Ronan.* He strode toward us, looking classically handsome. His black hair was combed back and looked slightly damp, like he'd just gotten out of the shower. He'd shaved, revealing the cleft in that strong chin. *Jerk.*

My eyes went to the boys' table and back again. The vampire Trainees all of a sudden seemed like a bunch of kids. Cute, sure, but just boys. While Ronan was a *man.*

And to him, I probably seemed as young and awkward as that table full of teenage boys. Young, awkward, and apparently gullible. I cringed.

He stopped to say a few words to each Proctor he passed. His manner was easy and confident. He wore jeans and a forest green sweater that was snug on his chest and arms. In just his T-shirt, I hadn't realized he had such broad shoulders. My cheeks flamed hot. That green would do killer things to the color of his eyes.

He turned to walk toward us. I reminded myself that he and Amanda were close. That it'd be *her* he was coming to see.

Most important, I had to remember the only reason I was here was because he'd *tricked* me. How could I ever trust someone who had the power to persuade me with just the touch of his hand?

I looked nervously at my breakfast. I wasn't finished, but there was no way I could swallow anything now. I pushed the tray away.

"You must drink." Amanda shoved the tray back in front of me. I stared at that thick, dark liquid. The thought of it should've turned my stomach, but, oddly, it didn't.

With a silent nod, I tossed the whole glass down in a few gulps. For some reason, I didn't want Ronan to watch me drink it.

Turning my back to him, I wiped my mouth, watching the

breakfast crowd disperse. Many Acari had taken their course schedules from their envelopes. Proctors milled around, talking to them, pointing, explaining, directing.

I still hadn't opened *my* envelope yet. I'd planned to, over breakfast, but I'd shoved it in my pocket and hadn't thought about it again since seeing all those boys in the dining hall.

"Your girls will need help finding their first class," Ronan told Amanda. He stood over me. I felt his presence like a solar eclipse.

"Oh, I've done this a time or two before." There was a smile in Amanda's tone.

I wondered how many years she'd been there. How many years were girls stuck on this island before they graduated off? I filed my questions away for another day. I didn't trust my voice at the moment, anyway.

Ronan still stood there. I stared at my hands, trying to breathe normally. I was angry with him, so why did I also feel so nervous?

"Annelise?"

Oh, God, the way he says that. Was my reaction to him real, or was he even now using some sort of spellbinding juju? I looked up, mortified to feel my face so hot. "Yeah, hi."

"Time for class." The green sweater *did* do crazy things to his eyes, making them look deep and vibrant and soulful. That gaze searched mine—or at least I imagined it did. Was it fraught with meaning, looking for answers? Trying to hypnotize me into doing something horrible? Or was he just impatiently waiting for the silly Acari to say something? He chuckled into the silence, and I wanted to disappear under the table. "You have looked at your class list, aye?"

"Um, no . . ." I fumbled in my coat pocket and pulled out the envelope.

"Most girls get four classes and a private study," Amanda said.

I brightened. "A private study?" My whole life, I'd longed to do a private study. My mind raced, thinking of all the possibilities. Theoretical mathematics. Deconstructionist philosophy. Or maybe it was a private tutorial having something to do with that Viking mythology book. I'd dabbled in a few Germanic languages, but would love to try Old Norse.

I tore it open. The paper looked expensive, like yellowed parchment with unfinished edges. What, did they think I was going to save it in my scrapbook or something?

I had to read and reread my schedule a few times for the full and truly effed-upness of it all to sink in. Phenomena class? Decorum? Combat? *Freaking* fitness? It was one part Baroque atelier, one part YMCA.

But it was the last item on the list that made me want to hurl. My private study. It was *swimming*.

"Swimming?" My voice cracked. The notion had taken a moment to register. It'd been the last thing I'd expected to face.

"Aye, that's your private study," Ronan said in a tone that brooked no disagreement.

Amanda stood and put on her coat. She was chuckling.

"But I don't swim."

"You do now." He crossed his arms in front of that broad chest. "And I'm your teacher."

CHAPTER FOURTEEN

"But, seriously." I jogged to catch up to Ronan on his way out of the dining hall. "I *can't* swim."

Just the thought of it was enough to freak me out. I despised it. Despised the sensation of being submerged, of water going up my nose and gurgling in my ears. It was just *wrong*.

To top it all off, *Ronan* was my teacher. *Ronan* would be the one sitting front and center at my carnival of lameness, ineptitude, and irrational fears. Clearly, the fates did not believe in the personal dignity of Annelise Drew.

Not to mention, this did nothing for my plan. How was I to excel and escape if I had to swim? I would never excel at swimming. "What happens if I can't learn?"

"You will." He held the door open for me.

I pulled on my cap and zipped up my coat, following him down the stairs, my mind racing. Surely there were Watchers out there who weren't great in the water. We were training to be emissaries for vampires, not mermen. "But if I don't, will I still be able to progress to the next level? I don't care how much you try to hypnotize me—I *really* can't swim."

"That's why you're in a private study. And I didn't hypnotize you." With a sigh, he stopped and faced me. "Now it's time for you to get to your first class. Do you know how to get to the science building?"

I stared at him. "I'm *so* not done discussing this whole swim thing."

He turned onto the path, ignoring my comment. "Never mind. I'm going that way. I'll show you."

"But wait." The path appeared to head *away* from the buildings, so I turned away from him and stepped onto the quad instead. The snow had transformed into shoals of dingy gray ice atop mucky gray gravel, and it crunched underfoot. "Isn't it this way?"

"Stop," he said abruptly. "Acari aren't allowed to stray from the path."

I gaped in disbelief. "You're kidding, right? Is that supposed to be a metaphor? Some sort of *Karate Kid*, wax-on, wax-off thing?"

He gave me that peeved quit-your-joking look he sometimes got.

Shoulders slumping, I reined in the sarcasm and rejoined him. "So, you're saying we have to take *every* corner around the quad, *every* time? Not just for naked midnight hazing runs?"

He gave a brisk nod and strode ahead. "No shortcuts."

"And if an Acari breaks the rule?" Catching up to him, I saw the expression on his face and quit that line of questioning right there. "Okay, I got it. I won't break the rules. But you've got to help me at least drop swim class."

Ronan raised his brows. "Have you learned how to swim in the past twenty-four hours?"

"No." *Duh.*

"Do you wish to drown during your stay on the isle?"

"Of course not. I—"

"Then you have no choice, Drew. There is no *dropping classes*. There is no *choice*. You do as you're told, and you survive. You *will* learn to swim. And, moreover, you will be the best."

Ronan had no idea what he was talking about. Surely I'd be able to fudge my way out of it. Because I not only couldn't swim, I *wouldn't* swim. I was terrified of choking, of drowning. Just the thought of it clenched my chest with panic.

I had to change the subject. I fished my course list back out of my pocket and shook it at him. "And what's with these other classes? Come on, I have to take a class in *decorum*?"

The word had come out louder than I'd intended. By Ronan's exasperated headshake, I could tell the irony wasn't lost on him.

"You may want to keep it down," he muttered, looking around. I'd caught the attention of one of the Initiates, and he gave her a nod. His friendly expression struck me as forced, but it seemed to satisfy her.

I toed a rock free from the path, kicking it a few steps ahead of me. "Decorum," I grumbled. "I'd thought you were putting me in some sort of gifted-and-talented program, and instead you're making me take a class in *manners*?"

"*I'm* not making you do anything. It's required of all Acari. The vampires find modern girls to be . . . coarse." He shrugged. "You should be pleased I got you out of piano."

"Piano would've been cool."

"So you'd think."

"And what's with combat? Are they sending me to war?" I tossed off a cynical laugh, but his curious stare silenced me. "Wait. They're not sending me to war or anything, right?"

"No wars per se." He was trying to assure me, I think. It wasn't working. "But you must learn to fight. Hand-to-hand sparring. Other necessary tactics."

"Fighting?" I felt the cold, prickly sensation of blood draining from my head. I'd been hit enough times in my life already— I'd hoped to put the whole getting-pummeled thing behind me. "You're going to make me fight? I can't fight."

"We'll train you."

I pulled the black knit cap from my head and raked my fingers through my hair. "Like, fight with the other girls? I thought we were training to be attachés."

"You'll be that and more. You must be ready for anything, at all times."

I clenched my hands, feeling a familiar dread wash over me. Needing to be *ready for anything* sounded a bit too much like my childhood. "But swimming? *Combat?* I can't do all that stuff. And I definitely can't fight the other girls."

He touched my shoulder. "You can and you will."

The contact was light and quick, but it was enough to halt my growing hysteria. I calmed a little, noticing I'd accidentally crumpled my schedule.

And then my body seized. I flinched my shoulder away from him. I didn't trust him or his supernatural touches. "Don't touch me."

He actually managed to seem confused and innocent for

a moment. *Bravo, Ronan.* Then he said, "You must learn to trust me."

We were approaching the group of buildings, and Ronan slowed his pace. "It's not all academics on this isle. Combat tactics, physical prowess—those elements are integral to success. This system is built to train girls just like you. Trust me on this, if nothing else. You can do it."

I tugged the cap back onto my head. I thought it might be a little askew, but I didn't particularly care at the moment. "Trust you? You're the one who got me into this mess in the first place."

He stopped on the path, looking at me thoughtfully. "Annelise, the swimming aside, I think you might be surprised at how much you enjoy your studies."

I scowled, remembering the scene in the dining hall. I wasn't exactly looking forward to witnessing my peers salivating over one another. "So, *boys* will be in the classes?" They'd struck me as a bunch of jocks, the lot of them. I wondered if they were as meat-headed as they looked.

"Just decorum and phenomena. Male Trainees have a different physical-education program."

"I'll bet." It seemed obvious that stalking potential victims, catching them, and then drinking their blood required a completely different skill set.

I shivered. Did the vampires in training know what was ahead of them? How did *they* feel about this whole messed-up scene?

I guessed I could ask one of them. My first class was phenomena, which Ronan had said was coed. I frowned. "What does one study in phenomena, anyway?"

"You'll find out soon enough. You're here." Ronan nodded

toward a stout, two-story stone building. It looked like a place you'd see on any college campus in the Northeast.

"Your only other class today is fitness." He pointed back the way we came, toward a building whose stark, rounded, and corrugated roof proclaimed it to be Standard-Issue Gymnasium, Circa 1970. "It meets three days a week, after lunch, two o'clock sharp. Combat meets there, too, on alternate days."

I *loathed* working out, and now I had five days a week of it? I turned my back to the gym. *One panic attack at a time.*

I nodded a wordless good-bye to Ronan. Hopefully he took my silent farewell for cool nonchalance, and didn't clue in to the fact that I was about to completely lose it.

Clutching my regulation black messenger bag to my side, I warily walked in for phenomena class.

Whatever *that* was. Something stupidly archaic and redundant, I was sure.

The blast of heat did nothing to ease the tightness in my chest. Old-fashioned radiators lined the hallway, and each one I passed was like walking through a pool of hot air. I followed the sounds of adolescent chatter coming from the end of the hall. The pinging and knocking of the ancient heaters tracked my progress.

I passed a few closed doors. They were the old kind, with big rectangles of wavy glass on the top half. The lights were off, and I thought they must be empty offices.

Something that looked like a library took up almost the whole other side of the hallway. I wished I had the time—or the guts—to peek in. If there was one thing I was looking forward to in this whole hot mess, it was accessing the old knowledge— and old books—of a bunch of ancient vampires.

I stopped outside the last door, my heart in my throat. The chatter was loud, and sure enough, it was girls *and* boys.

I was determined to take a seat at the very back. It was only a matter of time before I was identified as a nerdbot worthy of heckling. Until then, I'd lie low and do my work. Just like I'd done in Florida. Get in; get out.

Taking a deep breath, I entered. I swept my eyes across the classroom. Far from my fantasy of a genius academy, this was shaping up to be some sort of training facility for truants and delinquents.

And I'd bet *they* could all swim.

I scanned the seats, determined not to panic. What had I been thinking? *Of course* the back row was already taken. So much for part one of my plan.

First-day-of-school seat selection always felt so rife with meaning. Was one cool enough for the very back? Overeager front-row material, perhaps? Or was it to be the mediocre middle?

Avoiding all eye contact, I took the first seat I saw that had empty spots on either side. Unfortunately, it was in the very front.

I braced myself. It was only a matter of time now. I wondered if and when miscellaneous crap would begin to clip the back of my head, just as it had every day, in every class, in my dear old alma mater.

I was determined to stay focused. I needed to be stellar in my academic classes. Especially seeing as I was going to bomb swimming.

I unpacked my notebook very slowly. I imagined myself invisible.

A large body slid into the seat next to mine. Not *large*-large, but tall-large. My peripheral vision estimated an even six-feet, plus or minus. Black hair. I caught a glimpse of the gray sweater and black denim of the boys' uniform.

I slowly pulled a pen from my bag. Carefully opened my notebook to the first page, smoothing it flat. I was invisible, *and* very busy.

"Hey, Blondie. You're not one of *them*, are you?"

The body came with a voice, and it was addressing *me*.

CHAPTER FIFTEEN

I sat frozen. The jig was up. So much for flying below the radar. By *one of them*, the boy had surely meant "total impostor." Or "geek loser," maybe. Either way, it was only a matter of time before my identity as Drew the Dork was uncovered.

Here goes. "One of what?" Taking in a steadying breath, I looked up.

A surprisingly kind face met mine. He was also startlingly attractive. If I imagined a Japanese pop star, it'd be this guy. His features were chiseled and almost perfectly proportionate. His black hair was artfully tousled by a cut that I'd wager had cost him a bundle. A pair of black eyes and furrowed black brows seemed concerned with my response.

"One of *them*."

As if on cue, a girl's voice trilled from behind us, "What is phena . . . phenoh . . . phenomenals, anyway?"

Then I actually giggled.

Heat immediately flamed my cheeks. *What am I doing?* I put on my nonchalant, I-don't-care-about-you face. "Oh, *them.* No, definitely not."

There. Conversation concluded. I looked back down, getting ready to write my name very carefully in the top corner of my notebook.

Only he spoke again. "My name's Yasuo."

Social niceties didn't come easily to me. I could reel off the name of every American president, in chronological order, but, believe it or not, an ordinary exchange like this required my concentration. "I'm Drew," I said stiffly.

I felt Lilac enter the room. I looked up and there she was, the whole tall, honeyed length of her. I was in her sights, and she was slinking right toward me. I numbed myself, readying for the inevitable barb.

Shuffling his feet under his chair, Yasuo leaned, elbows forward, on his desk. Was he trying to look cool? Did he read the malice in von Slutling's eyes? Because here was his moment to throw me on the fire.

"Hey, Charity." She raked her eyes over Yasuo. "How cute. I see you made a little friend."

She'd lobbed him a softball. All he needed to do was sacrifice me and he'd earn the mother lode of popular points. I braced for it.

But Yasuo didn't say anything. It amazed me. He didn't smile, didn't look at her, didn't acknowledge Lilac in the slightest.

She gave a lilting laugh that made my flesh crawl. "Oh, that's right. The only way a boy will deal with *you* is if he doesn't speak English."

Yasuo sneered. "I'm from L.A., girl." He turned to me and said in a stage whisper, "That's so cool they mainstream the special kids here."

I bit my cheek to keep a laugh from exploding out. My shredded faith in humanity was momentarily restored.

Lilac narrowed her eyes. "What*ever*."

She swung away from us, and I had to duck to avoid getting clipped by her bag. It appeared our Lilac had a thing for wielding her accessories as weapons.

Yasuo and I cut looks over our shoulders, watching as she found a seat. Something had opened up in the back row. Go figure.

Yasuo turned back around, slouching over his desk. "Does she not get that I'm gonna be a *vampire*?"

I laughed at the joke, but it made me wonder about all the nascent hierarchies. If Watchers answered to vampires, and these boys were training to become them, what did that say about gender relations on our little isle?

"So, what'd you do to get queenie all riled up, anyway?" he asked.

"I was born." Our gazes connected. His eyes were twinkly and dark, and I let myself smile.

The door opened, and the difference between regular school and this crazy vampire island became instantly clear. The teacher walked in, and the room fell utterly silent.

I recognized him at once from the headmaster's talk. He'd been one of the guys who'd helped Ronan clear Mimi's body from the stones. He was cute in a brown, puppy-eyed sort of way. He didn't have the same menace as the headmaster, or as the other vampire I'd spotted in the dark. Was he a Tracer, like Ronan?

"I'm Tracer Judge," he said in an American accent, answering my unspoken question. "And I'm your phenomena teacher."

There was a little explosive giggle in the back. Some idiot girl who couldn't stop herself.

He grew still, pinning her in his sights.

Here we go. I'd seen what happened when these dudes were crossed. I held my breath, waiting for the evisceration.

But Judge surprised me by giving her a kind and knowing smile instead. "I'll bet you're wondering what phenomena is."

I swore I felt the room give a collective exhale.

"Think of it as a fancy word for *science.* Vampires may be an ancient race, but they've kept alive—they've *flourished*—by keeping abreast of modern technological advancements. Computers, forensics, explosives. We'll study all these things."

I forgot the kids behind me. I forgot Lilac and Yasuo. I even forgot about the whole swimming debacle. Tracer Judge had me at *forensics.*

I picked up my pen, poised to transcribe his every word, if necessary. Ronan had been right. I might just like my classes after all. This one, at least.

"We also study sciences of the natural world," he continued, sauntering to the back of the room. He caught students' eyes as he walked. "Anatomy. Physiology. The vampiric process."

It was creepy to consider why prospective vampires needed to study anatomy. But learning the vampiric process? *Cool.*

"Today we'll start with the most basic of skills." Judge opened a cabinet at the back of the room and retrieved a burlap bag.

I was mesmerized, wondering what could possibly be in there. The sack was big and lumpy, and by the way the teacher hefted it around, it seemed heavy. He'd just talked about topics in basic biology—for all I knew, he had a few heads in there.

Judge reached in, grabbed something, and slammed it on one of the jock's desks with a sharp *thud*. The boy flinched but then shot a cocky, dim-eyed grin, informing us that he was still, in fact, cool.

We all craned in our seats to see. My secret hope was that he'd laid down a protractor, and Meathead would be forced to perform a series of geometric calculations for us.

No such luck. But, oddly, when the teacher lifted his hand, what he revealed was almost as good. "Today I'm going to teach you the basics of lock picking."

Yasuo and I gaped at each other, wide-eyed.

"The first locks date from ancient Egypt four thousand years ago. They utilized a wooden pin tumbler that's the basis of technology still in use today."

Judge walked the room, placing a random assortment of items on each student's desk. I spied paper clips, forks, flat bits of metal, scissors, and a variety of locks. Padlocks, dead bolts, doorknobs—you name it.

"You were each given a set of tools in your kit."

"Did you get tools?" I asked Yasuo in a whisper.

"A tool kit works in the best of circumstances," the teacher continued. "But, unfortunately, the circumstances are not always best. Are they?"

Yasuo waited for Judge to reach the far end of the classroom before he whispered back, "Yeah, in a little leather roll."

"Oh. Duh." I smirked. "I'd thought that was, like, a nail kit or something."

We shared a quiet laugh, then felt Judge's eyes on us. I tensed, but the teacher only gave us a smile. Like he, too, felt expansive about all this first-day-of-school lock stuff.

Sitting there whispering with Yasuo, smiling with this teacher who, so far, seemed completely and utterly benign—it all felt so *normal*. I'd never felt normal. I kind of liked it. I was sure it wouldn't last.

"You have a torsion wrench in your kit." Judge made his way to me, where he set a knife, an empty soda can, and a padlock on my desk. "But, the fact is, you can shim most locks with any bit of metal."

I stared at the assortment on my desk in disbelief. It couldn't be that easy. He walked away, and I immediately turned to Yasuo. "A Coke can? Seriously?"

"Well, look around." He nodded to the back of the room.

A few students sat kicked-back and bored, spinning their padlock hinges or idly drumming with strips of metal. They'd been able to pick their locks the moment they'd received them. *Crazy.*

"I should've figured," I muttered. "Don't tell me. Are *you* a lock expert, too?"

Yasuo just waggled his eyebrows suggestively. Looking away, I bit my lips not to laugh. In-class bonding was one thing. But making the teacher's blacklist on the very first day was another matter entirely.

Judge came back to the front of the class. He leaned his hip against his desk, arms crossed casually in front of him. "Before today's class is over, you'll be able to pick your lock using only the materials in front of you. And that's a promise."

Forget swimming. I was going to pick a lock with a soda can and a steak knife? The prospect made me giddy.

I set to slicing open my empty can, actively not thinking about why *this* was a skill I'd ever need to cultivate. Now, if I could only see past the monsters hiding in the dark, beyond the mean girls, the whip-wielding Initiates, and all that blood, I could really get into this place.

CHAPTER SIXTEEN

I stood on the steps of the gym. I could do this. It wasn't even two o'clock on my first day, and already I knew how to shim a padlock, unlock a doorknob without a key, and crack the code on Master combination locks.

I'd even made a friend. After class, Yasuo and I walked to the dining hall and ate lunch together. And the food wasn't that bad—some sort of creamy fish soup that'd looked disgusting but was actually pretty tasty. Granted, Yasuo didn't make me feel all wiggly and agitated like Ronan did, but at least I could trust he wasn't using superhuman powers of persuasion to put thoughts in my head.

After the shock of so many positive events, I figured I could swing gym class.

What did they mean by *fitness*, anyway? I pictured something like an episode of *The Biggest Loser*. Hopping around, doing asinine things with body bands and medicine balls, while people yelled at me about my core.

I jogged up the gym stairs before I could think twice. I sensed these vampires had exquisite taste they'd refined through the centuries, and had envisioned a glossy, high-tech health club. I was sorely mistaken. I entered, and it was how I imagined an old-time boxing gymnasium might look. In Russia.

Damp heat and the smell of stale sweat greeted me. Blue mats were stacked in a tower in the corner, faded ropes hung from the ceiling, and a set of gray high bars loomed ominously along the wall. And, of course, in the very center, was a sparring mat.

I rubbed my forehead, letting my messenger bag slide from my shoulder to hit the floor. "Damn."

"Be careful, Annelise." I knew that voice. It sent every cell in my body standing to instant attention. "The vampires aren't overly fond of profanities."

Crap, damn, dammit to hell. What was *he* doing here?

"Ronan." I turned to face him, feeling ill. Seeing me swim was one thing, but he wasn't really going to witness me floundering around in gym shorts, too, was he?

"It's *Tracer* Ronan now."

The fish soup became a queasy slosh in my belly. I'd thought maybe Ronan and I were becoming less formal with each other, not *more.* He'd asked Amanda to look out for me. He'd seemed sincere when he'd insisted I trust him. Being friends didn't seem out of the realm of possibility. He seemed to care. Kind of.

His attentions had probably just been about seeing the girl he picked succeed. Maybe Tracers got extra brownie points if the Acari they'd recruited were the ones to excel. The thought made me sadder than I had a right to be.

He read the direction of my thoughts. "I'm your teacher now. We must respect protocol."

I looked at the girls gathering along the bleachers. Some had already changed into the navy gym shorts and T-shirts we'd been issued in our kit bags.

Was I missing something? Would I get to skip gym class for our private study? "Wait. Are you here to take me to swim class?"

"Our private study is later. I'm also your fitness teacher." He walked to the bleachers, leaving me there feeling like I might gag.

Then I thought: gym class, swimming . . . Would I get to see *him* in running shorts? Or maybe even in one of those teensy Speedos? The prospect cheered me a bit.

Scooping up my bag, I followed him, eyeing the other girls warily. I spotted Lilac and the scrappy heart-faced girl, plus some other familiar faces, including one of the French girls and someone from my dorm floor.

It struck me that there were a few predictable types on this isle. There were the Lilacs of the world, whose lifetime gym memberships had carved muscle from calves that somehow remained perennially smooth, toned, and tanned. With their perky ponytails, they looked like they might burst into a cheer routine at any moment.

There were also what I liked to call the *juvies*. They were fidgety and restless, like they were ready to bolt at the slightest provocation. Who knew what'd made *them* such hard bodies. Running from the cops, maybe.

And then there were the girls with something to prove.

They had carved biceps and probably enjoyed things like extreme triathlons and raw-egg smoothies, and dreamt of the day they could fight an upstart like me. In a cage.

The girls hailing neither from the U.S. nor the U.K. were a bit harder to pin down, though there were only a handful in that category. There were those two French girls. I'd also seen a few leggy, white-haired creatures, with frost blue eyes to match the ice that surely coursed through their veins. I'd nicknamed them the Valkyries, though there was no way I'd risk getting close enough to eavesdrop on whatever language *they* might be speaking.

There were a couple of oddballs, too, like Heart Face. That was the group I belonged in. No surprise there. I plopped onto the bottom bleacher with a sigh.

Ronan stood frozen, arms crossed at his chest, waiting for everyone to quiet down. I tried not to groan. It was no joke; he really was going to be my teacher.

"For those of you who don't know me, I'm Tracer Ronan."

Damn the little shiver I got at the sound of that husky, Scottish-sounding accent.

I wondered which type Ronan might be. Despite his good looks, he didn't strike me as the sort with a lifetime gym membership and a fondness for racket sports and wheatgrass shooters. Nor did he seem like an ex-con or a barbell-wielding gym rat. Might he be an oddball, too? There was that hot tattoo to consider—not every guy had Proustian ink on his arm.

He was explaining the rules, and I tuned back in, nervous about what I might've missed. "You'll keep a locker here," he was saying. "I expect you to be geared up and ready to go at the start of each class."

Some girl to my right already had her navy gym shirt tucked neatly into her navy gym shorts. Her brown hair was pulled into a bouncy ponytail, and she compulsively smoothed it, looking quite pleased with herself. If there were such a thing as a Step Aerobics Olympics, she looked primed and ready.

"Today's class will be a simple fitness assessment," Ronan said. "We need to see what kind of shape you're in. We'll be gauging things like strength, endurance, balance, and flexibility."

I slumped. Generally, whatever thoughts I gave to my body pertained only to its role as a vehicle for my head. In other words, I was so screwed.

Those frayed mats, the bars and ropes—they all mocked me. I remembered the whole miserable drill from high school. How many sit-ups, push-ups, pull-ups? I sucked at every single one of the ups.

"We'll start today with a fifty-yard dash."

The prospect made me surly. Hadn't I proved my jogging ability already? And if they were grooming us to become sophisticated vampire attachés, what good would climbing a rope do, anyway? I knew for a fact that rope climbing held no practical applications.

Ronan dismissed us to the lockers to get changed.

The only thing I hated more than gym class was *changing* for gym class. I frowned, refusing to meet anyone's eye. Locker rooms horrified me. *Mortified* me. Where else could a girl suffer the torments of her peers while also braving an encyclopedia of fungal infections?

I'd once learned the hard way that sneaking into a bathroom stall to dress was a magnet for harassment. So I resorted to my usual survival drill. Pick a corner locker, face the wall, change as fast as I could.

It wasn't fast enough.

I sensed Lilac's approach. Felt her hovering. Heard the tittering girls who already orbited her like a bunch of dim-witted moons.

Shit. Of course I was naked, but for my bra and granny briefs. My cheeks flamed.

"Oh, Charity! How cute they *were* able to find a training bra for you."

"How cute that they let a bunch of seventh graders in here," I grumbled, not risking turning around to face her. Instead I pulled the plain navy T-shirt over my head as quickly as possible.

"As if," she snapped. "Hey, they gave us razors, you know. You may want to shave before you make the rest of us vomit."

"That's the best you can do?" I stepped into the matching shorts. They were made of the same navy T-shirt material, and the whole outfit hung on me in the most unflattering way imaginable. I tucked in my shirt, hoping to give myself some shape. Plucking at the waist, I feared Lilac was right; if anyone needed a reminder of how small-chested I was, all they needed was to see me in this thing.

I sensed movement but was unable to flinch away in time. There was a quick *whish-whish* sound, and then Lilac's towel rat-tailed the backs of my calves.

It stung, but not as much as the locker room full of laughing girls.

I turned. Lilac's posse was staring me down, with her at the forefront. I wanted to show them all. "You'll regret that."

Lilac stood defiantly, her shoulders back in a way that

showed off how well she filled out *her* uniform. With a flip of her maple hair, she lifted her chin. "Bring it, bitch."

Then it hit me. As much as I wanted to escape, I wanted more to beat *her*. To show up Lilac and her stupid clique.

"Sure thing, von Slutling." This time, I was the one to let my shoulder bump hers as I stormed out.

CHAPTER SEVENTEEN

———✀———

A few weeks passed. Twenty-three days, to be precise. More than five hundred hours in which to get used to the image of Ronan in swim trunks.

And yet there I was, headed to the natatorium (the vamps couldn't just call a pool a pool), girding myself for yet another one of our *private studies.*

I had no choice, of course. Lilac was out for blood, and I'd do whatever it took to beat her. Which meant learning to swim.

I'd thought nothing could be worse than the sensation of water whooshing into my ears, but that'd been before I'd withstood the indignity of dog-paddling to Ronan with only my faded yellow noodle to support me. Serious humiliation time.

But, oddly, after a few weeks of lessons, the sharp spear of panic I knew at the smell of chlorine began to blunt. I still hated to swim, still couldn't swim, still couldn't ever imagine myself a swimmer, but neither did I think each dip would result in my certain and instant death.

I think it was the blood that did it. Drinking vampire life-blood was gradually eroding my inhibitions.

It was making me stronger.

Unfortunately, it wasn't making me any more social. I still kept mostly to myself, not branching out from my friendship with Yasuo, whom I hung with between classes and in our rare free time before curfew. And there was always Ronan.

Always it came back to Ronan. And those damned swim trunks. They had a dangerous way of making me forget he wasn't to be trusted.

I reached the natatorium, slamming my hip as I always did against the long metal bar that opened the door. "Ow!" The door hadn't budged. Rubbing my side, I tried again, this time pushing with my hands, but no luck. Someone had locked it. "What the . . . ?"

I ran my hand over my neck, trying to maintain calm. I had to meet Ronan at the specified time . . . or what? Somehow I doubted they had detention on this island. But how could I make class when the door was locked? I groaned. For all I knew, this was some bizarre new test.

I leaned in to try once more when a burst of voices alerted me. I ducked aside just as the door swung in and a crowd of Initiates bustled out. Immediately I felt their jangly, nervous energy, hearing tension in the subdued murmurs of the usually cocky older girls.

Two steely-eyed Tracers followed, whisking an awkward, canvas-wrapped object from the building. Unless it was some sort of rug—a large, lumpy, heavy rug—I knew it was a body they were disposing of.

I made myself as inconspicuous as possible, watching as a few more Initiates spilled out behind them. One stood out at once, stumbling along, holding another girl for balance. Her white terry-cloth robe hung open, revealing our standard black Speedo one-piece underneath. Something bad had to have happened for an Initiate to appear outside the pool in anything less than her full catsuited glory.

They swept past, and I saw she had a stunned, blank look in her eyes. Specks of pink foam clung at the corners of her blue lips. And I supposed *she* was the lucky one. Goose bumps crawled along my skin.

Ronan trailed the group, speaking in hushed tones to a Tracer in a wet suit, and I caught his eye. He said some last thing to the guy and came toward me.

"What was that about?" I asked at once.

"Underwater training." He kept walking, headed away from the pool, and I followed.

Did that mean our private study was canceled?

My initial burst of excitement paled, though, when I registered his words. Learning to swim was one thing, but I'd eventually be expected to do stuff *underwater*?

"Wait." I stopped in my tracks. I'd thought the noodle float was degrading, but the idea that I might someday face Ronan with my big lips and bug eyes distorted by scuba gear? I almost dreaded that as much as the terrifying prospect of swimming in deep water. "We have to do underwater training? Like scuba diving?"

My heart began to hammer just thinking about having to breathe through some hideous metal apparatus. *No way.* There was *no way* I was ever going to fling myself from a boat, or do one of those backward somersaults off the side, or whatever Navy SEAL nonsense they had in mind for us.

The girl who'd just hobbled out of there looked like death warmed over. Pink foam burbling from one's mouth struck me as a definite red flag. My mind flashed to a morbid vision of *me* with blue lips, looking half drowned.

"No oxygen tanks. You learn to hold your breath." He didn't break his stride, and I had to jog to catch up. "Some free divers are able to stay underwater for nearly twenty minutes."

"Hold my breath?" It came out almost as a shriek, and I tempered my voice. I hoped he'd said such a ridiculous thing for shock value only. "You're joking me, right?"

He shot me that flinty, quit-your-nonsense look, and I knew if Ronan were there with those hypnotic green eyes and that manly-man confident touch, I'd probably find myself jumping into a school of sharks if he asked it of me.

I spied Lilac and her cronies from across the quad. What was I thinking? Ronan's green eyes already *had* coaxed me into a school of sharks.

"It's all about overcoming the instinct of your body with the strength of your mind," he was saying, clueless to the direction my thoughts had taken.

I adjusted my gym bag on my shoulder. *Overcoming, instincts, strength* . . . I was momentarily sick of all of it and decided a change of subject was called for. "I take it swim class is canceled. How'd I get so lucky?"

"There's gore in the pool. We'll meet tomorrow."

"Jeez-usss." My stomach flip-flopped. *Gore?* He'd said it so simply, so baldly, like, *Hey, Drew, no pool time today—the pH balance is off, and, oh, there are some bits of small intestine floating about, too.* What could possibly have happened in the pool for there to be gore? And would I eventually be expected to face it? "You don't pull any punches."

He gave me another look, but this time the set of his jaw had eased, softening his expression ever so much. "Aye, I don't pull my punches, Annelise. It's best you learn right away that this island plays for keeps. It'd be a shame to lose you so early in the program."

I stopped in my tracks. "*A shame?* It'd be a *shame* to lose me? It'd be a total, freaking, catastrophically shattering *tragedy* is what it'd be."

He looked at me for a slow moment, then with the slightest of smiles, gave me a wink. "Aye."

Then I knew. I'd heard it in that husky accent of his. He would feel the loss. If something happened to me, it *would* affect him. A warm shiver rippled through my belly.

Perhaps I could learn to trust him after all.

Though the realization made things a little easier, nothing could erase that horrific word echoing in the back of my mind. *Gore. Ugh.*

We went our separate ways, and I headed back to the dorm with much to think about.

But then my ears perked at the sound of shouting. If I hadn't seen the source of the noise in the distance, I'd have thought some sort of vampire apocalypse had begun. But it was just them. *The boys.* And they were in the middle of the quad, tossing a football.

Apparently, not even discovering an island ruled by

vampires could stop a bunch of guys from wanting an excuse to run around, grunt, and swat one another on the butts. I slowed my pace, glaring at the lot of them. I guess *they* were allowed to stray from the damned path.

I felt a spinning in my head like vertigo, so much did the sight of them disturb me. A bunch of boys tossing around a football was so innocent, so all-American. And yet I'd just seen an Initiate's dead body being toted away. For all I knew, these guys were being trained to do whatever the hell it was that'd happened to her today.

I considered walking right by, but the closer I got, the more fascinated I became. We hadn't been on the island long, but already the vampire Trainees had begun to change. We'd been told it took years to progress through the vampiric process, but it was obvious in the strength of their throws, the ferocity of their tackles, and their surprising speed that these weren't the same guys of just a few weeks before.

The blood was affecting them already. And who knew what other rituals or . . . foodstuffs these boys included in their routine? *Shudder.*

But of course, I thought. Of course the blood was changing them. I'd felt its effects myself. Did *I* seem this different already? I made a mental note to study myself in the mirror the next time Lilac left me alone in the room.

I stopped to watch their game, cursing that I couldn't spring onto the grass with them. Not that I'd ever willingly exercise unless a gym class grade depended on it. But the snow had melted, and it would've been nice to feel the soft give of turf under my feet. I never thought I'd miss the hot Florida sun and the smell of freshly mown grass.

Scanning the group, I looked for Yasuo and found him, goofing around with a few of the other Trainees on his team. A shot of warmth reassured me at the sight, making it feel as though the sun had come out.

I sighed. Warmth, yes. But a far cry from the occasional shots of heat I knew at the sight of Ronan.

If only. How easy it'd be if I could feel attracted to my friend instead. Though, considering it, Yasuo would probably never see me like *that*. If the way I'd caught him eyeing the heart-faced girl was any indication, he seemed to have a thing for redheads.

Scuffling and loud grunts caught my attention. "Holy crap," I blurted, hopping back just as a knot of bodies flew toward me.

Guys rolled and cursed at my feet, scrapping and punching. For a moment, I thought it was a real fight, but then they sprang up, cuffed one another on the shoulders, and jogged back to the center of the quad.

I glanced back to Yasuo. He'd spotted me and gave me a wave when he caught my eye. He peeled away from the group to walk toward me.

But then my belly gave a little churn. Because one of his Trainee buds was coming with him. And his eyes were two laser beams, focused right on *me*.

CHAPTER EIGHTEEN

The guys were making a beeline straight for me. My chest got tight. I wanted to see Yas, but I definitely wasn't up to making small talk with one of the meatheads.

And Yas's new buddy sure struck me as having definite meathead potential. Like the other Trainees, this guy was a World Cup–caliber hottie. Unlike many of the others, though, his filled-out body told me he was probably old enough to vote.

And then there was his hair. I didn't generally notice blond guys—being blond myself, it wasn't a condition that'd ever struck me as particularly noteworthy—but his was the color of sand, and he wore it long and scruffy, like he'd just gotten back from championship surfing along some dangerous Australian reef. It made me nervous.

My gaze drifted to his, but he caught me looking and gave me such a jarringly laid-back smile, my eyes had to jump back to safe territory. I wanted to turn and flee to my dorm, but there was no backing away now.

"Yo, Blondie!" Yasuo loped the last few strides to me, giving me a brotherly clap on the arm. "You spying on us?"

"Oh, please." I rolled my eyes. "I have better things to do."

Yas nodded to his buddy. "You met Josh?"

"Josh the Vampire?" The absurdity of it struck me, and I had to stifle a laugh.

But then Josh the Soon-to-Be Vampire chuckled right along with me, and the easiness of it unsettled me. Because I was never easy. My life? Not easy. The scant people whose acquaintance I was beginning to value—Yasuo, Ronan? Not one of them was easy.

But this guy was easy, every muscle in his body relaxed, like he'd just had a massage. "Not Josh the Vampire yet," he said, and damned if the accent weren't actually Australian. "Josh the *Trainee*."

Once more I met his gaze, and this time managed to hold it. He had dirty-blond good looks to match a dirty-good smile. Yes, dirty. There was just enough twinkle in his smiling brown eyes to suggest there might be all manner of naughty-guy impulses rattling around that cute body of his.

I felt a little flush inflame my cheeks. "Where'd they find *you*? The outback?" I'd blurted out my thoughts before I could filter them.

But he only laughed it off—easily, of course. "Harvard pre-med." His voice gave a little upward lilt at the end, sounding something like *Hahhvid premid.*

Great. Another adorable accent. And this one had a pedigree. "What'd you do to end up *here*?"

Yas laughed. "What'd any of us do?"

But Josh only shook his head, answering coyly, "I'd need to know you better to say."

"Mm-hm." I chewed on that, my mind whirring with possibilities. Did he mean he was planning on getting to know me better? Or that he'd done something so horrific, he dared not confess to anyone?

"You hear that, Drew? Harvard." Yasuo shouldered Josh, as if I might have forgotten who we were talking about. These guys . . . they were overly physical, like a pack of gangly wolf pups. "I told him about you, and he wanted to meet the other smarty-pants on the island. Now you've got to stop saying how *all* us guys are meatheads."

Realization dawned. He'd probably just wanted to meet me because I was the weird smart girl. I'd never get away from it.

"No, I guess—" A fresh round of grunting interrupted me. We stopped talking to watch a throng of guys tackle another throng of guys, followed by raucous cheers. The dog pile gradually broke up, and the Trainee who'd been pinned at the bottom of it emerged with a bloody nose and what looked like a dislocated pinkie.

I looked back to Yasuo, raising my brows. "I mean, yeah. Yeah, I do still think you're a lot of meatheads."

Josh startled me by laughing. Wasn't he supposed to get pissy and walk away, grumbling about the freaky girl? The fact that he didn't made me panic.

Yasuo never walked away on me, either, but that was different. And neither did Ronan, but he was a teacher and had to deal with me no matter what. But this Josh, he was one of my peers, and his affability threw me.

I glued my eyes to the roof of my dorm peeking over the buildings in the distance. "Look, I've gotta go."

"We'll walk with you," Yas said.

"Yeah," Josh added. "To protect you from the dangerous meatheads, eh?"

"That's right." Yasuo put his arm casually around my shoulders, whisking me along. "Otherwise another *boy* might try to talk to you."

I elbowed him in the gut. "Shut up."

He let go, getting in step with Josh, laughing it off the way guys do. And simple as that, I had two male companions.

At first I was unsettled, but they made idle chatter as we walked. I could tell Josh kept slowing his pace for me, but I still had to do a quick half skip every few steps to keep up with my long-legged escorts. The meaningless chatter flowed, though, and it actually began to feel nice.

Before I'd come to this island, things had never felt *nice*. It made me wonder if this whole messed-up scene might possibly be worth it someday. I thought of the Initiates escorting the survivor from the pool. Recalled Ronan whispering with his fellow Tracer. There were relationships to be had, trust that could grow.

Very few girls ascended to Watcher status, but I imagined the higher you went, the tighter you grew. And if you actually did make it all the way, it must become something like a family. I'd never had a family, not really. The whole process was sick, sure, but there was something in it that had me yearning, a little bit, to be a part of something bigger than myself. Part of a family.

I tuned in when I felt Josh's eyes on me. "I told you, mate," he was saying to Yasuo. "She's not your typical sheila."

What did *that* mean? Had they been talking about me?

"Sheila?" Yas screwed up his face. "Is that a girl?"

Josh nodded, but his eyes were still on me.

I squinted at him, suspicious. "Are you teasing me?"

His gaze finally broke from mine. "Yeah, a sheila's a girl. Learn to speak English, mate."

"That's not English," Yasuo said. "It's Australian."

"Wait," I said. "Go back." I was so not done with the whole not-your-typical-sheila thing. "What were you guys talking about?"

Yasuo heaved a sigh, like I was putting him out. "I told Josh you came by to spy on the guys. To see what we're up to; satisfy your natural curiosity and all. But Josh guessed that wasn't your thing."

I put my hands on my hips, ready for battle. "How is spying a typical girl thing?"

"It's a fact," Josh said. "Ask any girl what superpower she wants and it's invisibility. Girls want to eavesdrop and learn secrets."

I glared at him, looking for the fault in such a random statement. Sentences that began with *it's a fact* tended to put me on my guard. "And what do guys want?"

"Guys all wish they could fly, of course." He gave me a mellow grin. "Really. There've been studies."

Was that why a guy would want to become a vampire? For the power of it?

I realized I had to hand it to Josh. He was a pretty pleasant human being, and even this random topic hadn't stopped the conversation from flowing. I shrugged, deciding to take the

ISLE OF NIGHT

bait. "I get that girls like gossip. But me? No way. Who cares about secrets? I just want to pass my next fitness evaluation. So no, I'd definitely want to fly."

"Who knows?" Yas said, tugging my braid. "Maybe flying would help with your pull-ups. I hear test time is coming up."

My mood plummeted. "God knows I need all the help I can get."

"You're doing palms away, right?" Josh asked, instantly intent on giving me tips. "You should practice with negative pull-ups. Start with your chin over the bar, then get used to the feel of lowering yourself back down."

Yas shook his head. "Like you're such a pro. Dude, I could kick your ass any day of the week."

"You bloody well can't." Josh flexed. "I'd love to see you give it a go."

"Jeez. Boys will be boys, vampires or no." I strode ahead, my dorm in sight, but both of them caught up to me effortlessly.

"And girls are more sensible?"

I looked at Josh to answer him, and caught his gaze sweeping up from where he'd been assessing my girl parts. *Oh no, he didn't.* I scowled, but he only laughed, his eyes glittering.

"Hey," Yasuo said, clueless to the minidrama going on beside him, "I still don't totally get why we need girl protectors, anyway. If we're going to be vampires and all." He hissed, holding pretend claws up dramatically.

He was goofing around, but still, it made me think. What fragility did vampires have that they needed girls who could do things like jump-start cars and do pull-ups and swim?

Those last two hit me like a bucket of cold pool water on my head, and were reminders I didn't need at the moment. Thoughtful, I drifted to the outer edge of the walkway, balancing on the rocks that lined it.

"Don't forget . . . do not stray from the path," Yasuo said, his voice reverberating theatrically. He gave me a teasing nudge.

I caught myself before I stumbled onto the grass. I shot him a look, suddenly not in the mood. "Don't joke around. A girl died today. In the pool."

"Harsh. She dive headfirst into the shallow end?"

It was a bad joke, and apparently Josh agreed. He had a serious look in his eye, his usual ease replaced by some darker concern. "Unacceptable, mate."

His reaction made me think he might be a little less knuckleheaded than I'd originally assumed.

"Yeah," I said, reluctantly agreeing. "This is serious, Yas."

"I get it, Drew. Serious as a heart attack. But if you can't have a sense of humor about it, well, you might as well give up right now."

I went on, ignoring Yasuo's trite wisdom. "A girl fell from ropes last week, too. Broke her neck, and I know she didn't survive *that*." I pinned Josh with a look. "Isn't that right, Mr. Harvard Premed? And then she was taken away, but to where?"

I caught Yasuo and Josh exchanging a quick look that I knew I wasn't meant to see. Did they know something I didn't? Were they holding something back?

I took a calming breath. "Girls have been dying. Not a lot, not yet, but a few have, and yet nobody talks about it. I haven't even seen any coffins."

"I don't imagine you would," Yas said carefully.

I leapt on that. "Because the bodies are used for something else?"

Josh put his arm around me and leaned down to my level. "Don't ask questions we can't answer." His tone was light, but I sensed something steely underneath.

A shiver crawled up my spine. We'd reached my dorm, and not a moment too soon. I spun to leave them. "Fine," I said coolly. "No more questions. Bye for now."

Yas called to me, "Aww, D, don't do us like that." He began to improvise words to the tune of "Don't Do Me Like That."

I stopped and turned around. The two of them seemed so bereft, for a moment looking simply like two bumbling, teenage boys, and I smiled despite myself. "Seriously, it's okay. I just got upset. But I really do need to go."

"I'd walk you in if I could," Yasuo said in playful earnest.

"Wouldn't we both?" Josh broke into a grin. "The mysteries of the girls' dorm. Do you all walk around in little towels, doing each other's makeup and things?"

I rolled my eyes. "Naturally. We sit around in silk nighties, having one big mani-pedi-gossip-makeover fest."

Josh put his hands to heart. "Oh, mate, she made a joke for me."

I didn't have time to analyze *that* crack when the heart-faced girl walked by. Her auburn hair caught the sun, looking like molten copper. Yas stared, and the faraway longing in his eyes startled me.

Josh elbowed him. "Earth to Yasuo."

Yasuo shut his gaping mouth. "Did you find out yet who she is?" he asked me.

"Give it up." I stared at the door where she'd just entered. "She's the one person on this island who's lamer than I am. I'm not quite convinced she's capable of speech."

"Cute, though." Yasuo waggled his eyebrows. "Cute but mute? Sounds ideal."

I gave him a shove. "Shut up."

Josh ignored our banter, focusing on me. "You're not lame."

For a moment, I believed him. But I snapped out of it quickly, wondering again what his ulterior motive might be.

I ran a hand through my hair, clearing my mind of the boys' nonsense. "Okay, guys. Now I really do need to go." With a quick wave over my shoulder, I walked away.

I didn't want to have to think about free diving or gore or boys named Josh becoming vampires. I didn't want to stand out or be noticed. I was on overload, and back in the room, all I wanted was to dig out the picture of my mom and stare at her until the world felt right again. Though I feared I'd have to stare a long time for *that* to ever happen.

I rarely risked looking at the photo now, and only when I really needed the strength. I'd just have to imagine my mom's blond hair, that yellow *Kill Bill* pantsuit. How would my mother have fared in a place like this? I was still alive, and I had to have inherited my survival instinct from someone.

I curled onto my bed, thoughts of my father pushing their way into my head. His violent tendencies were in me, too. His rages and casual brutality were there somewhere, twined into my DNA. And I really hoped *he* wasn't the person I had to thank for my success.

CHAPTER NINETEEN

I stood against the gym wall, scowling for all I was worth. It was time. The next fitness assessment had arrived. I'd been here well over a month now, and this evaluation was shaping up to be as much of a disaster as the first one.

Fifty-yard dash: laughable.

Rope climbing: catastrophic.

Sit-ups: comical.

And, really, who failed sit-ups? I mean, I'd thought I was doing fine. Until I saw the other girls, arms crossed over their chests, *chuff-chuff-chuff*ing rhythmic exhales like maniacal little steam engines.

I'd made minimal progress in the past weeks. Did girls get kicked out if they weren't able to climb stuff?

Pull-ups were next. The blood was making me stronger, but still, I'd yet to get my chin up over that stupid bar. There was a better chance I'd sprout wings and *fly* than do a pull-up.

I glared at Lilac, trotting through every challenge like a freaking show horse on parade. The sight of her made me livid.

I wanted to triumph. Needed to. But Lilac stood in my way. How would I advance to the next level with Lilac doing all she could to instigate my downfall?

In my peripheral vision, I saw Ronan approach, though I didn't need eyes to know he was there. I managed to feel him whenever he was close. Like he was a torch burning hot and bright, and I was a big hairy moth.

Inhaling, I turned to face him. I was beyond surly, and eager to cut him off before he gave me the talking-to that I sensed was coming. "What, Ronan? I mean . . . *Tracer* Ronan."

"You must focus, Annelise." His tone took me by surprise. It wasn't that of a scolding teacher, but rather the whispered advice of an ally.

"Focus? I'm sorry, but I've been sucking abysmally at every single one of your circuits, and it has me pretty damned focused, thank you very much."

"Language," he hissed.

"Yeah, okay, *doggone* focused. That better?" I scowled at him. "And as long as we're talking etiquette, shouldn't you be calling me *Acari Drew*, not Annelise?"

"Annelise is your name."

Something drove me to nitpick him on the point. "The Initiates and Guidons call me Acari Drew. Shouldn't *you*?"

"It doesn't suit you as *Annelise* does," he said, beginning to look a little flustered.

Now I was the flustered one. Why we were even having this conversation? "Whatever. It doesn't matter. It's obvious I'll get kicked out of here soon, anyway."

"Don't say that." His voice was gruff in a way that gave me a shiver. His words had come out snarly and decisive and, well, really manly.

I couldn't help but turn back to him. "Why do *you* care if I fail out of here?"

"You *won't* fail. Not if you try." He stepped closer. He smelled like fresh air, like the sea. For some reason, it made me want to needle him even more. Either that or curl myself close so he could wrap me in those muscular arms that were hard to ignore beneath the thin fabric of his athletic shirt. "If you try it, you can do it."

His voice was stern. A teacher's voice. Not the voice of anyone who planned on embracing me anytime soon.

"*No try, only do* . . . that right, Yoda?" The words had spilled out of me like acid. It seemed picking fights was all I was good for these days.

But Ronan didn't take the bait. Instead, his voice got warmer, kinder. "You can do it, Annelise. You can accomplish any challenge set before you. You're here for a reason. You're special. You were chosen. For a reason."

His words made my heart swell. I told myself it was just a pep talk, teacher to student.

For one cynical moment, I wondered if he was using his *special* voice on me. But he'd told me he'd been unable to use persuasion on me without touching me. And when he had touched me, it'd felt warm and strange. No, I'd know if he was using his powers. He'd said something nice, and it'd reassured me. It was as simple as that.

"But you must take it seriously," he continued. "You *can* do this. I don't care why or how. Do it for yourself. Do it to spite your father. Do it for me. For Lilac. But this is serious, Annelise. You *must* be serious. Failure isn't tolerated. Failure of any kind."

I thought about the girls who'd died. They'd been doing simple things—in the pool, in the gym. Simple, deadly things.

Ronan's advice was grave, like this was life or death. And I believed it might be.

"Hey, Charity!"

That piercing pep-squad voice brought me back to earth. A knot of girls was clustered around the bars. Many stood, hands on hips, shifting their weight from foot to foot. Waiting. For me.

"Your turn!"

Ronan knelt to tie a shoe that didn't need tying. "You can do it," he whispered. "Not everyone is perfect at everything. Do whatever it takes. But you *must* succeed."

I strode to the bar. *I can do it.*

I'd never managed a pull-up in my life.

Ronan believes I can do it.

I stood beneath the tarnished gray bar, heart hammering in my chest. Lilac was there, and the mysterious Heart Face, too, as well as a growing crowd of curious Acari, slowing to witness the crash.

I'm here for a reason.

My back was to the wall. Though I faced the entire gym, my eyes avoided Ronan. But I felt him. Across the room. Watching.

Failure isn't tolerated.

"I'll spot," a quiet voice said. I thought it might be Heart Face, but I didn't look to make sure. I couldn't risk catching anyone's eye.

It was just a bar, held aloft by two metal poles, each with a metal foothold. I stepped onto the first. Clinging tightly to one side, I hauled myself up, bearing all my weight on the one foothold, a couple of feet off the ground. I acclimated myself, letting the pole cool my damp palms. It had a sour, metallic smell.

Praying my sweaty hand wouldn't slip, I swung toward the other footrest. I gripped both poles now, spread-eagled over the ground, with the horizontal bar looming over my head. My thighs trembled as I stood there, and my heart beat double time.

I couldn't do it last time. What would happen if I couldn't do it again?

But I had to do it. Whatever it took.

Palms away, Josh had said. I sucked in a stabilizing gulp of air. Reaching up, I grasped the bar in my hands. I edged off the footholds and let myself drop. I dangled there for a moment, wishing for a miracle. A miracle where I'd somehow, suddenly become strong. Able.

For a moment, I believed this might happen.

Until I pulled, and didn't budge.

The other girls were gleefully anticipating my failure. I kept my face blank—I'd make them believe I hadn't tried yet. I pulled again.

"Any day now, Charity."

I hung there wondering how long I'd have to undergo this torture. At what point would I let myself drop back to the ground to accept defeat?

"She can't do it," Lilac purred.

I couldn't let her win. Not yet. Not *Lilac.*

I pulled a third time, and this time gave it all I had. I visualized my arms folding, my chin rising above the bar. Struggling, I rose a little.

Turning to Ronan, Lilac shouted across the gym, "She can't do it."

"What?" Ronan yelled back, though I was sure the neighboring islands had probably been able to hear Lilac crowing my defeat. Acting indifferent, he strode to the hanging rope. Someone gasped as he peeled off his shirt.

I gasped as he peeled off his shirt. He mopped his brow with it, as though bathed in sweat, but I knew he couldn't be. He stared at us, and I sensed attention migrating to him. Almost as though he were compelling the Acari to stare.

I dangled there, knowing I needed to do something, anything. *Do what it takes,* he'd said. But what?

He dipped into a bucket of chalk, rubbing his hands together. In a single, elegant leap, he mounted the rope.

All eyes were on him now. I knew I should pull mine away, but I was mesmerized. Ronan's legs were held in front of him in a pike position, his every muscle flexed, hard and still. His back, neck, abs . . . his entire body looked carved from stone. Everything but for his arms, which began to pump hand over hand, sending him flying up the rope.

I forced myself to look away. He was doing this for *me.* This was my one shot.

Shutting my eyes, I tried again. Pulled as hard as I could. I held my breath, afraid I might make a sound.

I felt a hand on my butt and then a hard shove upward. It was gross and intimate and startling. And it was what I needed to pull my chin up over the bar.

Do whatever it takes. That was the lesson here. Not everyone was perfect, but with luck and smarts, one could find a way.

I held myself there, letting a little bark of triumph escape me.

"She did it," someone called.

Once I was in position, I was able to hold myself there for a moment. Long enough for the crowd to turn and see me.

Long enough for me to steal a glance down.

But I didn't need to look to guess whom I'd find staring up at me.

CHAPTER TWENTY

M y hands slid from the bar, and I dropped to the mat.
"Why?"

Heart Face shrugged, and then turned and walked toward
the locker room.

I wiped my hands on my shorts. If I wasn't mistaken, I had
a red splotch on my ass, roughly the size of *her* hand. All these
weeks and she hadn't said a word to me. Why this? Why now?
What was her deal?

"It's not over, Charity." Lilac's gaze strafed from me to Heart
Face and back again, looking suspicious. She began to walk
away. Slowly, she turned her head, watching me from the corner
of her eye. It reminded me of a bird of prey. "You're going
down."

I had to believe clever trumped hot. That smart and determined would triumph over cruel and petty any day of the week.

"Then I'll take you with me," I said, and this time I felt the words resonate to my soul.

It wasn't until after class that I finally got a chance to catch up with my mysterious helper. "Wait," I called, running to catch Heart Face.

"Thanks," I said, catching my breath. She only looked at me, so silent and strange. "You know, for earlier."

She gave me a half smile and shrugged.

Was she capable of carrying on a conversation? There was only one way to find out. "I'm Annelise Drew, but people call me Drew." Well, *most* people. "What's your name?"

"Emma Sargent," she said, quiet as a mouse.

"Oh." I blanked, unsure what to say next. Sparkling chatter wasn't exactly my forte.

She began to walk again, and I jogged a couple of steps to catch up and asked the next logical question. "Where are you from?"

"North Dakota" was all she said.

Okayyy. She wasn't going to make this easy for me. She was quite possibly the one person on this island who was lamer than me. I liked that. "How'd you end up here, Emma from North Dakota?"

She gave another shrug. "Long story."

So she wasn't big on talking. I could hang with that. She'd helped me with my pull-up—at the moment, I wouldn't care if she requested we hold every conversation in pig Latin.

We were almost to the dorm when I mustered another question for her. "What class do you have before this one?" She wasn't in phenomena with me.

"Decorum."

"Oh, I have that one, too. I *hate* decorum." It didn't offer anything nearly as cool as lock picking. Plus, the teacher freaked me out. "Master Dagursson is supercreepy."

"We had to dance with him this morning."

I shuddered. "You're kidding. I thought we had a few weeks till the unit on *dancing*."

We reached the dorm and walked up to the second floor, but Emma stopped halfway down the hall. She gave me another of those stoic nods and disappeared into her room.

"Okay, then," I said to the closed door. "See ya."

Who was her roommate, and why couldn't I have been placed with *her* instead of Lilac? I sighed, knowing I was about to face that very demon.

I returned to my room and nearly gagged. It smelled like a lit match. Or, rather, a hundred lit matches. I looked around, expecting to find my bed smoldering or my toiletries melted and clothes singed. But there was just Lilac, guiltily sliding something into her bottom drawer.

What little gift had the vampires given her? If I'd received throwing stars, she'd gotten what—a box of matches? Candles? Incense? *Explosives?* I dared not consider the possibilities.

"It smells like sulfur." I eyed her critically. "Did you get a little visit from your pal Satan?"

"Anything to mask *your* stench, dweeb."

I needed to find out what was in her bottom drawer. I was certain she'd already rifled through mine. I hoped she hadn't discovered my iPod, though I imagined I'd have heard by now if she had.

I peeled off my coat and hung it up. Sliding the closet door shut, I spied a bit of charred paper in the trash can.

ISLE OF NIGHT

Was our Lilac a juvenile arsonist? Pyromaniac, perhaps? I only hoped she was well acquainted with the concept of impulse control.

As terrifying as the thought was, unless she'd managed to smuggle in a lighter, her gift from the vampires must involve some sort of incendiary device. I vowed to find out the first chance I got.

CHAPTER TWENTY-ONE

———— ⬦⬦⬦ ————

The next several weeks passed quickly. Our training intensified as the effects of the blood began to take hold. The drink heightened everything. My enhanced sense of smell especially freaked me out. It was as if I could smell the origins of things and not just the things themselves—like the scent of leather brought me back to the cow itself, to the grass it fed on, the field where it grazed.

My sense of myself in the world also became more acute. I was hyperaware of my feet connecting to the ground, mindful of the people around me, where they stood, and how far away.

Most startling of all was the power. We were all growing stronger, and our instructors thrashed those new muscles at every opportunity.

I'd never been so sore in all my life. But, oddly, sometimes the aches and pains were a plus. I loved plopping into bed, being so dead tired I fell asleep instantly.

Some nights the injuries were too bad to sleep. And God forbid the vamps let us have a bottle of Motrin. They claimed it messed too much with our blood. Instead, our instructors taught us stretches and acupressure points, and we were allowed to take all the ice we wanted from the freezer in the kitchenette. But bags of frozen peas only helped so much when your whole body rang with pain.

Add to that the fact that Lilac said some pretty weird shit in her sleep. Hearing your roommate murmur things like *Burn, sunny, burn*—whatever *that* meant—wasn't exactly sleep inducing.

Those were the nights I snuck out my iPod. I'd wait for Lilac's psycho sleep chatter to begin, and I'd dig out my treasures, cradling them like they were my blankie. I'd listen to music, regular music—alternative, soundtracks, eighties hits, whatever—and just that little bit of normalcy did a ton to alleviate the aches, fears, and uncertainty of the whole messed-up scene.

My iPod also stored books—I kept dozens on the thing— and I was able to read and reread my favorites under the covers, pretending I was a regular girl in a regular dorm with a regular roommate.

I gradually got into a routine, and things started to feel fairly normal and uneventful. If *uneventful* meant finding a box of extralong matches, a gold Zippo, lighter fluid, and various other incendiaries in your roomie's drawers, and *normal* was a word you could ascribe to a vampire-ambassador training academy-cum–charm school.

I headed to phenomena class, thinking just how much I was beginning to doubt the *ambassador* part of that equation. With all the brutal gym classes, I sensed that a Watcher was less an attaché than an agent in the 007 sense of the word.

VERONICA WOLFF

I cringed, spotting a clique rounding the corner on the path ahead. Apparently, my hatred was strong enough that just thinking about Lilac summoned her out of thin air. She and one of her high-class gal pals were headed straight for me.

But they were with *Josh*.

They were looking cozy, too, him with an arm around each girl. Was he just being friendly? Didn't he know they were evil incarnate? Who was flinging themselves at whom?

Rumor had it that he'd joked he'd eventually make his way through all the Acari. Yasuo couldn't confirm it, so I didn't give it much credit at the time, chalking it up to girls getting the hots for the cute Aussie.

But seeing him now, remembering how that naughty-boy leer had flickered in his eyes, I wouldn't put it past him. I'd thought he was, I dunno, interested in me. But apparently, Josh was interested in *everyone*.

Disappointed, pissed, flattered, relieved . . . I wasn't sure how I felt about it.

Lilac's laugh trilled across the quad. Either she was really amused by something he'd said, or she was just really working it. My money was on the latter.

Double-oh-seven indeed. Who better to be cast as Bond girls but Lilac and her sleek, slutty friends? Her crowd seemed especially interested in Josh, and I couldn't figure out why. He was supposed to be a Harvard guy. What would a bunch of dim-bulb girls see in him? I mean, Josh was cute, but so was pretty much every other guy on campus.

They got closer, and instead of making room on the path, I stood my ground, striding toward them with my head held high. I would *not* step aside for Lilac.

She and her friend glowered, but Josh greeted me with his usual wide smile. The glint in his eyes made him look like he had a secret.

He pulled away from the girls, moving to the side to let me pass. "Looking lovely today, Drew."

His voice was slow and intent, like there was some private subtext. And who knew? Maybe he was trying to communicate a message to me. Or maybe he was just flirting. Maybe this was how *all* guys acted.

Well, no, thank you.

I listened to Lilac's laugh and Josh's sexy Australian lilt fading in the distance. Theirs was effortless flirtation—something that was completely foreign to me.

I thought of decorum class, and how even that was difficult for me. Knowing when to smile coquettishly and when to avoid a man's eye. When it was proper to stray from formal titles, when to serve soup and with which spoon. Charm, poise, courtesy . . .

I gave a little shudder. If there was one thing to clear Lilac and Josh from my mind, it was thoughts of Alrik's decorum seminar. I'd hoped it'd teach me things like Martini Mixology or Baccarat 101, but I'd been sorely mistaken. Instead, we had to endure things like couples' ballroom dancing. *Ballroom*, for God's sake. I despised it, just as I'd known I would.

And the instructor, Master Alrik Dagursson?

Creepiest. Teacher. Ever.

He'd taught me three things thus far.

1. I hated couples dancing.
2. Some teachers were vampires.
3. Not all vampires were hot.

So much for the *Twilight* worldview.

I suspected that Alrik—or Master Dagursson, as we lowly Acari had to call him—was one of the old ones Ronan had mentioned. The name alone proclaimed him of Viking stock, though he'd lost the trace of any accent long ago. Instead he spoke with contrived, faux-classical inflections. Imagine Keanu Reeves delivering a speech while pretending to be a Knight of the Round Table, and you had the velvet sounds of Master Dagursson.

As for his looks? Maybe they only made cute vampires now, but this dude looked like he might've been an aging rocker before being frozen in time.

All in all, my vampire count was up to three. Headmaster Fournier. Master Dagursson. And the mysterious monster from the path.

I unzipped my parka and bounded up the stairs to the science building. I smiled. Thank God it was Tuesday. Tuesday meant Tracer Judge's phenomena class, *not* decorum.

I loved phenomena. And I adored the teacher, too. I'd come to realize that people like Tracer Judge were rarities on this isle. He was supersmart in an always learning, inquisitive sort of way. And though he was disciplined, he was thoughtful and forgiving, too. The good news was, he said if I stayed after class a couple of times a week, he'd teach me the basics of hacking Linux servers.

I was still smiling when I swooped into the room, plopping into my usual spot next to Yasuo. Still smiling, I looked to the lectern. But my face drained when I saw *him*.

It was the monster from my night run, and he was staring right at me.

CHAPTER TWENTY-TWO

"We have a guest lecturer today." Tracer Judge stood to the side of the podium, his usual easy manner replaced by stiff formality. "He'll be discussing topics in mathematics, and I think you'll find his qualifications beyond reproach."

Even though it was Judge who was speaking, I couldn't drag my eyes from the vampire. Though I hadn't seen clearly in the dark, I knew without a doubt it was him. The one from the path. I felt it in that penetrating gaze—in his very presence, an energy that hummed like a giant magnet.

"Without further ado"—Judge took a step back—"I present Master Alcántara."

"Thank you, Tracer." His eyes swept the room, and I could've sworn they came to rest back on me.

I sucked in a breath.

He gave a gracious half bow. Aimed in my direction. "I am Hugo De Rosas Alcántara."

Hugo De Rosas Alcántara . . . it rolled off his tongue, low and accented, sounding as smoky and seductive as a snifter of Spanish brandy. Every female jaw in the classroom dropped open.

"I was born in the fourteenth century in Madrid." He let the shocking statement hang, and a collective gasp filled the room. His response was a wolfish smile, curling one corner of his lips.

I felt Yasuo shift in his seat, maybe trying to catch my attention, but I couldn't pull my eyes from the vampire. I was mesmerized. He looked like he was about nineteen, and I focused on that fact, ignoring his impossible-to-fathom *real* age, which must've been six hundred–something.

"My grandfather was one of the original Knights of Alcántara. A chivalric order of the Middle Ages." Though unfamiliar to me, the way he'd said it implied something dark and dangerous. Sexy, even. Not unlike like him.

"But I was a precocious child. And a precocious boy yearns to make his own way." He shook his head ruefully, a quiet laugh rumbling in his chest.

His black hair was longish and wavy, and so thick it seemed permanently tousled. He raked a hand through it, leaving him looking like a rock star who'd just carelessly pulled a shirt over his head. "I forsook my family's militant ways. The wars *I* longed for occurred in the space of my mind, waging battles of words, ideas. Of formulas and numbers."

He began to stroll about the room, and his movements reminded me of a panther. Exquisite, but something that could kill you in a heartbeat.

"Mathematics is a particular passion of mine. It is precision. But it is poetry, too. I traveled to the royal court in Castile, seeking like minds. King Peter was young, like me. And, like me, he was a man smitten with new ideas. Soon I was appointed court mathematician. This was the greatest of honors, not given lightly by a man whom the peasants called Pedro el Cruel. . . ."

He stopped speaking, and it was like he'd become a thing carved of marble. Impossibly beautiful and utterly still.

My heart kicked up a beat. And then I worried, wondering if he could hear my heartbeat. Did vampires scent fear like other predators? Did a being like Master Alcántara perceive me as prey? To him, I was likely a brief flicker of consciousness and flesh that could be snuffed out in an instant.

He clicked out of his trance, his anima firing vitality back into those dark eyes. "But this is a story for another day. Today we speak of mathematics."

His tone of voice had become light again. I hadn't realized I'd stopped breathing.

"Some of you are quite familiar with mathematical concepts. Others, not as much. I ask that you *all* open your minds. Mathematics is all around you. The pattern of a poem, the shape of a leaf, your pop music . . ."

Master Alcántara strolled back to the front of the classroom, casually leaning against the top of the teacher's desk. Was it a trick that made it seem like his eyes were aimed straight at me?

My cheeks burned. Why did he stare at me as he mentioned music? I hoped mind-reading vampires were just the stuff of books, and that he didn't, in fact, know about my hidden iPod.

"You've become acquainted with crude infiltration and reconnaissance techniques—locks, wiretaps, hacking. Now, tell me: In what way can the most basic *mathematic* principles be applied to espionage?"

His eyes didn't waver from me. But there were other kids in the class. He was staring at me—I was sure of it now. But why?

Everyone else was silent. Were they looking at me, too? Was the question directed at *me*? I couldn't tell—nor could I bring myself to look away.

"Acari Drew, is it?" Master Alcántara gave me a half-lidded smile. "A *spirited* name. I like spirit. Tell me, Acari Drew, do you need to decline the question?"

My eyes felt locked to his. Like he'd hypnotized me.

"Yo, D." Yasuo's voice was a harsh whisper at my left side.

Tracer Judge cleared his throat. "Drew?"

The interruption broke the moment, jolting me back to myself. "Um, yeah. I mean, no. I can answer it."

I *rocked* at math. Only I was acting like a girl who hadn't studied her times tables. I forced myself to focus.

"Sorry. A way math could be used for surveillance . . ." I shifted in my seat, feeling pinned like a butterfly in a glass case. My words came out in a rush. "Well, a mathematician could use graph theory. For example, you could apply a mathematical structure to phone records in order to determine enemy cells. Like, if each node represented a caller, and you graphed it out, you could identify central players, hierarchies—that kind of thing."

"Very nice." Master Alcántara's eyes grew warm, lingering on me. I found myself uncomfortably aroused. A fly drawn to the deadly spider. "This sort of critical thinking"—he gave me a courtly nod, and I thought I might catch fire—"reflects an understanding of how the basic elements of learning become relevant in the world at large."

He expanded on the thought, but all I heard was *blah, blah, blah*, because he'd enthralled me. Like a snake charmer. And he still seemed to be staring. At *me*. Even now, I felt that glinting gaze like a buzz on my skin.

"And it's precisely the sort of thinking that will earn top honors and this semester's Directorate Award."

Finally, he glanced away. At the word *award*, I sat bolt upright. They gave out awards here? I wondered if I could win myself a single room.

"As you know, only an elite selection of young women will advance to the next stage of Watcher training." Master Alcántara scanned the room intently. "What you don't know is that the top Acari will earn the privilege of shadowing *me* at the end of this semester. On a mission off-island."

There was a collective gasp among the girls, while the low hum of guys' complaints rumbled through the room. An award available only to the female students, and the prize was a ticket off the island.

"To determine this semester's winner, there will be a test in one of the four disciplines. A challenge. Participation is voluntary, though we would expect any Acari with an ambition toward becoming a Watcher would choose to compete."

A bright light flared to life inside me. You bet I was going to compete. I'd spent the last twelve-plus years at the top of my class. *I* could win the award, win a shot at traveling off this rock. I didn't know what was more appealing—shadowing Master Alcántara or a chance at escape.

I'd win, spend some time with an ancient mathematician—a prospect chilling but oddly seductive, too—and then I'd find a way to run away. I didn't know where precisely *off-island* was, but surely I could sneak out and find a boat. I could make a break for it.

He smiled then, wickedly. "But Acari should strive to be the best in *every* discipline, be it languages or fitness or the social arts. And so we will not disclose the test subject until the semester draws to an end."

My bright light wavered. A test in fitness? Social arts? *Crap.*

I stole a quick look at the rows behind me. Only Acari were eligible, so my gaze skipped over the boys, weighing my female competition. There was the leggy Valkyrie who always gave Master Dagursson a run for his money on the dance floor. The gang girls who fought dirty, and the butch ones who didn't need to. There was Lilac.

Every one of them was stronger than me in the other subjects. But nobody could beat me in academics.

Did that mean I was a shoo-in? Surely they wouldn't choose a nonsense class for the test. How would you compete in social graces, anyway? No, it was sure to be something like phenomena. A topic in algebra, maybe. Or an essay test. Like, on Norse mythology.

"She who accomplishes these things shall find herself rewarded in a manner heretofore unfathomed." He seemed to direct the words at me, his eyes pinned once more on *me.* They glimmered, like he was a predator toying with dinner.

A thrill crackled through me, sweeping across my chest. Never had being good at school entailed the possibility of *unfathomably awesome rewards.* The thought of what that might even *mean* made my breath catch in my throat.

The combat, the stupid ballroom dancing—I vowed I would find a way to excel at all of it. Even so, I suspected that surely the challenge would be in an *academic* discipline.

I looked up and he was still watching me, almost expectantly. I shivered. *Could* he read my mind? Was he confirming my thoughts?

Anything was possible. Master Alcántara was a mystery, a myth come to life. Ageless. Unknowable. Terrifying. There was something in his gaze. A look implying we shared a secret I'd yet to uncover. It gave me hope.

And then poof—he was gone. There was a glimmering movement and then Master Alcántara simply vanished. It looked like a movie that'd been edited wrong: In one frame he flickered before us; in the next he didn't.

Voices hummed through the room, and Tracer Judge silenced us. "You heard Master Alcántara. That means tonight's homework, like *every* assignment you receive, demands your best effort."

I finally caught Yasuo's eye, and he *ooh*ed and wriggled his fingers in a playful spooky-voodoo way. I gave him a big smile, excited about my prospects.

There was fresh grumbling as talk of schoolwork brought us back to so-called reality. "I know this problem set will be difficult for some of you," Judge added, raising his voice over the din. "Which is why it's more important than ever to *show your work*. These are very basic proofs. You can work through them, and I want to see your thought process as you do."

More like he wanted to make sure girls weren't cheating.

The moment he dismissed us, students bolted from the room. Some seemed upset. Basic tenth-grade geometry would be hard for many of them, I realized.

I bit back a smile. I'd been taking my knowledge for granted, expending my energy feeling sorry for myself about gym class and swimming, but I had a leg up on everyone. I could recite geometry postulates in my sleep. Maybe Alcántara's test would be a complicated theorem.

And that had to be a lot harder than learning how to dog-paddle.

I *wanted* that award. And it was within my reach. I just needed to buck up and learn to swim or fight or do however many pull-ups it took to stay alive till the end of the semester.

I felt a person hovering over me and looked up to see Yasuo's bemused face.

"Well?" He stood there, brows raised, shaking his head ever so slightly. "Girl, don't tell me that vampire dude hypnotized *you* like he did everyone else."

I opened my mouth to protest, but floundered for words.

"Aww, hell, Drew. Seriously? Man, I can't *wait* till I get my vampire mojo." He spread his hands as though reveling in his own epic coolness. "Just wait. The ladies will love them some Vampire Yasuo."

I laughed. "They won't know what hit them."

He grabbed my coat and messenger bag from the back of my chair. "Come *on*. Are you gonna sit there all day? I'm starved. I want to get to the dining hall before all the good stuff is gone."

"If you consumed something beyond bread, butter, and Fruit Crush—whatever *that* is—maybe you wouldn't have such a hard time." Standing, I snagged my stuff from him, but didn't put on my coat. "You go ahead. Tracer Judge said he'd stay after."

And I thought it was just as well, too. Yasuo would probably sit with Josh, and after running into him and Lilac, I wasn't exactly in the mood to chitchat over cafeteria lasagna.

"You're missing lunch to work on that computer thing? You are such a dweeb, Drew. Didn't anyone tell you that blondes were supposed to be, I don't know, perkier or something?"

"Do *not* start on the blond thing, or I won't help you with tonight's proof."

"Oh!" His hands clutched his breast like he'd been stabbed. "Whatever, Geek Girl. Just hurry up, okay?"

He headed for the door, but I stopped him. I knew I probably wouldn't make lunch, but there was no way I'd miss my favorite dessert. "Hey, if they have that shortbread stuff—"

"Yeah, yeah. I'll save you some." Yasuo shot me one of those careless-boy nods as he loped out.

Tracer Judge stood by the doorway, looking eager to shoo people through. Spotting me, he asked, "Did you need something?" He sounded agitated, which was completely unlike him.

Maybe today wasn't the best day to stay after. Or maybe he just forgot. My heart fell, thinking I might have to dine with Josh and his pals after all. I slowly shouldered into my coat, not sure how to play it.

He sighed, scrubbing his hand over his face. "Ohh, right. I was going to . . ."

"Teach me how to do that Linux hack." I gave him a hopeful smile.

"I'm so sorry. I completely forgot. We'll need to—"

Footsteps called our attention to the hallway. My Proctor, Amanda, stood there, frozen. Her eyes went from me to Judge and back again. Despite her pinched brow, she was as stunning as ever, statuesque in a fitted wool coat, her skin shining like a dark, burnished stone.

"Cheers." She gave me a tight smile. "Lunchtime, then. Isn't it, dolly?" Her tone was light, but she seemed as preoccupied as Tracer Judge.

I didn't know what, if anything, was going on between these two, but I could take a hint. And the hint was *No Drews allowed.*

"You know"—I swung my bag over my shoulder—"I need to take a rain check on the programming thing. I totally forgot . . . I promised . . . I'm meeting someone for lunch. I heard it's pasta day in the dining hall."

A lame excuse lamely delivered, but from the relieved looks on their faces, it worked. I jogged to find Yasuo, then bounded down the stairs, keeping one eye glued warily on the path. I was still getting used to this cold-weather stuff, and didn't want to wipe out on any black ice. "Hey! Yas!"

He stopped, greeting me with a quizzical look. "What happened?"

"Well . . ." I hedged.

"He forgot, didn't he?"

"Something like that." I actually sensed it was something like that and *more,* but in my short time on the isle, Amanda and Judge had both shown me moments of kindness, and I wouldn't speculate about things that weren't my business.

"Sorry, Nerd Bird. You'll get your moment. Wouldn't want to look too much like teacher's pet in the first semester, anyhow." Yasuo's smile made the nickname affectionate, not an insult. He gave my shoulder a squeeze, and we strolled on toward the cafeteria in an easy, companionable way. "How'd a blondie like you get so dweeby, anyway?"

"Me? How about you? What's *your* deal, Yas? I mean, you seem pretty nice. How'd you end up *here*?"

"You mean, how'd a nice guy like me end up in a coven of ancient, bloodthirsty vampires like this?"

I chuckled. "Precisely like that."

"Let's see. Here are the headlines: Mother Kidnaps Infant Son, Flees Yakuza Lover for America."

I halted, stunned. It was the last thing I'd expected to hear. "*Jeez.* The Yakuza? That's like the Japanese mafia, right?"

He nodded. "Yeah, that's them. And the concept of *son* can be kind of a big deal. My biological father flipped when my mom left."

"What happened?"

"We hid. I grew up. He eventually found us." He forced a halfhearted laugh. "I blame the Internet."

There was obviously much more to the story. My voice was subdued as I pressed for more details. "And?"

Shutting his eyes, he took a shuddering inhale. "He killed my mother. And then I killed him."

In that instant, I saw the great darkness that flowed beneath Yasuo's smiling demeanor. He cleared his voice, and with it, the shadows cleared from his brow. "Next thing I knew, I was in a town car headed to an L.A. airstrip."

"The vampires?"

"Yeah, a Tracer named Gunnar found me." He shrugged. "I was curious. I had nothing left. It was either stay and face my uncle and his minions, or *this.*" We'd reached the dining hall and he gestured toward it. "This seemed the lesser of two evils, believe me."

"Oh, crap," I whispered. Ronan, standing on the stairs ahead of us.

"What is it?" Yas asked, immediately on guard.

I studied Ronan. We were supposed to meet at the pool later, but there he stood, holding a big box, looking very stern. "Ask not for whom the bell tolls. . . ."

"Uhh . . . *what?*"

"It tolls for me."

"Are you, like, speaking in tongues or something?"

"No." I sighed. "Nothing. Go on in, Yas. I'll see you in there."

I approached Ronan, alarms shrieking in the back of my mind. I looked skeptically at the parcel in his hands. "What's that?"

"It's for you." He handed it to me. It was heavy and awkward, and my muscles flexed when I took it from him. "It's your wet suit."

CHAPTER TWENTY-THREE

I hunkered down in my seat, slamming the door to the old Range Rover harder than necessary.

Eating lunch had been impossible.

Fitness class unending.

Today's slew of Lilac barbs particularly excruciating.

All day, two images replayed on an obsessive loop in my mind: the canvas-wrapped body of the girl who'd died in the pool, and the thick black wet suit that hung in my locker like a skinned marine mammal. Did the wet suit mean I was going to have to go underwater? Hold my breath till bloody foam came out of my mouth? Was I to face something that would claw me enough to bring bits of gore floating to the water's surface?

"Why can't we do like normal people and swim in the pool?" I asked Ronan for the umpteenth time. "I like the shallow end. Our lessons have been going great." Amazing how the threat of a nighttime swim in the frigid North Sea could make a pool seem infinitely less detestable.

I stared out the car window. Though the March sun set later than when we'd arrived in January, come late afternoon it always faded and the sky dimmed to a dull gray. "It'll be dark soon. Isn't it dangerous? Shouldn't we do this during broad daylight?"

"It won't be pitch-dark for hours yet." Ignoring my tone, Ronan buckled his seat belt with that calm detachment he'd perfected and put the car in drive. "And even if it were dark, it's a good exercise. You won't face ideal conditions in the real world. Best not get used to them now."

"Doesn't this send me from, like, zero to sixty? What happened to the noodle and my little blue kickboard?"

Abruptly, he pulled the car to the side of the gravel road. "The fighting will begin soon, Annelise. And then these girls will be your competitors in more than just the classroom. Do you truly want them to see you thrashing about in the shallow end?"

Fighting. Girls had died already, and yet Ronan was telling me the challenges hadn't even begun yet? I tried to work some moisture back into my dry mouth. "Um, I'd rather they see my wet suit and think I'm a badass. . . ."

"That's the way." He popped back into gear, turning onto a road I hadn't seen before. We bounced over a rocky trail rough and rutted enough to knock me back against the headrest.

Despite the madly jouncing SUV, Ronan elaborated in his typically cool Ronan fashion. "It's impossible to re-create natural conditions in a pool. Variables like temperature, wind velocity, currents, riptides . . . Visibility issues like murk, flora, black water—"

"Okay, stop." I put up my hand. "You're freaking me out.

Let's just start by mastering my float; then we can work our way up to murk. Which, by the way, I don't believe is a word."

I think he actually smiled. Too bad I was too panicked to savor it. It seemed we really were driving to a cove, with me really wearing a wet suit. There was no stopping any of it.

He hit a huge pothole, and I grabbed the looped leather handhold on the door. "How come *I* have to do this as a special study? Am I the only person who can't swim?"

"No, you aren't the only one who can't swim."

I waited for him to elaborate. Which, of course, he did not. "Well, why don't these other mysterious nonswimmers have to wear wet suits and go to Crispy Cove, too?"

"It's *Crispin's* Cove, and the other Tracers tutor as they see fit."

The wet suit was riding up my backside in the most unpleasant way, but there was no chance I'd be working out any wedgies in front of Ronan. I did have some pride.

Putting it on had been a humiliating and demoralizing chore. It was heavy, it was daunting, and it had the most maddening up-the-back zipper, which had taken me ten minutes to master. At first I'd fantasized about asking Ronan—perhaps in my best sultry-starlet purr—if he'd zip me, but reality had found me hopping and grunting with one arm behind my back instead.

I plucked at the thighs, using the bounce of the tires to scooch back in my seat in an effort to free myself from my impromptu neoprene G-string. No luck, and it made me churlish. "Well, why doesn't *Lilac* have to swim in subzero water?"

"Your wet suit will keep you warm. And Lilac has her own special study."

I sat upright, my mood brightening at once. "What's *Lilac's* weakness?"

Ronan turned onto a road even bumpier than the last. "Everyone is assigned a special study. None of them is your business."

This was. If I was ever going to best von Slutling, I had to find her Achilles' heel. I remembered the elementary German workbook I'd spied on her desk. "It's some language thing, isn't it?"

Ronan stared ahead, refusing to answer.

"Hmph." There went that conversation.

I stared out the window into the growing dusk, surlier than when we'd set out. I was trapped on this island, trapped in a too-tight wet suit, about to be trapped in freezing, black water. It put me in a complaining mood. "It's so dark here."

"Enjoy it. You won't realize you miss the darkness until it's gone."

"I doubt that." I chafed my arms. We were in the middle of nowhere, and the prospect of vampires running amok in the steely half-light turned my skin to gooseflesh.

"We're close to the pole. Just as there are months of mostly darkness, there will come a time of near-constant twilight. They call it the Dimming."

The word sent a shiver across my skin, even as a lightbulb went on in my head. We were near the Arctic Circle. Summer would be here before I knew it. Come June, there would be a sun that never set in a sky that was rarely bright. "The land of the midnight sun," I muttered. "And that's why vampires like it?"

"Aye, that's why. It enables vampires to move about, imagining the sun on their skin, but without risk of discomfort." His voice was laden with some heavy emotion that told me he spoke of more than just the loss of suntans and his daily dose of vitamin D. "So appreciate the darkness now, Annelise, because you'll miss it come the Dimming."

"Fine. I'll start missing it tomorrow. How about that?" My heart rate spiked as a gently lapping cove came into view. The gunmetal sky was darkening rapidly now, pressing down on water the color of night. He pulled to a stop beside a jagged boulder, casting the car into cold shadow. I clung tight to my buckled seat belt. "But for now, it's too dark for my taste."

"Annelise." He turned to face me. Dramatic shadows accentuated his stubble, the cleft in his chin, the shock of hair on his brow, like he'd become a charcoal drawing. "There is no putting this off. You must learn. And you must open your mind to the night. It, too, has lessons to teach. There's a Chinese proverb. 'Better to light a candle than curse the darkness.' "

"Thanks, Obi-Wan. I'll remember that as I drown."

He raised his arm, and I bristled, wondering if he dared try one of *those* touches again. I held my breath, but the moment passed.

Instead, he pointed to the shore. "Go stand by the water. Dip your feet. I need to put on my wet suit."

"You're coming in, too?" I knew instant relief. Though, thinking about it, it was obvious he couldn't let me go in the sea alone. My panicked brain just hadn't gotten that far.

Then another fact struck me. It meant Ronan and I would be in the water. Together. And he was graduating from swim trunks to a wet suit. A *skintight* wet suit.

He gave me a quiet smile. "I'll not let you drown, Annelise."

As shocking as it seemed, I truly believed him. Mustering a smile, I nodded and turned toward the water.

Large, softly rounded stones lined the shore, and I clambered over them. Venturing in the growing darkness, balancing on rocks, and even the naked feel of the wet suit—it all made me feel free, like I was a child again. Or, rather, like the child I'd never been. *My* youth had been strip malls and parking lots. But in the dark, in this place, Central Florida was a surreal and distant memory.

I hopped off the last of the big rocks and reached the water. Tentatively, I edged closer and closer to the quietly lapping waves. I wore a pair of skintight booties, and I scuffed them over the rounded pebbles of the shoreline, marveling at how the thick neoprene protected me from the elements.

Twilight had turned the sky a flat, slate gray. I inched closer, straining to see. Elsewhere I'd spotted crashing waves, but enormous rocks bracketed Crispin's Cove on either side, sheltering it from the larger surf.

"Ready?" Ronan materialized from behind a boulder.

I tossed off a mirthless laugh. "I was born ready."

Slipping a hand under my elbow, he began to usher me in.

"Wait, wait, wait." I dug in my heels. The water was completely black. "I'm not ready."

Taking my shoulders in his hands, he turned me to face him. "And that's your first lesson: You never will be. Now come. All I ask tonight is that you work on your floating. Can you do that?"

I suspected I could, but with his hands on me, I didn't trust the feeling. I frowned at my shoulder. "You're making me think I can do it, with that hoodoo touch of yours."

"Look at me, Annelise." His voice was deep and commanding, and I couldn't help but raise my eyes to his. My shoulders and neck grew warm and tingly, my brain muzzy. I felt like a melting pat of butter.

Abruptly, he pulled his hands away, and I was instantly chilled. "*That* was my 'hoodoo touch.'"

"Oh," I said meekly. The memory of his touch seared

through the fabric of my wet suit. I rolled my shoulders to erase the sensation. "Do you promise not to do that again?"

"The only thing I can promise is that you're more capable than you realize, and your mind more formidable than most."

"Because I'm so smart?"

"Because you're so stubborn," he snapped.

I laughed, thrilled for once to be something other than the weird genius girl. Even if it meant I was the aggravatingly willful one.

He reached for me again, cradling my head in his hand. There was no supernatural burn, just the warmth of a guy's touch. "I think you've spent a lifetime selling yourself short. Don't underestimate your ability to discern illusion from reality. You, Annelise, are one of the most cunning, one of the bravest young women I've ever known."

Emotion clutched my throat. For the first time in my life, I felt *seen*. Understood. Nobody had ever paid attention before. Never had I known such concern. I'd spent my life feeling isolated and alien and friendless. It was a shock to realize how much I'd been wanting someone to care for me. To give a shit.

He tucked my hair behind my ears, and though my body thrummed hot, I shivered. "Now, tell me," he said. "Do you think you can float?"

I didn't know what it was about Ronan's attentions, but he made me feel stronger, like maybe I was a better person than I'd realized. "Yeah, I guess I can do that."

He led me into waist-high water, and the wet suit felt strange and heavy, like a wall of cool was pressing in on my body from all around. With an arm around my shoulders, he eased me onto my back. "Relax now. Imagine your belly reaching to the sky."

I did relax. A little. Until he let go of me, and my feet plummeted to the bottom.

He righted me at once, patiently bracing his hand along my spine, his strong fingers careful at the nape of my neck. "Again. Unclench yourself. You've done it in the pool—this is no different."

I'd puckered my lips shut, but water, frigid and briny, still found its way into my mouth. I nodded tightly, grunting in a way I thought sounded very agreeable, considering the circumstances.

"Does that mean you're ready?"

I tensed, lifting my head in alarm. "I'm not doing it yet?"

He gently pushed my forehead back down again. "I'm going to let go again."

The moment he did, my feet dropped like cement blocks to the bottom. Instinctively, I caught myself, coming to a standing position.

"Annelise Drew." Ronan's tone was stern. He lay me back in the water, a little more roughly this time. "It's not much more than a meter of water. Relax. Breathing helps."

"I am breathing," I said through gritted teeth. I was doing all I could to keep my head above water. But still it gurgled in my ears and up my nose, making me panic.

"No, I don't think you are. You must let your head drop."

"Can't you use your googly eyes on me? You know, convince me to be a good swimmer or something?"

"You must do this on your own."

A wave lapped over my face and I flinched, and Ronan's hand slipped. *Oh, God.* Was that Ronan's hand on my butt? I froze, projecting my mind through the thick fabric of my suit.

That *was* Ronan's hand on my butt.

This had the unfortunate effect of petrifying my entire body. I felt my legs drifting down like a couple of dead logs.

Ronan's calm demeanor finally wavered. "Och, Ann, don't be such a wretch." He sounded impatient, exasperated, and maybe a little amused.

But rather than feeling chastised, I was flooded by a long-forgotten memory. It was my mother, calling me Ann. I'd never remembered that before. I could hear her voice so clearly, almost like she was in the water, too, whispering in my ear. It was a gift that warmed me, calmed me.

Nodding, I loosened my neck just a little, finally relaxing. "Okay. On my own." I shut my eyes, becoming aware of the gentle lapping sounds of the tide, and it soothed me. Inhaling deeply, I opened them again to the most magnificent sight.

A light was beginning to pulse low on the horizon. It was bright green and swirling, like some childish god had splattered a bucket of lime paint across the sky. I gasped. The aurora borealis.

"You see them? The northern lights?"

"Yeah," I managed. They humbled me, amazed me, left me speechless.

"Did you know that you're floating?" Ronan's white smile glowed eerily in the dark.

I realized then. I no longer felt his hands on me. I giggled, but it made me sink a little and so I stilled, blanking my mind as much as possible. My stomach bobbed back to the top, making me feel like a bit of kelp floating in the sea. The water in my ears, in the corners of my eyes, no longer bothered me.

If I could learn to float, I could do anything. I would learn to swim. Maybe even to fight. The award would be mine.

I thought about Ronan, wondering what training he'd

endured, why he'd chosen the life he did. What was his background? And, more important, why was he only a Tracer? Though they did seem stronger and sharper than most regular people—a by-product of drinking the blood—why wouldn't someone choose immortality? "Why don't you want to be a vampire?"

There was only the lapping sound of the water, and I thought he wouldn't answer, but finally I heard him utter, "Unbearable."

"Why?" My voice was a whisper.

"Because life would be only that, forever. To watch person after person perish while I lived on? A life of grief and loss. Unbearable."

"You sound like you know. Like you've experienced a loss."

"Aye, I have. As will you."

If it was so horrible, I didn't understand why he'd chosen to stay. Or why he'd continue to bring girls like me to the island. "If this life is so bleak, then why are you even helping me?"

Though hard to see in the dark, it seemed he stood straighter, tenser. "Someone has taken an interest in you."

My heart fell. That was the only reason? It freaked me out to think someone out there was watching me. But worse, I'd convinced myself Ronan was helping me because *he* wanted to. Because of me. "Oh," I said quietly, cursing the dopey teenage melancholy in my voice.

"And I confess . . ." He shook his head, as though regretting what he was about to say next. "You remind me of someone."

An old girlfriend? A lover? "Who?"

Abruptly, he turned his back on me. I dropped like a stone and righted myself, scrubbing the water from my eyes.

"That's enough for today." Ronan strode back to shore, his shoulders lurching from side to side, knees lifting high over the surf, getting out of the water as quickly as possible. *Away from me.* "Weather is coming. We need to get back for the evening meal. You must drink."

A higher-than-usual wave slapped at the backs of my thighs and I stumbled, awkwardly finding my footing. Whatever illusions I'd harbored about a regular guy helping a regular girl learn to swim were shattered with those three words: *You must drink.*

It was so aberrant, so repellant to take something that'd once flowed in another's veins and absorb it into your own. But what alarmed me wasn't the thought of having to drink that ropy, viscous fluid. It was that I couldn't wait to get back for it.

CHAPTER TWENTY-FOUR

———

We had a few lessons like that, and Crispin's Cove began to feel like *our* place, safe and familiar. I liked the fresh air and found I preferred the briny taste of the sea to the superchlorinated indoor pool. The black water didn't freak me out as much as it had in our first lesson, and I'd even graduated from floating to a solid crawl stroke.

Ronan and I toweled off, quickly peeling off our wet suits and changing in the dark, with me hidden behind one of the larger boulders for privacy.

I was tousling my hair, encouraging it to dry, and chatting some nonsense as we walked up the dorm stairs. They were waiting for us in the foyer.

I knew at once something had happened. Most everyone was there. The Initiates, the Proctors.

Had someone died? But then I thought *No, girls have been*

dying, and there is never any ceremony around it. I studied the crowd, my panic growing. Everyone was staring at *me*.

All the girls from my floor were there, glaring like I'd just drowned their pet kitten. Except for Lilac, who had a sort of gleeful malice dancing in her eyes.

I stood as still and expressionless as marble. My Proctor Amanda stepped forward. Her frosty greeting bothered me more than any evil stare Lilac could shoot my way. "Drew, why'd you do it? I can understand the photo, but did you seriously think you could keep an *iPod*?"

Slowly, I registered her words. *My mom's picture.* Confiscated. I stood there stunned, feeling gutted.

And the iPod? Now that I was entrenched in my new world, it seemed so stupid that I'd once valued something so ridiculous. But then a little bit of the old Drew flared to life. "It was just an iPod," I muttered to nobody but myself.

Unfortunately, Guidon Masha heard me. She cracked her whip, and though I was fully clad in my winter gear, her aim was lethal. The leather kissed my face, so precise that I hadn't known she'd broken the skin until I felt the warm ooze of blood down my cheek. "You will keep silent, Acari."

Cold nausea washed through me. I was in deep trouble. And who knew what punishments this freak show doled out to girls in trouble?

I glanced to Ronan, but he looked stricken, his expression one of such profound disappointment, I had to turn away. Before coming here, when I messed up, I messed up only for myself. But now, seeing how troubled he was, and Amanda, too, I couldn't help the sickening feeling that I'd let them down. That I'd failed them.

Lilac was biting back a grin now, and I glared openly at her. It was her fault. She had to be the one who'd narced on me. She'd rifled through my stuff, found the iPod and picture, and waited for just the right moment.

I'd never receive the award. Never get a chance at *off-island*. I doubted I even had a chance to live through the night.

If I survived my punishment, I'd take her down. I'd vowed it before, after my nearly naked midnight run. But this time it'd be more than an armful of snow I'd dish out.

"Sadly, when one Acari errs, all suffer." Guidon Trinity, the redheaded Initiate, was speaking. Her accent was crisp, like a well-bred Northeasterner, and it snapped me to attention. She'd struck me as a Lilac type, though a little classier, and I wondered what Swiss boarding school they'd plucked her from. "You will all go out, dressed as you are. You will be blindfolded, separated into groups, and driven to a point far from here. You will make your way back to the dorm. On your own."

I looked around. Everyone had donned their coats—perhaps anticipating just this sort of sadistic hazing—but some were missing their gloves or hats. *I* was missing my hat, and my hair was wet. Though the glares pointed in my direction were probably smoldering enough to keep me warm.

"We have rules for a reason," Trinity continued in that snippy voice. "They civilize us. Sometimes they teach you your place, and other times they simply keep you safe. You *must* follow the rules. And now we will teach you what happens when you don't."

She strolled around the group, eyeing each of us with disdain. "Rule one: no personal items. Acari Drew broke this rule, and now you all suffer the consequences. Rule two: Never go out after curfew. Rule three: Never stray from the path. Tonight you will be dropped far from here, *after* curfew, *off* the path, and you will see what happens to Acari who disregard rules."

"Out." Masha used her whip to herd us to the door. She looked to the Initiates and ordered, "Blindfold them. Acari, you've not eaten, and we won't feed you. Instead, you will be taken in four groups and dropped at different points on the island. Try to make it back alive."

Dread snaked through me, making me feel sluggish and heavy. Someone grabbed me roughly from behind, and a coarse strip of cloth was tied tightly around my head, covering my eyes. I felt a few shoves from behind, sensed the other girls moving around me, and I stepped forward with them, out the door.

As Ronan predicted, the wind was up, and a bitter chill slammed into me. My hair was long and would take forever to dry, and already my scalp prickled as body heat escaped from the top of my head. Moisture stung at my cheeks. *Snow.* I began to shiver.

Not only was I cold, but I hadn't eaten a real meal since breakfast. Even then I'd had only a yogurt. I drank at lunch, but I'd stayed after class to work with Judge, and hadn't had the time to consume any actual food. Just the thought of it made my belly ache with hunger.

I was a wreck already. How would I make it through the night?

They separated us into groups, shuffling us into what I assumed were those extralarge SUVs. Though I couldn't tell for sure how many of us were in the car, it felt like more than five and less than ten.

We drove. And drove. I hadn't realized the place was that large. Short of circumnavigating the whole island, I had no idea how we were supposed to find our way back again.

We drove into darkness as black as my thoughts. I didn't care about the iPod, but the picture was gone. The only photo I had of my mother, lost forever. It added a poignant twist to my despair.

The car was silent but for the sounds of shifting gears, rustling coats, and the heavy breath of frightened girls. The driver slammed on the brakes, and we were flung forward. There was a sickening thump as we hit some animal on the road.

I shivered. Definitely not a good omen.

The car slowed, bouncing over an uneven road. We stopped.

"Blindfolds off, Acari." It was Masha who'd spoken. I wondered who else was in the car.

I tugged the strip of fabric free, scrubbing my eyes where it'd itched my skin. I saw that Amanda had driven, with Masha seated next to her in the front. There were six other Acari, and my stomach lurched to see Lilac. But heart-faced Emma was there, too, and it gave me hope.

"Bitch," someone whispered, climbing past me to get out of the car. It was a black-haired girl I recognized from phenom class.

There were other whispers, too, and one stomp on my foot. The comments were all along the lines of "Thanks, bitch" or "What makes *you* so special?"

The group I'd found myself in was, apparently, both understanding *and* creative.

Girding myself, I was the last out of the car. I looked at Amanda, still in the driver's seat. Her eyes went to my bare head, her expression tight.

"Well," Masha said, leaning out the window. "What are you waiting for, Acari? Find your way home. And beware of the monsters."

Monsters? My thoughts drifted to Master Alcántara, as they often did lately. A reluctant, scared fascination rippled through me, remembering how his eyes had glowed on the night of my run. I wondered what other sorts of monsters might be waiting for us out there.

The wheels spun, crunching gravel, and darkness enveloped the SUV as it drove away. Taillights blinked out as it rounded a corner and disappeared.

It was dark. Really dark. Clouds concealed most of the stars. The barest hint of northern lights flickered low on the horizon.

Despite the darkness, I felt all eyes on me.

The wind whipped around us, and Lilac adjusted her hat. She pinned the other girls with a challenging stare. "Let's go, ladies. Except for you." She stepped up to me. I stood straight to face her down, but she still towered over me. "Let me break it down for you, Charity. I'm sure there's all kinds of shit waiting out there to eat us. And there's strength in numbers, right? But you got us into this mess. And we're not going to help you out of it."

"Actually, you got us into it when you tattled on me."

Lilac stared at me, that euphoric hatred putting a mad smile on her face. "A minor detail."

The other girls turned to leave. It was surreal to watch them tromp away into the night. As the reality of my situation hit me, I began to tremble, nervous and cold.

I could prove geometry theorems or translate High German, but ultimately I was just a suburban rat from Florida. I could die out here, alone and frozen.

But I'd learned to float in the sea. Surely I could find my way across the snow back home.

Emma came to stand by me. "I'll go with you," she said, quiet as the wind.

Lilac laughed then, a shrill, heartless sound. "Freaks." Her eyes narrowed to slits. "You follow us, and you're dead."

She spun and jogged to join the others, leaving us in the darkness.

CHAPTER TWENTY-FIVE

I plopped onto a rock. Wracked with shivers now, I folded into myself, rocking back and forth, rubbing my arms and legs. "I'm *freezing*. What are we going to do?"

"We're going to walk back," Emma said. She looked at me on the rock. "Don't sit. Move around."

I took her advice and hopped up, shaking out my arms and legs, desperately trying to generate a little heat. The movement made me light-headed. "Oh, my God, I'm starving, too. I haven't eaten since this morning. I mean, I drank—fortunately—but no food. How can I walk all that way with no energy? How long does it take to pass out from hunger? You'd think I'd know that kind of thing." My panic had me chattering *and* chatty.

Emma studied the sky, calmly taking it all in. "You think you're hungry, but you're not. That won't be the thing to kill you, anyway."

"Wow, cool. Thanks." Chafing my arms, I went to stand

near her. My gaze tracked hers, sweeping the cloudy night sky. I tried to approach the problem scientifically. "This place can't be longer than four miles from end to end. I think there are some large rock formations in the center of the island, so we'll need to hike around. Our biggest concern right now is the cold."

Emma stared at me in that blank way of hers. At first I'd found a sort of appealing serenity in her stillness. But now it was just driving me batty.

"Jeez, Emma. Aren't you freaking out?" I began to jog in place. "Why are you shaking your head?"

"The biggest concern is fear. Not cold. Fear is what kills." She began to walk away.

"Wait. Where are you going?" I jogged to catch up. It was pitch-black now, and I didn't want to lose her. If fear was what would kill me, I had a decent head start.

"Dealing with first things first," she replied.

Emma found the road we'd come in on, and we backtracked a few hundred yards. I had no idea what she was doing, but she seemed to have a plan, which was more than I could say for myself.

She halted. A dead rabbit lay at our feet.

Emma squatted, studying it. The top of its body canted at an unnatural angle from the rest of it. Other than that, it was remarkably blood-free, looking ready to up and hippity-hop away, if not for the whole snapped-spine thing.

"That must be what we hit on our way out here," I said. "Can't be very auspicious to have—"

She plucked the rabbit up by the ears.

"Gah!" I skittered back a few steps. "What are you doing?"

"You're hungry."

"Not *that* hungry." I gave her a wary look. "I've seen the survival shows. You're not going to make me consume larvae or urine or anything like that, are you?"

She didn't laugh or even pretend to answer me. Instead, she said, "This'll help the chill, too."

I didn't want to *begin* to think how Emma might use *roadkill* to keep me warm.

Rather than going back to our original starting point, she headed toward a rock face, barely visible near the side of the road. Dropping the rabbit, she reached behind her and pulled a ginormous knife from her waistband.

"Jeez! Where'd you get that thing?" It looked like a hunting knife. One of those things with a wooden handle and garishly serrated edges, used by guys with names like Cletus or Bobby Ray.

"It was in my drawer." She patted around the boulder, snapping off small branches from what little shrubbery grew at the base.

"So you just carry it with you?"

She nodded.

"Silly me," I mumbled. "*Every* girl should run around with a huge buck knife in her pants."

Emma took one of the branches and began to methodically strip it. "If they gave it, they thought I'd need it."

Now, *there* was an insight. It was my turn to go silent. Why wasn't I carrying around my throwing stars? Just because I hadn't been taught to use them yet didn't mean they might not come in handy. Maybe I could've speared Lilac in the back as she'd walked off.

Emma finished with that and took a larger branch. Kneeling in the dirt, she laid it on the ground and began to whittle it flat.

If each Acari had her own talent, I was dying to know what Emma's was. "Okay, Pocahontas. What's *your* skill?"

"I don't know. Common sense, I suppose." Unimpressed by the concept, Emma simply finished her whittling, removed her gloves, and began to dig in the pockets of her parka. "Do you have any lint?"

I was beyond questioning anything this girl did. As far as I was concerned, my life was in her hands. I dug in my pockets, scraping my nails along the fleece seams. "Sure, probably."

When we'd gathered a quarter-sized wad of the stuff, she unzipped her parka, slid her hand into her tunic pocket, and pulled out a little tube of Vaseline. I recognized it from the basic Dopp kit we'd been issued. She squirted out a gob of it, working it into the lint ball.

"Wow," I said. "I have *no* idea what you're doing right now."

"Petroleum jelly."

I saw it wasn't going to be easy getting information out of her. "Yeah? Vaseline is a petroleum product, and so . . . ?"

"Flammable," Emma said.

"Ohhh. Cool." I knelt beside her. She was going to make a *fire*. A fire meant light, heat, hot food, dry hair. I rubbed my hands together in anticipation. Emma wasn't exactly going to be leading any campfire songs, but I sure did like having her on my team.

I watched, mesmerized, as she created a small bow out of a stick, using a thin strip of fabric for the bowstring. She wound the bowstring around a thicker stick, stood that on the flat bit of branch she'd whittled, and, holding the bow, began a sawing motion with her hand. The stick twirled furiously, and Emma blew gentle puffs of air at the base of it, encouraging a spark to light the lint and the pile of shrubbery she'd nestled close for kindling. Next thing I knew, smoke tickled my nostrils, and a humble orange flame flickered to life.

She set to work skinning the rabbit, deftly wielding her knife in a way that made me happy we weren't enemies. As dinner roasted on a spit, she scraped the rabbit skin clean.

Just the thought of heat and dinner had calmed my nerves, and neither of us had spoken in a while. Finally, I broke the silence. "So, is this what the kids do for fun in North Dakota?"

She gave me a blank look.

"Sorry. Lame attempt at conversation." *Note to self: Emma is long on wilderness, short on humor.*

"I didn't know many kids." She was cleaning the rabbit pelt, and I had a feeling I was looking at what was to be my new hat. "It was just me and my grandfather on a homestead in Slope County."

I thought of my father and instantly assumed Emma and I had had similar experiences. "Did he hurt you?"

She looked baffled for a moment, then exclaimed, "My grandfather? Great Pete, no. Why would you think a thing like that?"

The girl thought nothing of dressing and eating roadkill, and yet she said things like *Great Pete.* Crazy. "Sorry. I didn't mean to offend you. I just assumed . . . *My* dad . . . Well . . . never mind."

That seemed to be enough of an answer for her.

All the knife wielding aside, she actually struck me as oddly innocent. I wondered how on earth she'd found herself *here.* I decided there was only one way to find out. "Emma, can I ask—how did you end up here?"

The boulder shielded us from the snow, which had been

falling steadily since we'd arrived. Warm, amber firelight danced around us. But Emma just stood and walked away into the darkness.

For a moment, I honestly believed she'd just left me there for good. But she came back, rubbing fistfuls of snow over her hands and forearms, cleaning off the blood.

When she finished, she drove some sticks into the dirt, making them into little triangles, and then draped the rabbit skin by the fire. She looked at me over the flames, her face an eerily blank slate. We stayed like that for a moment, just staring at each other, taking each other's measure. Finally, she answered my question.

"My grandfather died. Round about Thanksgiving. I ran the homestead by myself for a while. Then some men came. They tried things." She shrugged. "I protected myself. But the township saw it different. They locked me up; said I was only sixteen and needed to be put in a home. But then someone came for me. He told them he was a lawyer. But he wasn't. He told me about this place. And I came."

I stared, dumbfounded. In some ways, the girl before me was as new and pure as the snow falling around us, and yet she'd already lived a lifetime in just sixteen years.

Emma removed the spit from the fire. She'd impaled the creature with a stick, and it looked like a dark, glistening bunnysicle. "Rabbit's done."

I gave her a broad smile, reaching my hand out for a leg. I'd never tasted anything so good in my life.

We were just finishing up when we heard the rustling. We froze, our eyes meeting over the fire. There was another sound—guttural and hissing, like a growl from the back of a human throat.

Then we saw the eyes. They glowed red and rabid, lacking the ancient stillness of Vampire. Instead, this thing emanated chaos, fury. Hunger.

And it was looking right at us.

CHAPTER TWENTY-SIX

I t leapt at us from the darkness, its feral growl ripping through the snowfall's heavy silence. A hideous thing in the shape of a person, though whatever humanity it once knew was long gone. It saw the fire and flinched back a step, standing and panting.

Paralyzed by pure terror, I could only stare.

Its skin was crackled and black with decay, looking like thin parchment wrapped around a webbing of pure, lean muscle. Tufts of hair clung to its bald and peeling scalp. Red eyes stared at us, glowing from dark sockets.

The thing pulled back its lips. It had only a few teeth, all rotted. Except for the fangs. Two shining, perfect fangs. They looked long. And sharp.

Emma and I rose slowly, edging close enough to stand shoulder to shoulder. It began to circle us, keeping a wary distance from the fire. Emma slid the knife from her waistband, her progress so careful and deliberate, I barely even realized she was moving.

God, I loved that girl.

I'd mistakenly believed the creature was plodding. Or had seen the fire and was cautious. I should've known never to underestimate anything I encountered on this isle.

With a tearing shriek, the thing flew at us. At me.

I didn't have time to think. It grabbed my arms, and pain ripped through my body. Its nails sliced easily through my coat, piercing deep into my skin. They felt like talons that'd been sharpened to hard points.

I was screaming senseless things. Random words . . . *no, what, off, go, no.*

Adrenaline dumped into my veins. Its attack slowed, and I became aware of everything. The crackling sound of its skin as it opened its mouth, the rancid stench of its breath, the gleam of firelight on shining fangs. The warmth of my own blood seeping down my arms.

It dragged me a few steps back into the darkness.

"Stop!" I stomped my heels into the ground, trying to flail free of its grip. But those nails dug deeper. It was stronger than anything I'd ever encountered. Stronger, even, than my father. "Off!"

It leaned closer, and I thought it might bite me. A cascade of surreal thoughts swirled through my head. How strange to be taken this quickly. To be killed, to disappear from the world so easily. Eaten like meat, and without thought, as I might eat.

But the thing didn't bite me. It wasn't that merciful. It grabbed me instead, sniffing me.

I flailed, kicked, struggled—anything to pull myself free. But its grip was too strong. And then it began to squeeze.

Its foul limbs wrapped around me, squeezing tighter and tighter, until it was crushing the life from me. I couldn't drag in enough air to catch my breath. My screams became strangled.

My ribs creaked. I thought my hair was being torn from my scalp, trapped in the vise of the creature's arms. I heard a keening wail and realized it was me. Tears and snot streamed down my face as I gasped for breath.

My cries became choked whimpers.

But then I sensed movement. It was Emma, stabbing the monster over and over in the back.

She kept yelling "Git!" She might've been hollering at a bear.

Her attack reverberated through its body to mine. But the monster didn't feel anything, all her thrusting the mere pricks of a mosquito.

I felt its mouth on my neck. It grunted in frustration, pulled away. I sucked in a blessed gulp of air, but wasted it on a scream when the thing tugged my coat down like an eager lover to reveal my shoulders.

It leaned into me. Its mouth was so close, I saw the fine lines of its cracked and blackened lips.

And then it screeched. The thing abruptly pulled away, fury distorting its face. It looked like a demon, furious and raging.

It shoved me away and I stumbled, catching myself before I fell into the fire.

The monster spun on Emma. She shrieked, and it was a surreal sound, bright and trilling like a scream from a bad horror movie.

My mind raced. Something had stopped it. Something Emma did had angered it.

I remembered a conversation from what felt a lifetime ago. Proctor Amanda's words: *A stake through the heart does 'em in. That bit's true enough.*

I ran toward her. The thing clutched her as it had me, but now an intense rage fueled its hunger. It gripped her savagely, spasmodically clenching her body and tugging her clothes.

She tried to stab the monster, but that only enraged it. It swatted her arm and the knife went flying.

It landed somewhere in the dark perimeter of our little camp, and I bounded after it. Dropping to my knees, I hunted for it. Though I'd taken off my gloves to eat, I didn't feel the cold, even as my bare fingers raked through frozen dirt and muddy snow.

All I knew were Emma's whimpers and the horrifying noises the creature made. Its humming growl a sound of anticipation.

I felt the knife, and made the craziest laugh-cry sound. "Thank you, thank you, thank you."

The handle was thick, but my fingers and palm found their place, nestling perfectly along the slope, like coming home. The weight of it was foreign, and I wriggled my wrist to get used to the feel.

I sprang back up.

The monster had Emma pinned on the ground. Her legs were kicking slowly now. I hoped I wasn't too late.

A stake through the heart.

I had to hope a hunting knife would work just as well.

I realized calm had washed over me. Focus replaced fear. I was a machine and I would kill this thing.

I surveyed the creature's back. I tracked spine and ribs, its figure gnarled and knotty with age. With death. This thing had been human once.

I eyed its left side. Estimated where the heart might be. And I lunged.

"You fucked with the wrong girls," I screamed, plunging the knife in over and over. The shock of stabbing something of flesh and blood reverberated up my arm.

The thing squealed, a shrill, high-pitched sound like a stuck pig. It rose, slapping at its body, lurching drunkenly. There was a jerk-jerk of its body, and it stumbled.

The fire. We stood close to it. I leapt toward the creature and shoved it. It felt like a brittle thing now, splintery and light. Ready to be dust and ashes.

"Burn." I shoved it onto the flames. It shrieked, twitching and seizing as the meager orange flames licked at its skin. Its rags began to smolder, skin crackling like our rabbit on the spit.

My first kill.

My belly lurched, threatening to toss my dinner back up. I swallowed convulsively until the feeling passed. Because something primitive had clicked to life in the back of my brain. I needed to keep my food down. I needed to put the gloves back on my hands. I needed to push aside repulsion and dry myself by the corpse-fueled fire.

Because it was all about survival.

The knowledge was freeing. I felt exhilarated. Lawless.

I'd faced a monster, and the monster lost.

CHAPTER TWENTY-SEVEN

"So we navigate by the stars?" I stared up at the sky, mentally preparing myself for the long hike. I felt oddly serene. I hoped it wasn't shock.

The kill had intensified my purpose. I was focused, in the moment, and crystal clear about what needed to be done.

Emma was already walking ahead. "Not exact enough. We navigate by that." She pointed to one of the only lights visible in the overcast sky. "The North Star."

"Oh. Of course." I stared up at it for a moment, then ran to catch up.

I let her lead, and asked the occasional question about which path she was choosing and why. It seemed she might have as much to teach me as some of the vampires. I wondered if she also knew how to track game. Or people.

Without the blazing fire and scent of roasting meat, we didn't attract any other creatures that night. I was relieved, but knew some strange flicker of disappointment, too. I felt amped, my muscles tensed and ready for action. I had to wonder what was wrong with me.

We made it back to the dorms much faster than I'd expected. It was still full dark, and with the blanket of fresh snow, silent as the grave.

Masha scowled as she opened the door for us. I wondered whether she was actually bummed we'd made it back alive, or if she looked that dour for every occasion. Had she hoped that, right about then, we'd be something's midnight snack?

"The first to return," she announced as we came to the second-floor hall. A cluster of Initiates were gathered on the couches, waiting.

The first to return. We were the only ones who'd made it back so far. I bit my cheeks to keep from smiling. I'd show these Initiates I could be as stoic as they were.

Redheaded Trinity glared at us. Unflinching, I met her eyes. Never before had I let my gaze linger on her for so long. Her eyebrows and lashes were the palest shade of orange, making her dark eyes pop from her face. They were chocolate brown, and full of menace and hate. "Nothing found you?" She sounded skeptical and annoyed.

I stood tall, my chin up, even though all I wanted to do was collapse into my bed. Emma was a quiet presence at my shoulder. I'd relied on her in the wilderness, and she was relying on me now.

"Something found us. We killed it." I was proud of the matter-of-fact tone I'd managed, when what I really wanted to do was *squee* and jump up and down, telling everyone in great, dramatic detail all that'd come to pass.

"Truly?" Masha feigned a patient smile. I wondered if she thought she'd caught us in a lie. "What did this . . . thing look like?"

I met her eyes and refused to let myself look away. "It was human-shaped. With black skin, like a rotted corpse. Its eyes seemed to glow red."

I'd spent much time considering those eyes on our hike back. Vampires had the same basic body parts as the humans they'd once been, and our monster had struck me as a vampire that'd somehow gone wrong.

The Initiates still glared at us, and, feeling I had something to prove, I busted out the academic speak. "Though if the thing really had been a person once, I don't know how glowing eyes would be possible, biologically speaking. They were luminous, reflecting ambient light in the darkness, like a cat's might."

"It was a Draug," Amanda said.

It was a relief to hear my Proctor, a relatively friendly voice. I hadn't seen her leaning against the far wall.

My smile flickered at the sight of her, but I forced my face back to stone. "Whatever it was, it didn't seem . . . rational. It was fren-zied, seeming to operate without reason." I thought of the closest counterpart in my experience. "It acted like an angry gator."

Amanda nodded. "Draug are barely sentient. They are id."

I felt Emma shift. I doubted the concepts of *ego* and *id* were ones she and gramps had explored on the old homestead. I clar-ified for her benefit, but subtly. "So they act without thought," I said, rephrasing. "On pure impulse. Instinct."

"That's the way, dolly. They're hungry; they eat." The other Initiates frowned at Amanda as she spoke. I suspected they'd rather we be kept in the dark. "You're lucky it didn't eat you."

"It wasn't luck," Emma said, her voice uncharacteristically bold. "I had my knife. We fought it. Drew killed it."

A faint ripple of movement washed across the room as Initiates parsed this information. Her delivery seemed like it might've been disrespectful. But she'd simply spoken factually and without emotion. If they wanted something to reprimand, they weren't going to find it in Emma.

"Acari Drew took it down, eh?" Masha stared at me.

I forced myself not to pale. I wondered how many of these Draug *she'd* killed. I gave her a brief nod.

"Nicely done, Drew." Proctor Amanda didn't risk a smile, but her features did warm momentarily. That was something. I couldn't bear being hated by *everyone*.

I thought of Ronan. He must be furious. Would he hate me for sneaking my iPod? Worse, would he be blamed for it? I hoped my kill would at least make him proud.

"Very well, then," Trinity said briskly. "Go wash. You smell foul. But come back here. You'll not sleep tonight. You stand vigil with us. Waiting to see which girls come back."

Which girls. That meant they didn't expect everyone to return. Dread unfurled in my belly. I tried not to think how it was all my fault that everyone was in this situation in the first place. Tried not to think how any death tonight would be on *my* head.

Lilac's group returned not long after we'd finished dressing. Her eyes found me the instant she entered the common area and they lingered there, as cold and sharp as the edge of a knife.

She spoke for the girls as their leader, which was no surprise. What was a surprise was how they could've possibly made it back, and in such good time.

"Tell," Masha ordered.

"I burned them." Lilac pulled off her gloves. Black char marks smudged her fingers and the backs of her hands. *Fire.* Fire was how she'd kept everyone alive. Fire was Lilac's gift.

Them. She'd taken down more than one. I shivered. My unpredictable pyro roommate unnerved me more than any monster I might face in the dark.

IT'D DAWNED CLEAR, AND BRIGHT bolts of sunlight sent a million shards of crystal glittering atop last night's snow. The place looked like a winter wonderland. All the more obscene an atmosphere in which to hear the news.

The final group had returned. All two of them. The others had been slaughtered. By a single Draug.

The French girl with the pixie-cropped hair—I'd learned that her name was Stefinne—vomited repeatedly in a trash can in the corner. Her friend with the short bangs had been among the victims.

I'd been responsible for her friend's death. Me and my iPod and my mother's picture, too. Though I knew in that moment I'd have risked it all to keep alive any connection to my mom. But that connection was lost now, forever. I wondered if they'd destroyed the photo.

I wished *I* could get sick. To vomit and scream and weep. But I refused to let my face show any of it. Staring at Stefinne's stupid hair—dyed black, the roots growing in a mousy brown— I forced the thoughts from my head.

Her companion, a generically pretty Idaho girl, repeated the story. Meanwhile, the Initiates sank into the chairs and couches of the common area like they were settling in for movie night.

"It came. It took us one by one. We threw stuff at it." She was traumatized, covered in blood and scratches, speaking in a lifeless monotone. A tic in her cheek was all that told me there was a person in there somewhere. "Rocks. Tried to hit it. But it just kept grabbing girls. Like it wanted to hug them. Smell them. It pushed them down. Climbed on. Biting . . ."

With a sharp inhale, life slid back into her eyes, lighting her face with horror. "Oh, my God!" she shrieked. She began to shake and scream, as though still fighting the monster. "Oh, God! Make it stop!"

"Congratulations." At the sound of Lilac's voice, my head shot up. I saw her reflection in the window, hovering at my back like an assassin. She'd showered and somehow managed to look perfect in her gray uniform, despite the lack of sleep. "You must be so proud."

Amanda sprang from the couch, putting her arm around the Idaho girl's shoulder. "It's all right, dolly. You're back safe. How about we get you and your mate washed up?"

"Five down." Guidon Trinity looked at her nails. She might've been discussing a football score, for all the emotion that was in her voice.

Emma and I shared a quick look, then glanced away. Instinct told me to show no emotion, no allegiances.

Five girls. Dead. It was my fault.

Finally, we all dispersed. Numb, I staggered up to the room.

Crawling into bed was such a blessed relief—I didn't remember the last time I'd slept. I almost didn't care who my roommate was. Von Slutling could torch me in my sleep, for all I cared.

Her voice chimed into my consciousness, just as I began to drift off. "Watch your back, Charity. So many girls want to take you down, they're going to have to start giving out numbers."

CHAPTER TWENTY-EIGHT

⸺∞⸺

The gym lights flickered to life with a loud *click-click*. Yasuo stood in the doorway, looking skeptically at the heavy-duty fluorescent domes. "Are you sure we're allowed to be in here?"

"Ronan says we're encouraged to use the gym after hours. As long as it's before curfew and all." I slung my bag on the floor against the wall and pulled off my coat. I shot him a challenging glare. "Don't tell me you're backing out now."

"Trainee Yasuo Ito doesn't know the words *back out*." He joined me, shucking off his black wool peacoat. "I just don't get why you need me. Aren't you learning how to fight in combat class?"

"Yeah, sure. Combat rocks—or it will. They're still mostly having us do intro stuff, like basic fencing or tai chi forms." I climbed over the ropes into the ring. "I didn't exactly have an épée handy when that Draug came at us. I can't help but worry it was dumb luck that saved me."

Yas smiled. "Sounds like Emma was pretty cool about the whole thing."

I heard something in his voice. Emma was attractive in a refreshingly scrubbed, prairie sort of way. If it were the normal world, I might think about setting them up. "So you think Emma's cool, huh?"

"I don't know." He wandered around the gym floor, stopping at the hanging rope, giving it a tug, as if he might need to test it out. "I've never met anyone like her. Especially not in Hell-Lay, California."

I leaned over the edge of the ring, trying to get a good look at his face. "Are you blushing?"

"Guys don't blush."

"Uh-huh." I shoved against the side of the ring a few times, but the ropes barely gave. There were five of them, fully padded and sturdier than they looked. "Come on, then. Unless you're chicken. I want to see some of your good old L.A. street-fighting moves."

He prickled. "You think because I'm from Los Angeles and I'm Asian, I'm in some sort of gang?"

I gave him my *don't-go-there* look. "No. . . . I think because you're a guy who claims to have killed his Yakuza father that maybe you know a thing or two."

Smiling, he shook his head, and like that, the tension was gone. "Yeah, I guess I've got some choice MMA moves."

"What's MM . . . ohhh." Understanding dawned. "Mixed martial arts? That's, like, late-night, cable-TV, cage-fighting stuff, right?"

"Drew, I'm shocked." He hopped into the ring, his movements lithe as a cat's. Clearly, he'd done this before. "MMA is a highly respected form of fighting."

"Forgive me if I'm not acquainted with the vernacular." I stared as he bobbed from foot to foot, shaking out his arms. "Jeez, Yas, you are *such* a guy."

"I should hope so. Now get ready. I'm going to teach you my favorite move." He flashed me a brilliant smile. "*Ground and pound*, baby."

I approached him warily. "Sounds like a cooking thing."

"Nope. It's the thing that's going to save your ass someday. When you're fresh out of those ninja stars or you drop your fencing . . . foil, or whatever those wussy-ass swords are called."

I had to agree with him on the fencing. The moves were elegant, and I could see how repeating the same series of stances increased arm strength and built the foundation for stronger overall fighting. Only I'd seen the eyes of that Draug, and it'd wanted to eat me. All the hopping and feinting in the world wouldn't save me if I were caught off guard.

But Yasuo had dissed my throwing stars, and *nobody* dissed my throwing stars. "My weapon is known as the shuriken."

"*Wakatta yo.*" He shot me a look of exaggerated annoyance. "As in, *Duh, Drew.* I think I know what they're called in Japanese."

"Okay, okay, sensei. So let's ground around this thing." I stretched my arms in front of me, cracking my knuckles, but it kind of hurt, so I shook them out with a scowl instead.

"Ground and *pound*," he said distractedly. He'd begun to circle me like a tiger about to pounce.

It put me on my guard, and I squatted in a standard defensive posture, hands bracing the air in front of me. He was taking too long to attack, so I taunted, "What's the problem, Yas? Afraid to hit a girl?"

But then he pounced, and the breath whooshed from me as I hit the ground, shutting me up. I knew he wasn't my real enemy, I knew this was a friendly grapple, but still, adrenaline dumped into my veins.

Memories tumbled into my head. The breath whooshing from me when Daddy Dearest shoved me to the ground. The creak of my ribs when he'd grip me tight, flinging me into my room and slamming the door. I forced the images from my head. I'd survived my father and it'd made me stronger. That other girl wasn't me anymore.

Because now I had the tools to fight back.

We rolled on the floor. I scrapped and scratched, managing to get on top. I suspected he'd let me.

"Come on, Drew. Push me down."

I scrambled, painfully aware of how tiny I was compared to him. It would be that way with every fight for me.

"That's it." He began to shout encouragements. "Push me down. Pin me. Use your elbows. Hold me down."

"But you're too big." It was frustrating, and I snarled my anger at him.

"Get used to it. Everyone's bigger than you. Now shut up and use your weight." He slapped at my leg. "Use it *all*. Get your knee in my stom—"

I jammed my knee onto his belly, and he grunted. "Damn, D, not so hard. But yeah . . ." He shifted, grunting again. "Now use your other hand to pound my face."

I went at him, and he flinched. Laughing, he yelled, "Not for real!"

Finally, I got him down—one knee on his stomach and a fist poised over his face. "Pretty simple," I said, feeling triumphant.

"Yeah, until I flip you." With a single swing of his legs, Yasuo had me on my back before I knew what had happened. "You didn't keep your weight on me, D. You can't let up for a *second*."

We grinned at each other, panting to catch our breath. He straddled me, pinning my hands to the mat.

I froze.

It was pretty intimate, and I let my mind go there for a second. Yasuo was an undeniably good-looking guy. Plus he was nice, he was cool, and we got along.

And here we were, him astride me, leaning down like he was getting ready to kiss me. The smile on his face faded, and I could tell the notion had entered his mind, too.

I explored the thought, opening myself to feelings. But nothing came.

And then I imagined what it might be like if *Ronan* straddled me like this. If it were Ronan's legs wrapped around me, Ronan holding my hands down. Fire ignited from my belly all the way to my scalp.

He laughed, breaking the tension. And then he pretended to lay punches on my head with his elbows and fists. "Pay attention, Drew. I'm braining you."

"Huh?"

"Cover your head!"

"Right, yeah." I got right back in it, curling my arms up, covering my face.

"That's it. Always guard your head." He stopped for a second. My arms were still clenched over my face, and he rested his hands on them. But that feeling of intimacy had passed. I sensed it from his end, too—like he'd also played a scenario out in his mind but had felt nothing.

He jiggled my arms. "You're pinned. Do you know how you're going to get out of this?"

"No." I gave a spurt of kicking and wriggling, but Yasuo was solid over me. "I'm stuck."

He gently pulled my hands from where I'd clenched them around my head. "Now take this arm"—he gave my right arm a squeeze—"and wrap it through mine. Yeah, like that. Now grab my hand."

I did as he instructed, and, neat as a pin, I'd wrenched Yasuo's arm out to the side. "Cool!"

He smiled. "Not done yet, Blondie. You're still pinned. Your opponent will think you're struggling, that he's got you. But listen. If you're ever on your back like this, get to the ropes. *Scoot back*."

I did as he told me, shimmying toward the edge of the mat.

"More. Scoot back against the ropes . . . or the wall, or the trees, or *whatever* you're pinned against."

I scooched and wriggled until my head hit the bottom rope.

"Boom," he said. "You're there. The only way to survive is to get back on your feet. You've got my arm, but I think I've got you pinned and cornered. Now you have to sit up a little."

I glowered at him. "How can I sit up?"

"Just a little. Just brace your other arm behind you." He tightened his grip, and I squirmed. He was making this a little too realistic.

"You're getting off on this," I snarled. Struggling, I edged to the side a bit, doing as he instructed. "Shit, Yas. You make it . . . sound . . . easy."

I got my arm behind me, and once I braced on my elbow, it was easy to lever myself to a half-sitting position. He was still over me, but my shoulders were back up against the ropes.

"Yeah, you got it. Sometimes having your back against the wall is a good thing." He beamed. "Now free your leg."

I swung my leg away from under him. And then I laughed. These moves were a revelation. I could use my own weight, and then use my opponent's weight against him.

He nodded to my shoulders. "Lean against the ropes. The ropes aren't pinning you now, they're *supporting* you. Edge up, bit by bit."

I took it from there, the move instinctual.

When I got halfway up the ropes, he backed off, hands lifted in praise. "And up you go."

I high-fived one of his open hands. And then I collapsed onto the mat to catch my breath, half laughing, half panting. "That was awesome. Thank you. I now feel completely equipped to be mauled by the next Draug with dignity and grace."

He plopped next to me, and we lay there for a few minutes in companionable silence.

"Why'd you do it, anyway?" he asked finally. "Keep your stupid iPod, I mean. I get the family photo, but seriously, D. An iPod?"

"I know." I sighed, flopping my arm over my face. "But it was a *Touch*. It even stored books."

"Books . . . cool," he said sarcastically. "Until you die from your nerddom."

He'd struck a nerve. Girls *had* died because of it. I changed the subject at once. "What about you? You're here with me— aren't you nerdy by association? Shouldn't you be hanging with all the vamp-trainee-jock dudes? Your pal Josh is, like, home-coming king now, the way Lilac and her clique are always hovering around him."

He shrugged. "We hang out. Sometimes. Some of the guys are all right."

There was something tight in his voice that I didn't get. I wondered if it was fear. My questions spilled out in a barrage. "What's the deal with the Trainees? Do you compete like the Acari do? Are you scared of the other guys? I mean, aren't you scared of the whole *process*? Like, will it hurt to become a vampire? Does it mean you have to *die* first? And what if everything messes up and you turn into some sort of crazy Draug thing? Have they taught you how all that works?"

"You know I'm not allowed to answer any of that stuff, Drew." He sighed, and I heard the strain there. "But yeah. *Scared* is pretty much the word for it."

CHAPTER TWENTY-NINE

W eeks passed.
          I went to class. I got stronger. The end of the semester was in sight. Just a matter of weeks until the Directorate Award was mine.

Many of the girls were gunning for me, just as Lilac had warned, but Emma and Yas watched my back.

I dared not befriend anyone else. Girls were disappearing every day now, and the rumors that'd once abounded had all stopped, as though Acari were afraid even to discuss it, lest they might disappear in the night.

It was becoming clear that either you succeeded or you died, and I couldn't risk too many friendships when my very survival might depend on another girl's downfall. Friends were a new concept to me, and I didn't know how I'd handle the loss of one.

But I did let myself get close to the teachers. Oddly, we were really clicking. I'd always been smarter than my teachers back home, but these all had something to teach me, even creepy Master Dagursson.

I knew some girls were struggling. I could see it in class. But I was pouring myself in heart and soul. I was labeled a teacher's pet, but I didn't care. I think that might've been the only thing keeping other Acari from suffocating me with a pillow in my sleep.

The academics alone astounded me. There was no end to the knowledge available to me. Tracer Judge gave me a key to the phenom library, and I read whatever I wanted, whenever I wanted.

My morbid fascination with Master Alcántara continued to grow. I couldn't decide if he was totally appealing or totally terrifying, but discussing map coordinates with someone who'd actually met Descartes, the dude who'd *discovered* the X and Y axes? Now, that was cool. He only guest lectured once in a while, and every time reminded me how profoundly I coveted that Directorate Award.

It would be mine. I was working so hard. I *had* to win. I'd find a way off the island.

Even combat class had taken on new meaning. I headed there now, thinking how in all my years of dissing gym class I'd been so wrong. Since fighting the Draug, I'd become exquisitely aware of just how valuable my body was, of how physical aptitude was precisely the thing that would transform my mind into a killer weapon.

"Good afternoon, Acari Drew." My combat teacher, Watcher Priti, smiled as I walked in. Her language, like her posture, was ever elegant. "You're the last of my little birds to arrive."

I smiled back naturally. Because I *adored* Watcher Priti. She

was smart and strong and beautiful. It was like being taught how
to kill with your bare hands by a maniacal Padma Lakshmi
look-alike with a penchant for Chanel No. 5 and pert tennis
outfits. I was certain she was as deftly dangerous with her chosen weapon, a razor-sharp discus she called a chakra, as she was
with her charms.

"Just swooping in for my landing," I said, playing off her
nickname for us students. "I hope I'm not late," I added, even
though I knew I was. Just ninety seconds, but that'd be enough
to get most girls on toilet-scrubbing duty for a week.

"We've not begun yet." Priti was pulling padded vests from
the storage locker. "If you're already geared up, you may join the
other Acari on the bleachers. We're doing blade work today."

She flashed me a broad smile, knowing how much I loved
anything with a blade. We'd yet to move beyond simple attacks
and defensive techniques, but I knew the day would come when
I'd graduate to my throwing stars.

If only this were all there was to being a Watcher. But, sadly,
the island was so much more insane than cool phenomena topics or learning how to sword fight. I was mastering all sorts
of illegal, immoral things—breaking and entering, hacking,
exploding, stealing. Killing.

It appeared I had three choices in life:

1. Be the best.
2. Be a victim.
3. Be on the first boat out of here.

Though I knew option three would be a lot harder than it
sounded, I was still gunning for my eventual escape.

And yet . . .

A tiny part of me had begun to mourn the thought of leaving. Some of the people around me were beginning to feel like a makeshift family. I'd always dreamt of belonging, and if I ascended to Watcher, I'd become a part of something bigger. I'd have a place.

I was mesmerized by Watcher Priti and studied her hungrily, eager to emulate her. She was elite and shown so much respect. I'd spied the affectionate smiles she'd shared with some of the Tracers—they were close-knit and trusting.

What I wouldn't do to have Ronan smile at me like that. He hadn't smiled at me since the Initiates discovered my iPod.

If—rather, *when*—I escaped, I'd be saying good-bye to all that. Good-bye to Ronan. Good-bye to a shot at the sense of family I'd always longed for.

There was my training to consider, too. I couldn't deny I was enjoying every minute. It'd been chemical compounds for me in the morning, and was shaping up to be a knife-wielding afternoon. I was learning new things. Learning how to be strong.

But I was also learning how to be a woman. Which is partly why Priti held such fascination for me. Growing up without a mom, with a front-row seat to my dad and the Yatch, I didn't know much about femininity, about how the power of it went beyond styled hair and a good pedi. I'd spent these past months studying Priti's every move, knowing she had far more to teach than merely combat techniques.

As a result, I found myself standing straighter. I practiced on the Trainees, letting myself hold their gazes, just to see how they'd react. And the reaction was generally positive. I'd never realized before how simpleminded boys could be.

I heard faint whispering from the bleachers but ignored it, feeling hostility aimed my way. It bugged a lot of the girls that I was one of Priti's favorites. She was so elegant and lovely, I guess other Acari felt she should've snubbed a wallflower like me right off the bat.

And I don't know why she hadn't. Maybe I was a project for her. I worked hard, got hurt a lot, but never said anything. Maybe she sensed that, too.

I glanced over at my waiting classmates. They were watching our little exchange, envy and hatred in their eyes. I decided to prolong it. "Is today the day you let me try your chakra?"

Priti laughed. "You know it's not, little Acari." She eyed my bag. "But I see you brought your shuriken."

I hugged it close to my side, thinking of my throwing stars tucked safely inside. I took them most everywhere now, like Emma with her hunting knife. "How can you tell?"

"I can see it in your eyes." She chucked my chin, and her lithe five-foot-eleven frame alongside my meager five foot two must've been a comical sight. "And by the way you're clutching that bag."

"Does that mean you'll finally let me use them?" I'd been dying to learn how to throw them, but Watcher Priti said I still needed time.

Her face bloomed into a gorgeous, pearly smile. "Do you think you're ready?"

"Ohmygosh, really? Today?" I restrained myself from jumping up and down in giddy anticipation. "Yes. Totally ready."

"Today, then." Lowering her chin, she sharpened her tone. "And now I think it's time you took your seat, Acari Drew."

Class was unending. We worked through a circuit of standard sword and dagger exercises. Shoulder and arm warm-ups, weight work, footwork, basic defensive maneuvers. All interminable. My only thought was for the four perfect stars in my locker.

I was at the kendo station, practicing a standard series of lunges, arcing swings, and footwork. The long bamboo sword felt like an extension of me, and I repeated the moves by rote.

"Very nice, Acari Drew." Priti snatched the end of my sword in midair. She eyed me speculatively. "I know you enjoy our sword work. Shuriken may have sharp edges, but they're very different, you know."

Was this her lead-up to finally letting me throw them? "I'm sure," I agreed quickly. I'd agree with anything; I just wanted the stars. I was so eager to try them.

She narrowed her eyes in challenge. "I'm not sure you're listening to me. You must prepare yourself to miss the mark. Many times."

"I'm ready."

She didn't look like she agreed with me, but nonetheless she told me, "Go get them."

I raced to my locker and was back before Priti could have a chance to change her mind. I met her at the target station, a throwing star in my hand, the others wrapped in velvet at my feet.

I raised my arm, ready to throw. Nervous excitement jangled through me.

"Patience, Acari Drew." She stilled my arm, giving me an

amused smile. "Shuriken is an art form. The exercise mental as well as physical."

She wrapped my fingers around the star. It was cold, sharp. Not so much larger than my palm. "Feel the weapon. *Shuriken* is Japanese for 'dagger in hand.' Feel the edges. More than any knife, it is an extension of you. Nothing separates you from the steel. No artificial handle, no imperfection of the blades."

Priti took my shoulders, guiding me into position. "When you throw a knife, you must worry about distance. Not so for the shuriken. Yours have six points. Six opportunities for the weapon to hit its mark."

She squatted a bit, standing behind me, bringing herself to my eye level. "Now look at the target. You aren't just throwing *at* it. You are extending yourself, your will, your *power*, toward it."

I'd been contemplating that bull's-eye all semester. But I opened my mind this time. I extended my energy toward it. As though the target and I were connected by the finest thread.

"Yes," she whispered. "You see it, don't you? Watchers are taught a mantra. Listen, and hear the words." She cradled my arm extended before me. *"I am roots in the earth. I am water that flows. I am grounded. I am Watcher."*

Slowly she pulled away. "Now breathe. Feel the ground at your feet. Feel the weapon as a part of your hand. Relax and feel the connection."

I did. My head rose, my shoulders dropped slightly. I felt lighter.

"That's it, Acari. Stay relaxed. Always relaxed. The movement isn't merely in your arm. It's not just a flick of the wrist. You must draw energy from the ground beneath your feet. Let the energy flow up from the earth and through your body. Into your arm. Your movements should be fluid. When you throw, you cast the shuriken from you as though riding on a wave of power."

I did. I felt it. The soles of my feet were grounded to the floor. I was connected to the earth. The sensation of power rose from below, through my feet, shooting up my body, tingling all the way to the tips of my fingers.

I felt her whispered breath in my ear. "Now."

I threw.

The star flew from my hand on a wave of power. And then clattered to the floor.

I heard a couple of girls behind me snicker.

I felt my face turn beet red.

"Again, Acari. Without pause. You must try again and again." Priti patted my shoulder and walked away. I heard her shout a crisp order to one of the other girls, but her words didn't register.

The only things that existed were me, my shuriken, and the target. I tried again. Again I heard the disappointing *ping* of metal hitting the ground.

I tried over and over. And each time my star bounced off the target, clattering to the ground.

I felt the other students gathering their things, heading to the locker room. I kept my back to them. I didn't care if I had to stay all night. I was determined to get this.

Again and again I tried. *Ping. Ping. Ping.*

Until.

I knew the moment the shuriken left my hand that it was the one. I'd felt it. It had flowed straight from me. Riding on a perfect wave. I felt it going directly for the target, like a line being reeled back home. It hit and it stuck.

I heard a single pair of hands clapping for me. Turning, I saw Emma smiling at me. I realized I hadn't really seen her smile before. It warmed that heart-shaped face, opened it up. She was pretty.

She glanced at the clock. "You'd better git," she told me in that *Fargo* accent.

Many of our classmates had already showered. They sat waiting for Watcher Priti's final words.

I tucked my stars carefully in their velvet wrapper and headed to the bleachers. I'd have to skip my shower and change later.

"Hey, little piggy." Lilac made exaggerated sniffing sounds. "Disgusting. I can't sit near this." She and her crew shifted to one of the rearmost bleachers.

I smiled. High school barbs and minidramas meant nothing to me. I'd learned how to throw like a ninja.

Watcher Priti came to stand before the class. She was fresh-faced and glowing, looking statuesque in a white jumper. It was hard to imagine she was capable of great savagery, though I knew she surely was. A woman wasn't elevated to her rank without a flair for cold, calculated combat. I had a picture of her in my mind, beaming her pearly smile while beheading wayward Draug with her chakra.

"Wonderful news, little birds. We've determined the subject area for this semester's Directorate Award."

Heart kicking into gear, I edged to the front of my seat. This was it. She was going to tell us what our big, end-of-semester challenge would be. Math? I wondered. Some computer-programming thing?

"It will be a single-elimination tournament format. You will face off against an Acari challenger. If you lose, you're out. If you win, you face the next Acari. You do this over and over until either you lose or you win the tournament."

I hung on her every word, my mind racing. A tournament? But what would we compete in? Were they going to give us some sort of all-around trivia challenge?

Watcher Priti gave us her signature smile. It meant good news for me; I knew it. "This semester's chosen discipline is . . ."

I held my breath.

". . . combat."

CHAPTER THIRTY

I sat on my bed, leaning against the wall, forcing myself to concentrate. Dinner had been almost impossible. I'd made myself drink—with an upcoming combat challenge, I'd be a fool not to—but that was about all I'd managed.

Master Alcántara had said participation in the competition was voluntary. I could back out. But then I'd lose my shot at traveling off this rock. At escape.

Besides, I wouldn't be surprised if one's decision to enter or not enter the challenge weren't part of the whole test. Watchers were the best of the best, and Acari were expected to be driven, to be contenders.

I'd just never thought of myself in that way before. Motivated and determined, yes. But a contender?

I slammed my Norse book shut. It was no good reading anything tonight.

Combat. Just the thought of it made me ill. Of all the things to be forced to compete in, they chose combat? And what did that mean, anyway? We'd dress up in armor and spar? What would the rules be? What constituted winning? Would girls get hurt? Would girls *die*?

But of course they'd die. Girls were dying in training; getting offed in the heat of competition would be a given.

"You're looking shifty, Charity." Lilac slammed the door to our room and slung her bag on her bed. "Panties in a twist over the upcoming fight? What a shame you suck at anything to do with gym class."

She flopped on her bed, and for a moment we just stared at each other. It was such a mockery of regular dorm life, like two roomies in for the night, ready to gab. Then she pulled out her lighter, and I heard a clicking sound. *Flick, flick, flick*—over and over.

And she called *me* a freak. "Why don't you do us a favor and set yourself on fire?"

She fingered the neck of her tunic. I'd almost forgotten her scar, but her tugging revealed more of that raw, rippling skin than I'd ever seen. She already *had* caught on fire once in her life.

It chilled me to consider what might've happened. More chilling, though, was the fact that, despite having once suffered third-degree burns, she was still drawn to all things flammable.

She snapped the lid to the Zippo shut. Pinching it between two fingers, she wriggled it before me. "Rumor has it they'll let us fight with the weapon they gave us. Sort of like our specialty."

It made my flesh crawl to consider why Lilac might want to enter a sparring ring armed only with her lighter. I let my eyes travel back to the ridge of disfigured skin on her neck. "So, how'd you get *your* specialty, Lilac?"

"My mother brought this girl home once," she said in a musing voice. She traced the edge of her scar, and the movement was dreamy, almost sensual. "Just some foster trash, but Mummy decided she was her little ragamuffin. Decided she was my new sister. But she wasn't."

"Umm, okay. You didn't like your foster sister—there's no surprise." Was that why Lilac had borne me such instant and irrational hatred? "So is this a wealth thing? Is *that* why you hate me so much?"

"Oh, it's so much more than that. You're a *dead* ringer," she said, and her choice of words gave me a shiver. She scowled at my hair. "Little Sunny, with her sweet blond hair."

"The kid's name was *Sunny*?" I knew a flash of sympathy for this anonymous child. I had enough baggage around the whole blond thing, I couldn't imagine having to bear the name Sunny in addition.

Lilac grinned. It was the first time she'd ever smiled at me, and it made the hairs on my arms stand on end. "Sunny, Sunny. She fooled everyone. But not me. Everyone always asked why I couldn't be more like her." Her grin turned into a sneer. "Poor girl, but so pretty and so bright."

"So that's it? You had a foster sister who looked a lot like me, poor but smart, and it didn't vibe with your rich-and-stupid routine? Or did you just hate that your *mummy* liked this Sunny better than you?"

Repeating the name made something click. I'd heard it before in Lilac's psycho sleep chatter. Foreboding made my skin crawl. "Wait. Is this Sunny, as in *Burn, sunny, burn?*"

Lilac narrowed her eyes, but the smile didn't leave her face. "Poor Sunny. The house burned down with her in it."

Blood turned to ice in my veins. Lilac was always calling me a freak, but as far as I was concerned, she was the only mutant in this dorm room. She must have incinerated her foster sister. And now she dreamt of incinerating me.

I doubted I'd ever sleep again.

I forced my voice to remain calm. "So, you gonna burn me while I sleep, Lilac?"

"No," she said in a matter-of-fact tone. "I'm going to burn you in front of everyone." And then she leaned over to unlace her boots.

"Over my dead body," I said.

"Oh, it will be. And, apparently, I can even win a prize for it."

The Directorate Award. "Careful, Lilac. People might think you're overconfident."

"You know I'm stronger than you are," she said. "How many of those pretty little stars did they give you? Four? I saw you in class today. In your lame hands, they'll be about as deadly as Christmas ornaments."

I bristled. She could diss my hair but not my weapon. "You know nothing about my shuriken, von Slutling."

Her laugh trilled through the room. "Listen to you, freak. Shur-i-ken . . . sure-ya-can . . . sure-you-*can't*."

Little did she know, her posturing only firmed my resolve. "Don't you have homework or something? You can burn down the dorm, sleep with every last Trainee, and spin-class your way to Watcher status for all I care, but it won't do any good if you fail out of German."

I'd hit a nerve.

She curled her upper lip in a flat-eyed snarl. Flowing hair plus that signature blank viciousness, and von Slutling looked like a lunatic Playboy Bunny. "What do *you* know?"

A lot more than you, I wanted to say, but I kept my mouth shut. I talked big, but I honestly didn't want to get torched in my sleep.

She snagged her German workbook from her bag and swung her legs onto her bed, and we proceeded to ignore each other.

Reaching onto my desk, I snagged Sun Tzu's *Art of War* and was immersing myself in wisdom that seemed just-almost useful, when I heard it. A quiet *shlish* sound.

I glanced over, but Lilac was slumped, looking sound asleep over her grammar homework. My eyes went to the tiny fold of paper that someone had slid under the door.

Was it for me? I sat up straight, on alert. Or was it for Lilac? I wasn't sure which would be more of a coup.

I waited, but Lilac didn't move. Miraculously, she slept on, breathing evenly onto the pages of her workbook. I decided to make my move before a stiff neck woke her up, and I tiptoed out of bed.

Grabbing the paper, I shuffled back to my bed, ready at any moment for von Slutling's eyes to fly open in an accusing stare. But they didn't.

As it turned out, the note was for me. It was scrawled in furtive, barely legible script that looked like a boy's handwriting.

Drew,

Something's happened. They said I might not live until morning.

Meet me by the gates, near the stones, tonight at midnight.

Please. I need you.

—Yas

I stared. His words chilled me to my bones.

I might not live until morning.

What did that mean? Was he dying? Was he going to be in a fight? Had there already been one? I had no idea what the situation could possibly be. The Trainees kept their business pretty top secret. We girls had no clue what happened behind their locked gates.

Yasuo needed me. But tonight? After curfew? All the way across campus, past those creepier-than-creepy standing stones, all the way to the gates of the boys' dorm? I dared not think how many rules *that* little scenario broke.

I glanced at the note, and four words popped out at me:

Please. I need you.

Ultimately, that was what convinced me. I had a friend and he needed me. *Me.* Nobody had ever needed me before.

Come midnight, I was going to break pretty much every rule available to me. I was venturing to the forbidden heart of Vampire central.

To the standing stones and the castle on the hill.

CHAPTER THIRTY-ONE

I lay in bed, waiting for time to pass. Apparently, this was to go down in the Drew Annals as the longest night ever.

I didn't know what was going on. Yasuo basically said they might not let him live. But *they* who? Vampires? Trainees? I didn't know what good *I* could do—I just knew he'd asked for my help, and I needed to be there for him.

I'd only been to the stones once, but Emma and I had seen the castle in the distance on the night of our epic walk. I thought I could retrace our steps. I considered getting her, or at least telling her where I was going, then immediately thought better of it. Yasuo was already in trouble, and if I got caught, I would be, too. Best to keep Emma way out of it.

And *what if* I got caught? Before, it'd just been an iPod and a photograph, and look at what'd happened. Then there was Mimi—all she'd done was talk back to a vampire, and Headmaster Fournier had turned her into a puddle of carnage. And now I was considering breaking pretty much every rule in the book.

They wouldn't look kindly on it. Leaving after curfew? Straying from the path, going near the boys' dorm, to the standing stones? I was toast if anyone caught me.

I was toast if *Lilac* caught me.

Her breathing was steady and deep, but was she really asleep? If I went, I'd be giving her the perfect opportunity to get rid of me once and for all.

But Yas needed me. Tonight. There'd been no doubt in his message.

I slid on my boots. The weather had gotten warmer, so I pulled on my lightweight fleece jacket instead of my parka. I needed to be able to fight or to run, if necessary.

The last thing I did was grab my shuriken, wadding up the whole bundle and shoving it into my jacket pocket. I really needed to figure out a better way to carry them, like a ninja-star holster or something.

The lights were out across campus, but the moon was bright and a great shaft of white light shot across the quad. It was empty, desolate. I wondered what monsters might be lying in wait.

What was I doing? What happened to Acari who broke the rules so flagrantly? I was certain they must suffer a fate worse than death.

But Yasuo was in trouble. He wanted my help. Out of all the people he could've asked, he'd chosen me. Shivering, I zipped my jacket to my throat and snuck from the dorm.

I stayed on the path all the way across the quad till I reached the science building. It was empty, and its blackened windows reminded me of the Draug's dark eye sockets. I had the eerie feeling the building watched me, that those windows might've blinked to life at any moment, glowing red, to witness my fall from grace.

This was it. The end of the road. My heartbeat thundered in my ears. I was entering the unknown, the forbidden.

But I thought of Yas. His life depended on this.

I stepped from the path. The first transgression in a night sure to be full of them.

Fear drove my feet forward, eating up the uneven terrain. I didn't slow my pace—if I was going to be mauled, I might as well present a moving target. Occasionally I spun, jogging backward to judge my direction in relation to the North Star. Emma had taught me well—I was on track, heading what I estimated to be due southwest.

I reached the standing stones sooner than I'd anticipated, a grim half-moon encircling one edge of a grassy courtyard. Girls had swarmed the area on that first day, but now, desolate in the shadows, I saw that the stones were even more massive than I'd thought. The castle on the hill loomed just beyond, and I didn't dare think what might be watching me from within its walls.

The yellow LED numbers on my standard-issue watch read 23:47. I was early. I needed to occupy myself until Yasuo came.

I bounced on the balls of my feet, pretending it was to keep away the cold, but really it distracted me from the fear that was twining its way up my spine, making me feel I might never be warm. I started to walk around, and before I realized, I found myself walking toward the stones. They called me. As though a superficial veil had been cast atop my conscious mind, urging, *What harm could it be to get a closer look?* It was a pull I felt deep in my belly.

And yet a tiny kernel of animal instinct nestled in the recesses of my brain was sounding an alarm, shrill and insistent. *You are prey. You must run.*

But I couldn't run. I had to help Yas.

My eyes were only on the center stone. It was where Headmaster Fournier had stood on that first day. The stone on which Mimi had met her death.

It drew me, and I walked to it. Placing my hand down, I braced myself for the shock of cold, but it was warm.

"Little Acari, so far from home." Cool breath tickled over the skin of my cheek, a gentle breeze in the spring night. "Do you come looking for me?"

My skin shrank two sizes, my flesh rippling into goose bumps. I recognized the sultry voice, the accent. I knew whose face I'd see when I turned.

Oh, shit. I was so dead.

I swallowed hard, somehow managed to find my voice. "Master Alcántara."

The sight of him stole my breath. His thick, black hair gleamed. His mysterious, dark eyes glittered. He was beautiful, an apparition promising charm, enchantment, seduction. But more than that, he radiated *power.*

I'd expected anger, a confrontation, but some other emotion played on his face. He looked wicked, playful even, and it terrified me.

He tilted his head, contemplating me. "I felt your approach. The flame of a torch cutting through the endless black of night."

Pure terror swept me. I'd broken the rules in the biggest way ever. He was one of the main vampires, and he'd busted me. What horrible punishment would I suffer?

I waited for him to lash out at me, but he just stared, consuming me with his eyes. Why was he being so casual? Was he toying with me before he struck?

He traced a finger down my cheek. My skin felt hot under his touch. "Did you sense me, as I sensed you? Did you seek me, as I did you?"

Breathing in and out was a struggle under that penetrating gaze. I was panting, worried I might hyperventilate. My reply was deliberate, my words slow and measured. "You sought me? The stones . . . they pulled me closer."

His eyes lit. "You felt it, did you not?"

Did he not know for certain? I'd just assumed vampires knew *everything*. That if they summoned a human, they'd know without a doubt that human would come running. I gave him a wary nod. "Yes. I guess I felt . . . drawn."

He grew more intense, if that were possible. I focused on not flinching away from him. On not getting sucked into the depths of those exotic, coal black eyes. Carefully, he brushed a strand of hair from my brow. "Like seeks like, Annelise."

I concentrated on slowing my heartbeat, deepening my shallow breaths. I refused to faint. I might wake in some horrible dungeon. Panicked at the thought, I blurted, "Sounds like a personal ad."

His laugh reverberated off the stones. "Truly, you amuse me."

I smiled back cautiously. Why hadn't he killed me yet?

He cocked a brow, his grin once again mischievous. "*Like seeks like*. Perhaps it could be a law of quantum mechanics. What say you? Are you here merely because the universe dictated the actions of yet another mindless bit of particulate matter?" He stepped closer. "Or were you, Annelise the woman, drawn to *me*?"

My mind worked frantically. What the hell was he talking about? Physics? Was he a predator toying with his meal? Or were these the words of a man? "Are you asking as my teacher?"

He laughed. "Poor, befuddled child. How must it be for you? Is it a pleasure, for the first time in your life, to feel a true challenge?"

I didn't think it'd be a pleasure when he finally got around to slaughtering me. But playing along seemed to have the added benefit of keeping me alive, so I answered, "You keep me on my toes. I'll grant you that, Master Alcántara."

"I knew you would enjoy the island." He cupped my cheek and I froze. His skin wasn't clammy like I'd imagined it might be. Instead, the flesh of his hand was firm and cool.

I forced myself to remember he was a killer. A monster. Breaking our connection, I made myself blink.

He stepped back. He sat on the stone and gestured for me to join him. "Tell me, *cariño*. Have you given thought to how it is you find yourself on our isle? Think you that paltry *Tracer* found you?"

His comment brought me back to myself. I remained standing. "You mean Ronan? He's not exactly what I'd call paltry."

Master Alcántara's face and voice sharpened. "Acari, I told you to sit." The shift in his expression was sudden and terrifying.

"Yes, Master Alcántara," I said, sounding like I'd been hypnotized. My mind watched as my body sat automatically.

"I caution you, Acari, not to get attached to your Tracer."

I cleared my throat, fighting the sensation of helplessness. "I'm not attached to Tracer Ronan."

"Do you truly believe *him* capable of finding *you*, out of all the girls in the world?"

"But that means . . ." That meant a vampire had found me. Chosen me. *This* vampire.

Ronan told me he'd been asked to watch out for me. I knew now: The one keeping an eye on me had been Master Alcántara.

"Understanding dawns on your face as vividly as the sun in the sky." He touched a finger to my chin, and fear thrummed through me. He could snap my neck as easily and thoughtlessly as plucking a flower.

A low laugh rumbled in his chest. "You betray every thought. I see I must teach you guile. For once you are silent, Annelise. Have you nothing to say?"

What were all these words he was saying to me? They freaked me out. "I'm just . . . confused. I mean, surely there are other girls in the world who know a thing or two about math."

"None such as you." He canted his head, and his attentions made me intensely uncomfortable. "You are the full package, as they say. I've suffered centuries of dim-witted beauties. Or girls with looks so repellent as to negate minds that shone like diamonds. I seek strength, too, and yet have had my fill of Amazons whose brawn lacks loveliness and grace."

I stared dumbly. What was I supposed to say to this little revelation? *Thanks. You're smart and cute, too?*

"But you, *querida*, your mind is luminous. You, a crude but radiant light. Your courage, your edge . . . Nurtured in a hothouse of cruelty, you've grown into a rosebud with deadly thorns."

"Thanks . . ." My words faltered. I was uncertain what to do. Uncertain what was expected of me. I opened my mouth to say more, but didn't know what.

"Do I frighten you with my words? You'll be unaccustomed to men, I think."

"Yes." I inhaled deeply. That was a good train of thought to cling to. "That's it exactly."

And speaking of boys, just where was Yasuo? It was surely well past midnight now. Had he seen Master Alcántara and been scared off? I was all alone with him, and I thought I might suffocate from the tension.

"I don't usually talk to a lot of boys," I added.

He gave me a look that I prayed was more *kindly uncle* and less *here's a live one for me to deflower.*

Master Alcántara stared up at the moon. "How many nights I've sat beneath this sky. How many stars have circled, how many times?" His gaze swung to me, pinning me. "And now I sit here with you."

Crap. It was the *deflower* one.

I made myself look away, staring blindly up at the stars. Looking anywhere but at the vampire. I had to keep my wits. This scenario couldn't end well for me. I'd seen the movies. When Dracula got the hots for a girl, it always ended with him draining her dry.

"Perhaps it means you're meant to win my award," he mused.

The vampire mesmerized me, but mentally I pushed back. Mustering my wits, I dragged my mind from its spiral. "Yes, I'd really like to win," I said, speaking as though I were addressing any teacher. "I've been working very hard. I feel I've made good progress, too. Plus, I'd really like to take a trip off-island."

And how. More than ever, I knew I had to do whatever it took to get the hell out of here.

"Is that why you've come looking for me?" His voice rose, waiting for some response.

I cleared my throat, imagining it cleared my head, too. Why *was* I there? Master Alcántara hadn't summoned me—*Yasuo* had. Award or no, I had the strong feeling I needed to clarify. What if it was *Alcántara* who'd sent the note, and this was all some elaborate test? "That's not exactly why. . . . It's . . . I was given a note."

He laughed, but I wasn't sure if it meant he was amused or angered. "I see you are incapable of lying. Do you know you just saved your life, little Acari? I dislike lies—I kill for less."

I swallowed hard. "I'm not a liar."

"I had to make certain." He gave me a courtly nod, as if granting me a point in a chess match. "Now tell me of this note you found. No"—he stopped me with an upraised hand—"I think *I* shall tell *you*. For I know more of it than you do."

My belly turned to ice. Had Yasuo been found out? Was he in trouble? "How do you know about the note?"

He shook his head in mock sympathy. "Poor, sad Acari. I will *always* know more than you do."

He studied me, and I wanted to squirm under his gaze. "Though you like that, I think. You've always dreamt of being instructed by one who knows more than you. It's why I wanted you. You relish learning—you're amused by the not knowing. You are *seduced* by it. Ever desirous of those moments your curiosity is finally gratified."

He made it sound like a sexual thing, and my heart thudded in response. I became aware of his arm pressed against mine. What was happening? I felt out of control. I was drawn to him against my will. Because I didn't want him. Did I?

"Your note isn't from young Yasuo. Though I have been watching him. Just what is it about that child that appeals to you?" He tilted his head in brief, almost aggravated, speculation.

"What do you mean?" I asked warily.

Master Alcántara inhaled sharply, visibly shoving thoughts from his mind. "Your note is from Lilac. Yes, she laid a trap for you."

Fury flared, roiling like acid in my belly. It made sense now. Of course it'd been Lilac. She'd had someone plant that note.

But then I felt cool relief quick on its heels prickling through me, loosening muscles I hadn't known I'd tensed. "So Yasuo is safe?"

"You are fascinating to me, *cariño*. To endanger your life, to risk a prize I know you covet . . ." His look implied I might yearn for something—or some*one*—more than just the Directorate Award. "That you'd jeopardize it all, and for someone you met mere months ago."

"Yasuo is my friend. I thought he was in trouble."

He stared as though I were a particularly entrancing specimen of butterfly. "I value loyalty. And it is why you won't die tonight. Any other girl caught as you have been would be made an example. But I find I want to spare you."

He stroked my hair, easing closer. I became utterly still, thinking for a moment that he might kiss me. I held my breath. Did I want him to kiss me? I didn't think I did. But still my eyes kept returning to those perfect lips.

Absurd notions flooded my head. Did vampires even kiss? Did they simply bite? Did Master Alcántara have fangs, and how is it I'd never seen them? Would his mouth be soft or hard? I felt my cheeks flame red, fearing he could read my every thought, but I couldn't stop my mind from its musings.

He licked his lips. As though in answer to my unasked questions, they parted suggestively, flashing a glimmer of fang.

"Don't be mistaken, *querida*." His whispered words held me in thrall. But this time I was unable to push back, unable to look away. He grazed a thumb lightly over my lower lip. "My mercy has a price. But I've decided you shall owe me."

CHAPTER THIRTY-TWO

I've decided you shall owe me.

The words replayed in my head as I adjusted my sparring uniform, securing the black wraparound top into a snug knot at my waist. They'd haunted me all night, echoing in my dreams. They repeated over and over as I pulled my hair into one long braid down my back. As I tugged on the metal mesh face guard and gauntlets.

Watcher Priti had announced that today's class would be spent practicing for our final combat tournament. Today's weapon would be a Celtic short sword, with an additional dagger strapped to each student's calf.

I did a few squats, making sure everything was in place. I generally felt good about my sword work, but Master Alcántara's words distracted me, and that was bad.

I've decided you shall owe me.

Owe him *what*? I knew enough about vampires by now to surmise that couldn't be good.

And then there'd been our weird conversation. His declarations had been almost intimate—that he'd sought me, that he'd chosen me. I'd found him mesmerizing. But creepy, too. The guy was technically dead, and yet he'd touched me like we were on some kind of date. Stroking my hair, cupping my cheek, rubbing his thumb along my lip. I shivered.

"You scared, Charity?"

Lilac. All day, I'd been trying to ignore the feel of her eyes boring into my back. Heaving a sigh, I faced her. "Of you? Hardly."

She was silent. If Master Alcántara hadn't told me already, the look on her face would've spilled the truth. She'd been giving me the same suspicious glare since we'd woken up.

She was shocked to see me alive.

She'd been the one to lay the trap. She'd convinced me Yasuo's life was in danger, knowing that leaving our dorm at midnight would mean almost-certain death.

It was time to show von Slutling she was messing with the wrong girl. I plopped next to her as we all gathered on the bleachers. "I hope I didn't wake you when I got in last night."

I nonchalantly tightened the empty scabbard at my calf. "And don't even think about tattling like you did with the iPod. There's no way you can prove I went out after curfew." I gave her my most sparkling smile. "You wouldn't believe what goes on at those standing stones at night."

Her shocked, gaping stare almost made my unsettling interlude with Master Alcántara worthwhile.

"It's time, Acari." Watcher Priti called us to attention. She went to the sparring ring and leaned a small chalkboard along-side. "Find your name listed among the pairs of challengers. You should already be familiar with our combat-sparring rules."

She was right—I had them memorized. The Rules of Combat:

1. Half point given for generalized contact above or below waist.
2. Full point given for "critical points" contact (eyes, groin, etc.).
3. A match lasts five minutes or until five points are accrued.
4. Knockout blow is an instant win.
5. Full-body throw executed in the first ten seconds is an instant win.
6. Only time elapsed, points earned, instant win, or unconsciousness may stop a challenge once begun.

I scanned the board and found my name three lines down. *Drew vs. Claire.* It was the pretty Idaho girl who, with Stefinne, had been the only other Acari to survive her group's night hike.

She glared at me.

Great. My buddy Claire. She'd had me in her sights—and had been Lilac's bosom buddy—ever since that night.

Two students were stationed at the weapons locker, handing out our short swords and daggers. We didn't get the real thing for sparring. Instead, we were issued special blades that had the heft of real steel but with blunted edges.

Girls clustered in a circle in front of the locker. The humming sound of their whispers reminded me of a swarm of bees.

Lilac stood at the center, the tall and leggy queen of them all. She caught my eye. "Good luck," she told me brightly.

I gave her a wary nod. Her words had come out too friendly, and it worried me. I wondered what she had up her sleeve.

But I didn't have time to give it much thought, because the matches began soon thereafter. The first two challenges went quickly, neither lasting the full allotted time. The first winner finished with five points to three, in an impressive two minutes of combat. The second scored a knockout blow to the back of her competitor's skull in the first minute. For a moment, I'd thought Priti might need to call for the Tracers, but the girl shook it off and staggered from the ring.

It was a shock seeing girls go at one another so brutally. But in our sparring, no body part was off-limits. In fact, contact with sensitive anatomy—kidneys, head, kneecap, groin— earned higher points. Priti told us, as I'd been told so many times already, that this was because there were no handicaps in the real world. Real opponents would aim precisely for something like our eyes, and so we needed to prepare accordingly.

"Acari Drew versus Acari Claire," Priti announced, calling us to the mat.

I climbed into the ring, bobbing on my feet, shaking out my hands, rolling my shoulders. I'd secured my sparring dagger at my left calf, and held my short sword in my right hand, swishing it, testing its weight with diagonal slices.

Idaho Claire stood in the other corner. She had a few inches on me, and some wiry, nature-girl muscles, but my small size made me fast, and I felt pretty good.

Watcher Priti struck the gong and the tournament clock reset, its numbers blinking to 5:00 for the challenge countdown. She struck the gong again, and we met in the center of the ring.

Claire hopped from foot to foot like a monkey, but I concentrated on the feel of the mat beneath me, repeating Priti's mantra in my head. *I am roots in the earth. I am water that flows. I am grounded. I am Watcher.*

She sprang at me and I dodged her easily, imagining myself as a tree swaying in the wind. *I am roots in the earth,* I thought, marveling that I *did* feel grounded. My posture stable and steady.

I extended my weapon, and she came at me again, our swords meeting with a loud metal clang. The impact resonated up my arm, but I gave it no thought. I concentrated on my connection to the mat. I was unshakable, unflappable.

The key to successful combat was simplicity. A true fighter frowned on showy flourishes, avoiding elaborate footwork and unnecessary displays.

Mindful of this, I shuffled forward, my sword waving before me just enough that I could maintain a visceral feel for its weight, its length. I'd yet to attempt my first strike, and it made Claire overconfident. *She* couldn't resist the flourishes and showed off with a quick feinting attack that I easily parried.

It was a foolish move. A short sword seemed light at first, until you were forced to extend it for any length of time. I read the strain of her efforts in the pinch of her brow, in the way she held her right shoulder.

With a rapid step-step, I was in Claire's space. I slammed my sword into hers, sliding up the steel and catching her hilt with the tip of my blade. With a deft twirl, my blade wrenched her sword loose. It flew from her hands, over the ropes, clattering onto the gym floor.

I heard a whoop, and knew it must've been Emma cheering for me. Nobody else would have.

Claire's face twitched. She was going to lose, and she didn't like it. I glanced at the clock on the wall: 4:37. I wondered whether I could set a class record.

But in that moment, she plucked her dagger from its scabbard and leapt at me. Her erratic movements slid past my defenses, and she managed to connect with my hip, her blade slicing deep along my side, all the way down to my thigh.

I sucked in a breath—the pain was instant, extreme. A shock.

Claire had a real dagger. A razor-sharp one.

We stared at each other for a moment, our eyes wide. She'd been given a real blade with a real edge, and we both realized it at the same instant.

Emma screamed, "Stop the fight! She has a weapon."

It didn't matter. Rule number six: *Only time elapsed, points earned, instant win, or unconsciousness may stop a challenge once begun.*

I hopped back to the ropes, regrouping. There were 4:17 left on the clock. My hip throbbed and my thigh stung with each movement. She'd managed to slice down my whole left side.

She studied me, grim satisfaction lighting her eyes. Though blood wasn't visible on the black uniform, the fabric clung to me, my flesh soaked with it.

I saw the moment Claire decided to kill me. I watched as her face hardened, resolve steeling her features. She gave me a smile. And then she leapt, this time slashing and yowling like a wildcat.

My back was already against the ropes and so I scooted sideways, ducking from her.

There was a cold gust of air. It sent a shiver up my injured leg, so wet with blood. I heard the heavy gym door slam shut. Someone had entered. I spared a glance.

I'd never seen them before, but I could tell at once they were vampires. They stood rigid, unmoving. Watching me with eagle eyes.

I knew instinctively: The scent of blood had called them. *My* blood. I sensed their hunger.

Peeling the uniform from my thigh, I bobbed around Claire, back toward the center of the ring. The blood was flowing now, and I gave up trying to staunch it with my hand.

Time had slowed. An interminable 4:02 was left on the clock.

I needed to keep calm. My sword was blunt, but I was smart and I was strong. *I am roots in the earth. I am grounded.*

I went on the offensive, and my abrupt attack momentarily startled Claire. I managed to get in a hit, slamming the flat of my blade against the side of her head. It made a dull slapping sound.

Clutching her head, she shrieked. Her eyes shrank to tiny, glittering stones. She came at me with renewed fury. Frantically, she sliced at the air, sloppy movements aiming for whichever part of me she could find.

I raised my sword, blocking her. I felt the gym door open and shut again. The Tracers would be gathering, preparing to roll my body in canvas and take me away.

I pushed it from my mind. I was pure focus. My feet felt glued to the mat beneath me. I was only the sword in my hand and the dagger flying at me. I parried her every strike.

I gripped my sword hilt in my right hand, bracing the blunt

top half of the blade in my left. Holding my sword diagonally before me, I edged toward Claire.

She shifted, gripping her dagger with both hands, like a baseball bat. And then she swung, hitting the very center of my blade. The metal snapped, my blunt practice sword unable to withstand an assault from high-grade steel.

Jogging backward, I tossed the broken tip from the ring. I spun to face Claire, jabbing at her with the ragged tip of my blade. I parried her strikes with what was left of my sword. But my stubby, blunt-edged weapon was no match for hers.

She slashed wildly at me, catching me on my forearm. Pain sheared up my arm. My hand opened reflexively, and my shard of a blade slipped from my sweaty palm.

The cut felt like acid searing down to my bones. Tears threatened to blur my vision, but I blinked back hard.

Blood dribbled down my arm. Wiping it from the back of my hand, I snatched the dagger from the scabbard at my calf. I tested the edge with my thumb. *Blunt*.

The door opened again. I didn't need to look. I could feel by the stillness in the room that vampires continued to gather. I wondered if Ronan was out there, too, witnessing my impromptu bloodletting.

I quickly shifted the practice dagger from one hand to the other, drying my sweaty palms along my uninjured thigh. I was just about done for, and I could see in Claire's glittering eyes that she thought so, too.

I was settling the useless weapon in my palm when one last, desperate option came to me. Instead of grasping the hilt, I took the blade between my fingers, finding its balance. The steel was cool. I imagined myself just as cool.

I am water that flows.

With a deep inhale, I threw, imagining the dagger riding on a wave of fluid power. It struck Claire just above the sternum. But the dull blade didn't penetrate.

Still, it had hit hard, and she rubbed her chest. She kicked the dagger away, and it careened off the mat to the floor below. She looked manic, half laughing, half snarling. "You'll pay for what you did."

I had to remain calm. I had no weapon. But I had my hands. There were 2:01 on the clock, and my life was in the balance.

Blood dripped down my leg, and I left smeary red footprints on the mat. The cut on my leg was deep. My hip and thigh were on fire.

Vampires swarmed the gym now. They looked like statuary posed along the periphery—a gallery of men carved from pale granite. My mind flashed to an image of them feeding on my lifeless body. It galvanized me.

I am grounded. I am Watcher.

I would survive. More than that, I would win.

No longer bothering to wipe the blood from my hands, I strode to Claire. I imagined myself powerful. I *was* powerful.

I flew at her, grabbing her blade arm with both hands. We grappled, kicking and kneeing and snarling. Claire wriggled in my grip, trying to point her knife toward me.

I wrenched her wrists back. Our legs tangled. I hooked my ankle under hers, thinking if I tripped her, maybe I could twist her arm enough to knock the dagger free.

She stumbled. My hands were slick with sweat and blood, and her arm slipped from my grasp. She fell.

But instead of hopping back up to continue the fight, she just lay there. I nudged her with my foot, half expecting a trick. She flopped onto her back.

I stared down at the body of Idaho Claire and the dagger that had caught in her throat.

Watcher Priti struck her gong. "Acari Drew scores a win."

My second kill.

CHAPTER THIRTY-THREE

everal days later, Ronan found me in the phenom library.
I'd curled into an oversized leather armchair and sat, staring out the window at the rainy day. My days blurred together,
and I hadn't seemed to be able to get back to normal. Accidentally killing your classmates had a way of doing that to a girl.

I idly rubbed my scars, concealed under the fabric of my
leggings. They itched like mad, but that was okay—I imagined
it a sort of penance for killing Idaho Claire.

My skin had knit together shockingly fast, a side benefit of
drinking so much vampire blood. Amanda had seemed pleased,
and more than a bit surprised, by how well and quickly I'd
healed. I guess I vibed with the blood. *Great.* Did that mean I
was no longer completely human, either?

I nestled deeper in the chair. More than ever, I wished I still
had my iPod. I was in a classical-piano sort of a mood. That or
Metallica.

"Where've you been? It's time for swim."

Ronan stood in the doorway. Not even the sight of his solid biceps peeking from the sleeves of a damp, clinging T-shirt cheered me. In fact, the effect was just the opposite. I needed to stop looking at him like that. I was terrified the day might come when Master Alcántara noticed me noticing.

I tore my eyes from his shirt. "Jeez, Ronan. Don't you get cold?"

"It's May." He walked into the library, raking the wet hair from his face.

Enough time had passed since the incident with my iPod, and things were slowly getting back to normal—whatever *that* meant—between us. But life was cheap on this island, and I couldn't let myself forget to maintain emotional distance. And that meant I *really* needed to stop ogling his clothes like I might develop X-ray vision. I turned my head, staring back out the window instead. "I think the hottest it's been is forty-four degrees."

The rain was coming down in buckets, as it had all week, and the bleak weather wasn't helping my outlook. Though the sun was setting much later than when we'd arrived—nightly sunset was well after nine p.m. now—the sky never seemed to get bright. It just morphed through shades of white and gray. "If this is the *Dimming* you told me about, well, it sucks."

Ronan ignored me, scanning the floor by my chair. There was nothing but my bag, a small stack of books, and my kicked-off boots. "Where's your wet suit?"

"But it's raining."

"Good. Then the water won't bother you so much." He gathered books to reshelve them. "The final challenge is a week away, and you must be prepared."

"Why do I need to practice anything?" I shifted to watch him, flopping my head against the back of the chair. "I seem to have a knack for getting girls killed all by my lonesome."

"You won," he snarled, knowing what was on my mind. I'd been in a funk since Claire's death, and I sensed Ronan was beginning to tire of my mood. "Would you rather you'd been the one to die?"

"Of course not." I glared at him. "Forgive me if it takes a while to get used to the fact that killing my fellow students is part of the curriculum."

"It is. Wake up to it."

"But it was just sparring practice," I protested, feeling myself getting riled again. "And somebody switched the blades. Shouldn't there be an investigation or something? Some sort of consequences—detention, at least?"

Though I didn't need to dust for prints when it was obvious who'd been the brains behind it. Lilac. My only surprise was that she'd allow someone else to take me down when she was so keen to.

Ronan shrugged. "Actually, the Initiates thought switching the practice blades was a clever bit of strategy."

My jaw dropped. "Clever? They thought that little blood-bath was *clever*?"

"I told you, Annelise. It's win by any means. And this is the last I'll speak of it." He strode to me, holding out his hand. "Now get up."

I sighed. He was right—I was here, and I'd best get used to the fact that all that compelling training with Priti would have some very real-world applications. But it didn't mean I needed to swim, not today and in the rain. Our competition would take place in a ring, not the pool.

I stared at his outstretched hand, fighting the urge to clasp it tight. His grip would be warm and strong. "Seriously, Ronan. Can't we take a day off? Please? Swimming is the last thing I can bear at the moment. How's swim going to help me, anyway? Combat challenges take place in a ring."

"Combat challenges can take many forms, and I'd have you be prepared for all of them." He leaned down and snatched my arm, tugging to me standing. "There are no days off. Now come."

"I'm up, I'm up. Man, you're being harsh." I pulled away from him with exaggerated annoyance. "How, exactly, will swimming help me? Unless you plan on holding my head under and putting me out of my misery. Which isn't a bad idea, actually."

"Annelise." His voice was stern, and it made me look at him. "Get your other boot on," he said more gently. "I have some ideas."

Apparently his ideas involved me treading water in a freezing cove while holding my hands over my head.

"I thought you said this would help me be a better fighter." I sank below the surface of the water and scissor-kicked back up. Coughing, I wiped my face against my arm. Though I'd become a decent swimmer, I still couldn't stand the feel of water on my face.

Ronan stood in waist-high water not too far from me. He could've stayed on the beach—I don't know why he didn't—but I appreciated the gesture of support nonetheless. "You need to build core strength." He nodded at my arms. "Arm strength will help with your throwing stars."

"Not if I'm too sore to lift them. You're killing me." My shoulders burned. My neck ached. "I can barely hit the target anyway. What good will strong arms do me?"

"You are capable of hitting the target. You simply need to learn how to keep a consistently calm mind."

"I'm drowning in here. Spare me the Zen crap." Gradually, my elbows slipped closer to the surface. Water splashed in my face, and I spat it out. "Seriously, Ronan. Can I be done now?"

He turned his back on me, diving away. I didn't get why anyone would *choose* to swim in this water. His head bobbed back up, and he slicked the hair from his chiseled face. I imagined it was what he might look like emerging from a hot tub.

I scowled even harder.

"You're done," he shouted, kicking away from me on his back. "Get out. Go run. I want five laps along the beach."

I was cranky and sandy and totally beat by the time Ronan and I walked back to where he'd parked. But I'd had a lot of time to think. "So, if I win, I get to go off-island with Master Alcántara."

Ronan opened the van's rear doors. "Yes."

Snagging a towel, I scrubbed my face hard, erasing the memory of water splashing into my eyes and up my nose. "What's his deal, anyway?"

"Master Alcántara?" he asked, incredulous. "His *deal*?"

My mind went back to that night. The vampire's strange words; the even stranger feel of his touch on my face. "Yeah, by the stones—" I stopped myself.

Ronan stared hard. "By the stones, *what*?"

I bent to pull off my swim booties, hoping he didn't notice how my face was flushing. I improvised to cover up the blunder.

"By the stones . . . on that first day . . . I'd wondered what other islands there are around here."

I stood up, tossing my booties in the back of the van. Ronan was looking at me skeptically.

I shrugged. "I just think it'd be cool to travel off the island with someone like him. Did you know he met Descartes?"

He slung his towel over his shoulder, then crossed his arms over his chest. It made his upper body look even more cut than usual. "Beware Hugo De Rosas Alcántara."

"Are you saying I should bow out of the challenge?"

"I'm saying no such thing. The girls who don't enter the competition are fools who won't survive the year." He stared hard at me, weighing his words. When he spoke again, it was slower, gentler. "Don't for a moment think the choices you make aren't a part of your trials on this island. You *must* participate in the challenge. But you must also maintain distance, Annelise. Alcántara is Vampire, centuries old and lacking in the human mores to which you're accustomed. Imagine yourself a professional. Because that's precisely what you aspire to be. Not a special pet or project or plaything for Master Alcántara. Don't let him lay claim to you."

His mini speech stunned me. "But he's one of them. One of the main vampire dudes, right? I can't just *stay away* from him."

"No, you cannot." Ronan reached behind his back to undo the Velcro on the neck of his wet suit. I kept my eyes strictly above chin level. "But you can keep a polite distance. Speak when you're spoken to. Don't stare him in the eye." He paused to glare at me. "As you seem to feel free to do with me."

I laughed, taken aback, and Ronan gave me a grudging smile. "I'm serious, Annelise. This is life or death."

I wasn't ready to die. Which meant I had to be ready to kill. I suspected the Directorate challenge wasn't so much about competing with the other girls as it was about eliminating them.

Ronan reached around his back, and with a tug on the long toggle attached to his zipper, he began to peel the wet suit from his arms. It revealed his tattoo, stark on his pale, chilled skin. *Le seul paradis c'est le paradis perdu.*

The sight of it, its possible meaning, held me transfixed. "What is it you've lost?" I asked quietly.

We stared at each other a moment. "Turn around, Annelise. A little privacy, please." He didn't sound angry, just tired.

I walked around to the front of the van, peeling off my own wet suit and pulling my sweats over the damp Speedo I'd worn underneath. I clambered into the front seat.

Ronan slammed the rear doors shut, then walked around and climbed in. He put the key in the ignition, but just sat there, staring at the steering wheel.

Finally, he said, "There are many things I've lost. Many people. Perhaps you'll one day discover life here is not what it seems."

I studied his profile, desperate to understand his meaning. "Then why do you stay?"

"It is where I belong."

His reply had been simple, but it was no answer. Something held him on the island. Something more than just habit or home. I could see it in his eyes, green and sad. But clearly he wasn't going to tell me.

I changed tack. I felt a connection with Ronan—I always had, despite his powers of persuasion that'd gotten me into this mess. "Why do you do this? It's more than just someone asking you to look out for me. Why have you been kind to me?"

He glanced at me. He looked so bleak in that moment, I wished I could touch him. Just a simple hand on his shoulder.

"I told you once before. You remind me of someone," he said. "A girl who'd been smart, like you."

I *had* been right. We *did* have a connection. But who did I remind him of? An old lover? High school sweetheart? Electricity pulsed through me, but I managed to keep my voice calm. "Who?"

"Acari Charlotte." He leaned back to stare out the windshield, his hands extended in front of him, resting on the wheel. "My sister."

My heart fell. Not a lover. I reminded him of his *sister*. I supposed it beat football teammate or pub buddy. But still. The sentiment was lovely. Heartwarming. Nauseating.

"She trained to be a Watcher. She didn't last a month."

I swallowed hard, keeping my cool. "Your sister?"

"She was a lot like you. Defiant. Misunderstood." He looked at me, and the desolation in his eyes made me forget myself for a moment. "She tried hard, but there was something in her that was too . . . gentle. These girls, they scent weakness. Charlotte never had a chance."

I glanced down, unable to hold his gaze. My heart broke for him.

But embarrassment skewered me, too, making me feel ashamed. Ronan had lost his sister, and yet I couldn't get away from my own selfish disappointment. I'd thought he was going to tell me something else. I'd thought he'd felt a different kind of connection with me.

I felt him reach for me, his movement tentative. He traced a single finger along the line of my face. His touch was warm, and it made my throat clench. My body tingled, but it wasn't because of any supernatural powers. It was because this was *Ronan*, and he was touching me.

I dared a glance, and his hand cupped my cheek as I turned to him. The eerie twilight made his hair appear darker, his eyes deeper.

"But Charlotte wasn't nearly so beautiful as you."

The air whooshed from my lungs. My body prickled to life, heat spreading through me. Ronan had called me beautiful.

He sighed and pulled away from me. "You are lovely, Annelise. And you are strong. I believe you can win this. But you must believe it, too."

I gave him a tight nod. Ronan wasn't a vampire. Not a monster, not a Draug, not an undead creature of the night. He was a guy, and he thought I was beautiful.

Granted, he had some crazy powers that made him more than your average person. But he'd believed in me when nobody else had. Even if he had used his supernatural mojo to get me here, it was because he had faith in me. Believed I could do it. Part of me suspected that maybe he even thought I'd realize some sort of potential here.

You are lovely, Annelise. And you are strong.

He put a finger beneath my chin, tilting my face up. "Are you ready?"

I knew he spoke of the fight. But in my fantasy, he meant more.

"Yes," I said, my voice barely a whisper. I was discovering uncharted territory, and I'd survive to see it to the end.

It wasn't until we'd driven almost all the way back to the dorm that I found myself once more capable of speech. Our conversation had felt special. That feeling hung between us, and it gave me courage.

I couldn't allow what'd just happened to let me forget what this was all about. That this, more than ever, was life or death. Ronan was serious about me winning, and it'd bolstered me. Made me serious, too. "So, fire is Lilac's special gift?"

Ronan stared straight ahead. "Fire is her *skill*," he said in a flat voice. "Lilac has a different gift."

I sat forward. I'd just assumed her thing was being some kind of pyromaniac. If she had a different talent, I had to know. "What is it?"

He hesitated. "I shouldn't tell you."

"I know, I know," I said impatiently. "But now you have to tell me."

"Truly, Annelise." He caught my eye, his face like stone. "Disclosing confidential information is a breach of *Eyja* law. They'd think nothing of slaughtering me for it."

"I understand." My heart was a heavy weight in my chest. What hideous thing was he concealing from me? "Please, Ronan. You have to tell me. What's her gift?"

His grip tightened on the steering wheel. "Pain."

"She knows how to give it?"

He shook his head. "She doesn't feel it."

CHAPTER THIRTY-FOUR

⸺◇⸺

I never thought I'd be jealous of von Slutling, but by the third day of the challenge, I'd have given anything not to feel pain. I'd never ached so badly in my life. Not even in my first weeks of training.

At least this was it—the final day. And thank God, because I couldn't keep up this level of fighting, even with the blood to sustain me.

Naturally, they hadn't considered holding the fights in someplace as mundane as the gym. Instead, we girls were duking it out at the standing stones, atop the massive, flat center slab.

Matches happened throughout the day, with each winner advancing to fight the next. And Vampire, Initiate, Acari, Tracer, Trainee—*everyone*—had gathered on the lawn in front of the stones to watch.

Everyone was waiting for the semifinal fights to begin. For *my* fight to begin.

I reached my arms in front of me, trying to loosen my stiff back. I was so tight, I thought the muscles might snap. A deep unease had me clenched and agitated. "Those vamps . . . they've got a sense of drama. I'll give them that."

"What?" Emma touched her ear to let me know that she hadn't heard me over the buzz of the audience.

I shook my head. "Never mind."

Yasuo was with us, and it was reassuring to feel a tall, strong guy standing by my side. He gingerly poked at my right ear. "Jeez, little D. How'd you manage to bruise your *earlobe*?"

I flinched away from his touch. Getting pinned on a mat in the gym was one thing. But being pummeled into a gargantuan granite plinth was a whole other story. Just the thought of facing it again tightened my chest. "It's that stupid rock."

Emma leaned close. "You're almost on."

"Thanks for the reminder." I tried to muster a sarcastic smile, but feared I'd missed the mark.

"She beat the hell out of those first two girls," Yasuo said, looking into the distance.

I followed his line of sight and found Lilac. She was sashaying through the crowd, a bevy of bright-skinned acolytes trailing her like the wake of a luxury yacht.

Josh was also swept along in her tide, and I caught him looking at me before he could turn away. *Whatever.*

"I pity the girl who has to face *her* in the semis," Yas added.

I nodded. Lilac was looking like a shoo-in for the finals. "Some girl named Antje gets that honor," I said. There were only four of us left in the semifinals, and I was surprised the vamps were having me face off against a Lilac underling instead of my known nemesis. Ronan's speech had made me realize how much attention the vampires paid to the comings and goings of Acari. I supposed it was one way to pass eternity. "Wonder of wonders, it's not me."

"Either way, we still have to get you ready." He looked at Emma. "You brought the tape?"

Nodding, she pulled a roll of white medical tape from her pocket. I automatically held my hands out for her to wrap them.

Emma touched my left pinkie, and I gasped. "Ow."

"Looks bad," she said, examining it. The finger was a repulsive shade of purple and poked unnaturally from the rest of my hand.

"I landed wrong." I felt the bone trying to knit back together, and although I healed fast, it wasn't *that* fast. "I think it's broken."

"Ya think?" Yasuo asked.

I stuck my tongue out at him.

Emma gently traced the line of the bone from the hand up to the fingertip. "Do you want me to bind it?"

I nodded, rolling my aching shoulders. "Tape my whole body, while you're at it."

Yasuo was still watching Lilac work the crowd. "They say the last girl who fought her died, like, thirty seconds after the fight began. Could be you facing that shit in the finals. If you beat that Mia girl."

"You mean *when* I beat Mia." My voice came out weaker than I'd intended.

"You don't *have* to fight," Emma cut in. "A lot of girls have stepped down from the competition."

Emma had bowed out the moment she saw her name pitted against mine on the fight bracket, and I feared the long-term consequences of her decision. "I wish *you* hadn't stepped down."

It was no secret Emma and I were friends, and a match between us would've made for the sort of drama the vamps craved
like catnip.

"I have no interest in traveling, and so saw no need to fight."

I rolled my eyes, exasperated. "It's about more than just
traveling, Em. I worry it's a mistake not to fight."

The barest lift of her eyebrows was my only answer. Otherwise, she remained intent on her work, her hands working
deftly over mine, taping up my wrists and knuckles.

I went on, beating the dead horse, even though it was too
late to change anything. "We could've figured out a way to look
like we were fighting, but both get out of there alive."

"Yeah," Yasuo chimed in. "You'd take a few hits for Emma,
wouldn't you, D?"

I nodded enthusiastically. If anyone knew how to take a few
hits, it was me.

"They'd know," Emma said simply. "It's better this way."

I gave it up, knowing she was probably right. It would've
been a big red flag if we'd both walked away from our fight
when pretty much every other bout ended with a couple of
Tracers toting away the loser.

And Emma wasn't the only one who'd backed out, either.
Only about thirty Acari had stepped up to begin with, and then
some dropped out once they saw just how serious the combat
was. As far as I was concerned, those girls weren't thinking
about the big picture. They didn't want to get off the island as
badly as I did.

I needed to escape. When I contemplated my future, killing
teenage girls didn't strike me as the most sustainable thing for
me to be doing in the long term.

"Just be careful." Emma calmly ripped the tape and smoothed down the edges. "Girls are dying, Drew."

"Thirteen girls dead in twenty-one fights," I agreed quietly.

"Not exactly stellar numbers," Yasuo said.

"And those are the ones we saw die." Emma's eyes met mine and we grew still. She pinned me with that stoic stare. "Who knows where the others were taken, or if we'll ever see them again?"

"Ambassadors, my ass," I muttered, spotting Master Alcántara in the crowd. "They're training us to be *killers*."

Which meant there was no room for error. Unlike the sparring we did in class, the tournament had no point system, no time limits. There was only one rule: The last girl standing won.

Emma sighed, turning my hand over in hers. "How does it feel?"

Holding my breath, I carefully wriggled the fingers on my left hand. The pinkie and ring finger were bound together, but the rest were mobile, if not sore.

And *sore* was an understatement. I was battered and bruised, and didn't know how much longer I could go on. "Feels good," I said, lying.

"It's not too late. You can pull out."

"Didn't we just have this conversation?" I'd spoken to her, but my gaze had drifted to the stage, where Alcántara was looking at the day's fight bracket. I shivered, feeling a wave of that nervous-morbid-excited fascination. "Because you know I can't."

Finding fresh resolve, I glanced from Emma to Yasuo. "Look, guys. I need your support. I've made my decision. I'm going all the way."

"That's it. Hand it over." Yas grabbed the tape. We both shot him a look, and he said, "You'll see."

He took Emma's hand and looped the roll on her finger. "Hold that," he told her, and pulled down a long strip. He twisted the stretch of tape into a tight coil, ripped it free, then began to wind it around the knuckles of my good hand. He flashed us a smile. "A little Muay Thai technique. Now you just tape over this, and you've got some extra power."

I flexed my right hand into a fist. It did feel extra strong somehow, like a medical-tape version of brass knuckles. "Nice."

He gave Emma a broad smile. "We're gonna make D here a fighting machine."

I laughed. "Not exactly the words I'd use."

"Come on. You *creamed* Stefinne. She was beating you to a pulp, then suddenly . . . BAM." He punched fist into hand. "Using the hilt of your sword on her temple—genius, D. *Knockout. Acari Drew advances to the semifinals.*"

"Luck, I guess." My smile went weak. *Knockout* was a kind word for it. One could also use phrases like *bump off, take out, do in*, or perhaps choose one of the more formal -*ates*, like *eliminate, assassinate, annihilate.*

But even more unsettling than adding another kill notch to my belt was the fact that I didn't think it was luck so much as it was something weird happening.

First, I'd earned a first-round bye, which was a fancy way of saying there'd been an odd number of girls, so I got to sit out the first set of matches. To win the bye, I'd answered a trivia question, and it was like it'd been catered just to me.

What's the largest possible prime number? Poor girls had been tearing out their hair, when I clearly was the only competitor who would've known there's a simple proof to show there is no largest prime.

And then there was my fight with Stefinne in the second round. She'd been beating me soundly, and just when I began to panic, the oddest thing happened. Stefinne had me in a choke hold, a dagger in her hand, and was hauling back for the death-blow.

But then she simply . . . zoned out.

It was the strangest thing ever. One moment she was in her eyes. The next moment, she was empty.

It'd given me the chance I needed. Sliding my sword from where it had been pinned under her leg, I clocked her on the side of the head, knocking her cold. Despite her hatred, I really hoped she might've just been knocked out, might live to see another day, but a couple of Tracers appeared to whisk her away, and I knew that was the last we'd ever see of her.

I shouldn't have won that round. But I did. And then I spotted Alcántara in the audience, with that wolfish half smile on his face.

Now it was time for my next fight, and it was against Lilac's bosom buddy Mia. Part of me wanted to win on my own merit. But there was another part that hoped for more vampire intervention.

Yasuo spoke, tearing me from my thoughts. "You all right, D?"

Rather than answer, I felt compelled to look at the stage. Master Alcántara was staring at me across the platform, his eyes glowing strangely. Inhaling, I gave my rattled head a shake. "Yeah, I'm okay." I managed a smile and then flexed my hands. "Just contemplating how remarkable it is that one of the most painful things ever is to punch a bunch of soft flesh."

"That Mia chick is *so* not soft," Yas said. The three of us watched as she worked through the obscenely limber stretches she did at the start of combat and fitness classes. She had long, stick-thin limbs. Her collarbone, every vertebrae, every rib, stuck out. Her black hair was pulled into a gleaming bun. "Look at her. Girl doesn't *eat*."

"She was a classically trained ballerina," I said.

Emma frowned. "Strange."

"Tell me about it."

"How'd she end up *here*?" Yasuo shuddered. "And what turned her into Skeletor?"

"Word is, a pesky drug habit. Girl moves to big city; girl meets meth. . . . You can imagine how the story went from there."

Yasuo grimaced. "Eeesh."

"Don't be fooled." I pointed at her as she folded herself in half, wrapping a hand around each foot. "That right there is lean muscle wrapped over bone."

Emma nodded. "Drew's right. I've seen her in class. She's strong."

The gong sounded. My turn.

Rolling my shoulders, I took a deep breath. I felt my friends patting me on my back as I stepped toward the stone. "Here goes nothing."

We both climbed on, and Mia stared at me from across the platform, pure loathing in her eyes. She inhaled deeply and dramatically, then fluttered her hands and bent her legs in a fluid karate form.

Great. Classically trained in both ballet *and* martial arts.

We were allowed one weapon. Mine was a pretty little switchblade that fit my small palm perfectly. I'd contemplated fighting with my shuriken, but wasn't good enough yet for them to be practical.

I stared in horror as Mia bent to pick up *her* weapon. She'd chosen the kama.

"Seriously?" I couldn't help a spurt of nervous giggling. Basically, a kama was a sickle that old Japanese men used to mow down rice, and young ones used to mow down enemies in back alleys. "You have got to be kidding."

She shot me a look of total disdain. We waited for the gong to sound again, signaling the official start of the fight, and Mia used the opportunity to whirl her sickle overhead with the same balletic movements she used in her stretches and forms. She took a long, graceful step toward me. "It's a weapon of the ancients. Used only by those with *sophisticated* training."

She wanted me to find her act daunting. But, really, all her waving around was just starting to annoy me. "It's a damned grass cutter."

"It's an art." She did some cranelike pose, rising up on the ball of one foot with that sickle raised over her head. Her pose was elegant and fierce, and she looked like a painting. She cawed her version of a karate *kiop*, but to me it just sounded like an injured monk.

"Spare me." I'd had enough of these boarding-school dropouts and their posh attitudes. I sheathed my knife.

Whispers rustled through the crowd. Disarming oneself before a fight was not exactly conventional behavior.

The moment the gong sounded a second time, I barreled straight for her. Who says you need to be sophisticated to be a good fighter? Or tall, for that matter.

I squatted and I dove. Straight for her knees.

Mia yowled. The kama flew from her hands. I felt her knee hyperextend as she pitched to the ground. We landed with a grunt.

"Hold . . . still." I pinned her legs. She began to kick, and I twisted, hitching higher, diving onto her belly. Her body was freakishly thin, and it felt like it might snap under mine. "Not so fancy now, Mia Ballerina."

The total crudeness of my moves had thrown her off. Even though I couldn't fist my injured left hand, I managed to land a bunch of hits to her belly and ribs. Her abdomen was washboard flat, and despite all the tape, my hands throbbed from the abuse.

"You won't win." She struggled under me, getting a hand free.

I leaned back as her fist whooshed by me, just missing my chin. I grabbed her arm, trapping it under mine, and wrenched her elbow. "Oh, I think I will."

I had no plan other than this primitive beating. If things went foul, I had to hope my guardian-angel vampire would bust out some supernatural mojo to help me.

"You won't." Mia pulled her arm free. And then she laid a bruising backhand across the side of my face. "Because you're trash."

Time stopped.

In that instant, I was ten and my dad was backhanding me for sitting in his chair when he got home after a bad day. I was fourteen, and he didn't like my eyeliner. I was nine . . . I was twelve . . . I was fifteen . . .

You're trash. I'd heard it, over and over. I'd been smacked. Disregarded. I'd been in the way. *Trash.*

But I wasn't trash. I was better than that. I had an iron will.

I knew who I was. I'd have shut down long ago if I didn't. I'd still be in Florida, flatlining in front of the TV, a Coors tall boy in my hand.

I was Annelise Drew, and I counted.

I'd hit and been hit. But, in that instant, I became a fighter.

Mia swung to hit me again, but I snagged her arm in midair. I held her wrist and I squeezed. I imagined that ballerina-thin bone snapping in my grip.

Relax, Acari. Priti's voice sounded in my head. *Breathe.*

All my life I'd watched people lose control. And I wouldn't become one of them. I would probably kill Mia, yes. But more than that, I would *defeat* her.

I breathed. I was aware of adrenaline pumping through my veins, urging me to act, but I disregarded it. I held myself in check.

I also felt the blood. I hadn't had any since morning, but I'd been taking it regularly, and it'd made me much stronger than I'd been just a few short months ago. I called to it now, summoned that strong feeling I always got after drinking. I felt my own blood coursing through me, pictured my tensed muscles flush with it, imagined oxygen flooding my cells. I found an inner power—the gift of the blood.

Squeezing my thighs, I held Mia immobilized beneath me. I unsheathed my blade with my left hand. I held it to her throat and smiled. "Surrender, Mia."

She bucked and spat, clawing at my face with her free hand. "No way."

"Not very classy for a ballerina." I pressed the knife harder, until a drop of red trickled down her neck. "I will give you one more chance. Do you yield?"

"Fine." Her body went limp. "I give up. Just get off me."

Knowing the Tracers would appear at any moment, I stood. Stepping away from her, I turned toward the crowd. Their indrawn breath alerted me, the looks on their faces telling me all I needed to know.

My knife was in my hand, my arm already raised, as I pivoted back to her.

Mia had rolled to her feet. She held her kama overhead, poised to cleave my shoulder.

I didn't think; I just threw. I summoned the blood, pictured the blade sinking between her ribs so clearly that it was surreal when it actually did.

Mia dropped to her knees. She clutched her chest. Shock mingled with the hatred in her eyes.

The gong rang. "Acari Drew advances to the final round."

CHAPTER THIRTY-FIVE

Yasuo, Emma, and I stood together, ready to watch Lilac's semifinal match. The winner would face me, that night, in the final round.

My body trembled. My ears rang, my hands throbbed, and pains and twinges riddled my body. And yet unspent energy coursed through me. I'd fought—*truly* fought.

"You okay?" Emma asked.

Her voice brought me back to myself. "Yeah, actually. I'm okay."

"You won't be, if you have to fight *her*." Yasuo nodded at Lilac.

The fight hadn't begun yet, but both contenders stood on the platform, stretching out, bouncing on their feet, psyching up. Her opponent looked nervous, but Lilac just looked ready.

"Lilac might not win." Emma sounded tentative.

I gave her a halfhearted smile. "Thanks, Em."

"Not win the semis?" Yasuo shook his head in disbelief. "Are you kidding? Von Slut-thing's going to butcher that girl. She's *owned* every single one of her opponents."

He was right. Tracers had gathered by the platform, standing by.

Emma stared in wonder. "Where do they take them all?"

"You tell us, Yas," I said. "You're the vamp in training. What happens to the not-quite-dead girls?"

Emma grew preternaturally still. "I wonder if this whole thing isn't just a way for the vampires to cull the weak from the herd."

Yasuo rolled his eyes. "Thank you, Farm Girl." He turned his focus on me. "Enough speculation. Now, listen up, D. All signs point to you fighting Lilac tonight. You need a strategy."

I nodded weakly, feeling ill. Strategy wasn't good for much when your opponent didn't feel pain.

"What's her deal, anyway?" Yas asked, and we all turned our eyes to her.

Lilac was long and lean, with that maple hair pulled back into a sleek braid. She looked entitled, confident, and gorgeous, in a vanilla sort of way. I shrugged. "Rich . . . white . . . boarding school. I don't know."

He snorted. "Maybe she learned all her crazy-ass moves playing field hockey."

"It doesn't matter." Emma roused to life. "You could beat her."

Good old naive Emma. She had no idea what I would be up against if Lilac won the semifinals.

The gong sounded. It was time for Lilac's match.

The girls stepped to the middle of the platform. It was Lilac versus a tall Valkyrie-looking creature with close-cropped hair, perfectly cut biceps, and cheekbones that went on for days.

The gong sounded a second time, and Lilac sprang from her corner, swinging her weapon over her head. My friends and I laughed nervously, seeing that she'd chosen a shinai, the long, bamboo sword we used in Japanese kendo practice.

My blood ran cold. "What the hell is she planning to do with *that*?"

"That won't cut anyone," Emma said.

"Duh." Yas shook his head. "But that thing's got reach, and she's got power. Sorry, D. I don't get how any of your blades will do you any good. Not that girlie little switchblade, and not those stars, either."

A third gong tore my eyes from him.

We stared at Lilac's opponent on the platform. By the way she writhed around, clutching at her neck, it looked like Lilac had just jousted her in the throat.

"It's over already?" Emma whispered. The fight had gone on for less than ten seconds.

Priti's voice was clear above the crowd. "Acari Lilac advances to the final round."

"Crap," Yasuo muttered.

I looked at Lilac, and her gaze was waiting for me. We locked eyes. She looked eager, raging.

I wanted the Directorate Award. I wanted off the island. But did I want it badly enough to face a girl who was more physically adept than me, who felt no pain, and who'd held me locked in her sights from day one?

My body went cold. "Looks like I'm fighting Lilac."

"You can do it," Emma said.

I kept my face blank, but inside I was freaking out. "What if I can't stop her?"

"You've been able to do it in these last matches," Yas said. "Pretend this is just another one."

But it wasn't, because von Slutling was like the Terminator. "You don't get it."

Emma leaned close. "Lilac may be the best fighter in our class, but you can outsmart her."

Yas nodded agreement. "You're smaller, D, and that makes you wily. Defensively, you're solid. Plus you have that fancy brain of yours. Outthink her."

"No, seriously, guys. You don't get it." They both opened their mouths to protest, but I cut them off. "Lilac doesn't feel pain."

That shut them up.

I regretted it instantly. Ronan had sworn me to secrecy. But I told myself not to feel guilty—information like that was too huge to keep to myself. For all I knew, this was the last time I'd talk to my friends; I had to warn them. "But you can't tell *anyone*."

"Yeah, yeah," Yasuo said, waving off my statement. "I get it. It's a secret. But how did you—" Understanding dawned in his eyes. "Ronan told you, didn't he?"

Now I felt guilty. Who deserved my allegiance more? Ronan, who had flashes of understanding but who'd also been the one to bring me here? Or Yas, my best bud, who'd one day have a big set of fangs gleaming against his undead skin? I shouldn't have opened my mouth.

I gave him a tense nod and was grateful when Emma broke the silence. She was looking at me in utter disbelief. "But everyone feels pain. Everybody feels something. Eventually."

I glanced at my enemy. She was greeting her well-wishers in the audience. Bruises and scratches covered every inch of visible skin, but still she slinked around like a cat. "Not von Slutling."

"How can she not feel pain?" Emma sounded perplexed.

"Rare genetic disorder? Mommy drank too many in vitro cosmos? How the hell should I know?"

Yasuo's eyes widened in question. "But you're still going through with it?"

I came close to saying no. It would've been so easy. But I sensed Master Alcántara's gaze on me, and that morbid fascination shivered up my skin. It left confidence in its wake.

I was the best student. *I* had the most potential. The award belonged to me, though doubts nagged at the back of my mind as I wondered how much I was driven by pride, how much by the urge to escape, and how much I simply wanted to beat the crap out of my roommate. "I am."

Yasuo sighed. "Then let's do this thing." He turned and openly studied me. "Okay. Headlines." He crossed his arms over his chest, determined to distill the whole situation to fine points. "The girl's got height on you. She feels no pain—whatever that means. And her gift is fire?"

"Her gift is pain, and her *skill* is fire."

Yas threw his hands up. "What the hell does that mean? Fire? Dude, you're psyched she's not busting any of that out here."

"How do you know she won't?" Emma asked.

Yasuo countered, "How could she? How would someone here even fight with fire?"

I'd wondered the same thing. "I don't know. Flamethrower?

Though I definitely would've seen it if she'd been hiding *that* in our room."

"She could spit flames," Emma said. "Like in the circus."

Yasuo stared at her, his eyes wide. "Girl, you amaze me. Were you raised in a barn? Oh. wait. You were, weren't you?"

Emma shot him one of her rare smiles.

Were they flirting? "Guys, can we get back on topic?"

I could've sworn Emma blushed.

"Let's talk weapons," Yasuo said. "You're not going to use that knife again, are you?"

"Do you have a better idea? A knife suited me just fine in the last fight." My tone was a little prickly. I considered myself pretty decent at blade work.

Yasuo put his arm around me, but he kept his eyes glued to Lilac. He leaned down, talking low. "Yeah, Drew, you're good. But this fight . . . it's going to go fast. You're going to grapple. Von Slutling's not exactly going to flash her exposed back like your Draug did."

"Why not use your stars?" Emma asked.

"Who says I don't have them? A little duct tape, a couple makeshift pockets, and voilà." I hiked up my wide-legged sparring pants and waggled my ankle. "I stowed them on the side of my boots."

"Neat." A smile flickered on Emma's face and was gone. "But isn't that against the rules?"

"The rule is *'Acari may carry one weapon into the ring.'* Get it? *Carry.* Like, in your hand." I smiled innocently. "I'm just following the letter of the law. That's what they taught us to do, right?"

It was evening by the time our fight rolled around, the sky

an eerie half-light, like the sun was shining in from another room. Master Alcántara stood between Lilac and me on the platform. His mischievous smile told me he was enjoying every minute of the spectacle.

Alcántara said something to her—I'd have done anything to hear—and then he came to me.

"Cuídate, cariño." His whisper was mellow and sultry with promises. Goose bumps shimmered over my skin, and I had to blink hard to clear my head. He chuckled, low and throaty. "That's it. Keep your head. Sharp wits are deadlier than any blade."

The palm of the hand that held the knife began to sweat. Was this all some sort of cruel lesson that combat came down to wits?

I panicked. I'd picked the wrong weapon. A switchblade would be worthless. Especially against that long bamboo sword.

Watcher Priti sounded the first gong.

CHAPTER THIRTY-SIX

L ilac and I bounced on the balls of our feet. I was going to let her make the first move so I could get a sense of her strategy. I needed to understand as much as I could about her mind-set beyond the fact that I resembled some kid from her past whom she'd apparently hated, then murdered.

Lilac ran toward me, swinging that sword, long as a pole. The crowd was silent, and the scuff of her feet on stone echoed around her. Her attack was abrupt, erratic.

"Easy, Cowgirl." I skittered out of her way, careful not to topple off the stone in the first five seconds of the fight. I'd already seen three girls fall to the ground and knock themselves out. There was no way I was ready to get whisked away by a Tracer.

I concentrated on the hard rock under the soles of my boots. *I am roots in the earth. I am water that flows.* I whispered a new mantra, for good measure. "I am stone."

"Down," she yelled, leaping for me.

I bounded forward and met her halfway. Our bodies slammed into each other, and she grabbed me close.

She whipped the backs of my legs with her shinai. The sharp sting of it stole my breath. She lashed me again, snarling, "You're going down."

I couldn't let her get momentum. Ignoring the sizzling on the backs of my thighs, I hugged her closer. Clutching tightly to her, I slashed my switchblade in a wild arc. "Taking you with me."

It caught her leg, grazing her. She didn't flinch. I swung again, slamming my arm into hers.

Her sword slipped from her hand, and she screamed, "Bitch!"

"Language, *Slutling*." I kicked her weapon, sending it spinning off the stone.

She reached around and grabbed my braid, tugging hard, trying to wrench me down. "You're a freak."

I stumbled, catching myself before I fell. Jangly pain shot from an old neck injury. I cried out.

"Oh, did that hurt?" she purred.

Wriggling in her grip, I whispered for her ears alone, "They say you don't feel pain. Maybe you'll"—I flexed my muscles, curling into her, slashing my knife at her face—"feel this."

She blocked with her forearms, grunting with the impact. A half turn, and she grabbed me in a neat hold. Then Lilac bit my arm, hard.

Even through the fabric of my shirt, the pain was startling, unnatural. The knife sprang from my hand. I didn't see where it landed, but heard it clattering off the rock.

I wrenched my arm free, the blood pounding where she'd sunk her teeth into me. "I hope you've had your shots." I shook it out, and then, thinking fast, kneed her. It wasn't a solid hit, so I grabbed the shoulder of her shirt and pulled her down to knee her again. She made an *oof* sound.

Rubbing my arm, I backed up to regroup. "What's your problem?"

Yasuo had been right. But for some spatters of blood by Lilac's feet, my blade had been almost worthless. The throwing stars seemed a ridiculous option now, too. Though that also meant Lilac wouldn't have time to pull any lighters from up her sleeves, and that was reassuring.

"*You're* my problem." She squatted, circling me.

I needed to buy time to catch my breath, but instead spread my hands and feet, ready for her. "*You're* the freak."

"I'm done with you." She leapt for me, and once more our bodies slammed together in the middle of the stone.

Talking stopped as we grappled, landing a few hits and then separating again. We did this a few times, elbowing, kicking. Using feet and nails. I tasted blood in my mouth and felt a sharp stab with each inhale. But we kept at it, that sloppy thrashing, relentless pounding.

The sky was darkening to gunmetal, and somebody began to light torches. Fire flickered to life all around, casting sinister shadows on the stones, on our faces and bodies.

The crowd remained silent. The only sounds were our grunting and the hiss and pop of flame.

I didn't know how much time had passed, but the combat was becoming too grueling. I felt myself beginning to flag and knew I needed to end it.

Time for Yasuo's ground and pound.

"Now," I snarled, hooking my ankle around Lilac's. I swept

her feet from under her. We toppled back. Her head hit the stone with a hollow smack. "I'm ending this *now*."

Her eyes glazed for a moment, but then she snapped back to life. She bucked and shoved. "Get off me."

She writhed onto her belly and almost crawled free, but I caught her between my knees, pinning her arms at her sides. I shoved her face onto the rock. *"No."*

"Off!" She bucked wildly, screaming. "Don't touch me!"

Scooting higher, I shoved her hair aside for a better grip. At the feel of that silky maple braid, I thought again. I snatched it up and wound it around my fist, wrenching her head up and back. "I *hate* your fucking hair."

I slammed her head against the stone. Pulled her head up again; slammed it again. I heard the crunch of her nose. She moaned, blood spilling down her face. It was a dark smear on the gray stone.

"I smell your blood, Lilac." And I *did*. It invigorated me. I thought of the vampire's drink. That thick, ropy liquid had made me powerful, made my every sense razor sharp. "I'm stronger than you."

Letting go of her hair, I inched down, wrenching her hands behind her back. She'd always mocked how smart I was. But I'd show her. Smart girls won. "You made fun, *stupid* girl." I jabbed the sharp edge of my knuckles over and over into her kidneys. "When you . . . should've . . . been studying . . . your . . . anatomy."

She was moaning now, breathing shallowly, facedown on the stone.

I staggered to standing. Leaning down, I grabbed her feet and dragged her to the edge of the platform. I kicked her, but she only teetered there. Shoving with the ball of my foot, I began to nudge her off.

Flush with triumph, I glanced at the crowd. I wanted a glimpse of Yasuo and Emma. I also wanted to find Ronan—I wished I could know the look on his face.

The audience drew in a collective breath, and I looked down. Lilac stared up at me, those pretty hazel eyes drained of humanity, her stare as cold and flat as a killer's. Blood streaked her face, her mouth and chin covered with it. When she spoke, her voice was hoarse, and bloody spittle flew from her mouth. "You always think you're so fucking smart."

Too late, I felt her fingers dig into my ankle. They were slender and long, clawing around my boot.

Lilac toppled from the stone. And she pulled me with her.

It was a long drop to the ground. Dense brush grew around the back edge of the stone platform and it broke our fall.

She landed on her back, and I sprawled on my hands and knees over her.

"Shhhhit." My left knee exploded in pain, and for a moment, white lights danced in my vision. I breathed hard through my mouth, trying to scramble from her.

She snatched at my legs, grabbing me around the waist, trying to wrestle me back to the ground. "You're dead."

I felt the crowd shift. Felt silent eyes watching us from alongside the ancient monoliths.

Shoving her against the platform, I clutched her close in an obscene embrace, trying to land awkward punches on her ear. "Not dead yet."

"I'll kill you. With everyone watching." She rolled me over in the brush, slamming me against the bottom edge of the stone.

VERONICA WOLFF

There was a deafening crack. I thought it was thunder peal-
ing overhead. Or gunfire.

"What the—?" I looked to the sky.

She head-butted me in the jaw. My chin snapped shut, and
I felt a shard of tooth scrape down my throat.

"I don't know what your damage is . . ." I freed my arm,
and, hugging her close, rolled her over me. "But I am so sick of
your shit." Bracing myself, I thrust my shoulder into her chest,
ramming her against the base of the platform.

Air chirped from her. She caught her breath. Clawed at my
hair and ear. "You're the—"

Another thunderous crack, and the ground beneath us shuddered. We sank deeper into the brush, tangled tight with each
other. There was a distant pinging sound, like gravel falling down
a well.

"Stop," she shrieked.

I clutched her neck close to mine, thrusting my knee over
and over into her belly.

She scratched at my face, digging her fingers into my cheeks,
trying to pull me away. "Don't touch—"

The ground jolted. Lilac and I froze, entwined.

There was an earsplitting crack. A massive crevice split the
ground along the base of the platform. A great, black chasm
spewing the stench of stagnant water and stale air.

The sound of skittering gravel, far away. Closer, the heavy
scrape of rocks sliding. And then the earth fell away.

Lilac and I tumbled into blackness. Tumbled down to hell.

CHAPTER THIRTY-SEVEN

W e landed with a splash. *Water.* It was deep, and I clawed my way to the surface, heart exploding in my chest.

Instinctively, I began to tread in a panicked, spastic dog paddle. "Oh, shit. Oh, shit."

I swam awkwardly to the side and pulled myself out, scrambling away from the edge as fast as I could. I braced myself on all fours, panting to catch my breath. I shook with shock and adrenaline.

Closing my mouth, I made myself breathe through my nose. I needed to be steady, keep my head. Get my bearings.

We were in almost total darkness. It sounded like Lilac was crawling from the water about twenty feet away. I couldn't see her. I blinked hard a few times. We'd landed in a vast, underground cavern. I thought I imagined red eyes watching me from the shadows.

Calm down. I forced myself to breathe evenly—in through my nose, out through my mouth—and tried to slow my pounding heart.

The air was close, the smell of it stale and dank. Other than the dripping water and the sound of our heavy breathing, there was silence.

My clothes clung to me, but I realized they weren't cold. Either the water was warm or I was too freaked out to notice the temperature. I looked back at it. Smoke rose from the black surface.

It wasn't seawater. It smelled sulfurous, its taste alkaline as it dripped down my face. *An underground hot spring.*

I looked at the slash of dim light overhead. The sun was setting, and yet its faint glow seemed bright in contrast to this tomb.

Glimmering eyes appeared, peering down from above. I startled.

Lilac cackled. "Fight's not over, bitch."

I leapt to my feet. "Then come and get it, Slutling."

I could see her now, emerging from the blackness, striding toward me. "Oh, I'll get some. It's just too bad I can't burn *you* like I did Sunny."

"Dream on." My legs felt like rubber beneath me, and I locked my knees to stay upright. I'd lost my knife, but I still had the shuriken in my boots. Whatever good *they'd* do. I held my arms in an attack stance. "Let's get this over with. I'm hungry for dinner."

The sound of flames whipped around us. We both froze. Vampires were leaping into the cavern, torches in hand.

"Proceed," a male voice said. It had the hint of a French

accent. I glimpsed Headmaster Fournier, his elegant features distorted in the brightness of his torch. He carried our original weapons.

I could see much more clearly now that there was torchlight. A network of tunnels extended all around us, reaching into blackness.

Metal rings were attached to the walls, and the vampires nestled a torch in each one. I shivered to think what this place might've been used for in the past.

Fournier put Lilac's shinai down by the water's edge. Next to it, my switchblade. Orange light glimmered along the blade, and I wondered if an attempt to retrieve it was worth the risk.

I wasted too much time thinking. Lilac acted first, diving past me, grabbing her long bamboo sword.

I snapped to attention and went for her as she was rolling to her feet. My plan was to tackle her as I had Mia. Her weapon would do no good at close range.

She turned and ran from me. I knew a moment of triumph. Then a moment of confusion, when she raced to the torches. And finally shock, when she held her bamboo sword in the flames.

The shinai blazed to life. I gasped, hopping back. "What the—?"

She cackled. "Looks like I'll get to burn you after all."

The fire *roared*. It was the sound of hunger, of fury, and it pervaded the cavern, echoing along the close walls. It consumed the air around us. The chemical stench and soaring height of the flames told me she'd soaked her weapon in lighter fluid.

"You're insane." I stepped back to let the initial hit of fluid burn off. I bent my arm, tucking my nose into my elbow.

"No, I'm *smart*." Lilac walked toward me, a look of angelic calm on her face. "Everyone's always going on about what a genius you are. But all your books won't mean jack when you're dead."

How true that'd been for Sunny. The thought was chilling. I backed away from her, my mind racing for a plan. "Easy, now. Wouldn't want to burn yourself."

I backed up some more, but she kept coming. I bumped into the cave wall. It was cool and damp. "Self-immolation is really a very messy way to go."

Lilac loomed in front of me. Using both hands, she held her sword aloft. "Let's see how brightly you glow in firelight."

Edging along the wall, I hopped away from her. "I think you hit your head too hard."

"I didn't get to watch Sunny burn." Flame sputtered as she gave a few experimental swings. She laughed. "But I *heard* her."

"Do you want me to yield?" I asked, even though I had no intention of giving up. I sidestepped some more, until I butted into a corner.

From my peripheral vision, I saw people streaming from the depths of the cavern, spilling from its tunnels, torches in hand. I wondered if Emma and Yas were there. Or Ronan. Would they watch me burn to death? I'd stagger around, bathed in flames, like something from a movie. My throat clenched.

Think, think. But I saw no way out. I stalled. "I give up. You won the I'm Insane contest—okay, Lilac?"

"It's too late." Lilac smiled. She swung her sword.

I ducked. She'd aimed too high, and I felt the blazing *whoosh* of her shinai as it whirred overhead.

"I hate you," she snarled. Fresh rage distorted her face. "I hate your hair. I hate your clothes. I hate your stupid face."

"My stupid face, huh?" My heart galloped in my chest. There were only so many times I could duck. I tried to summon the feel of the blood, but my mind was racing too fast. "Now, there's a new one."

Think.

But I didn't have time to.

She trapped me, grabbing me with her left hand, holding her weapon in her right. She reached back with her flaming sword and I ducked, anticipating a strike.

It was the wrong move.

She let go with her left hand, swinging in an uppercut, punching me on the chin as I squatted. My teeth clacked together, and the impact rang through my brain.

I didn't have a second to gather myself.

Lilac grabbed a fistful of my shirt and slammed me back against the cave wall. "I smelled my skin burn once. And now I'll smell yours."

It took only a second to realize she'd pinned me against her fiery sword.

I didn't catch fire. Not at first.

CHAPTER THIRTY-EIGHT

I shrieked. Hysterical thoughts cascaded through my mind, rapid-fire wishes for some fantastical miracle to occur. *Maybe my wet hair won't catch. Maybe my uniform is fireproof.*

I writhed, but Lilac was bigger than me. She'd used an elbow to restrain my arm, but I still had one hand free. I wriggled, clawing at her face. "Get off!"

She bore down on me, using all her weight to hold me against the damp stone. "I always wondered what Sunny looked like when she burned. How soon did she fall? Were her eyes open or shut?"

I felt heat growing at my back. It rocketed straight from a simmering warmth to excruciating intensity.

Think, Drew, think. I grasped at Priti's mantra. *I am Watcher. I am Watcher.* But the words were meaningless. I was too frantic, too panicked.

My hair had been soaked through, but it began to smolder and hiss. Steam rose in a cloud from my wet uniform. The steam became smoke. I got a whiff of it. It singed my lungs, and I turned my head from it, coughing.

Smoke curled up from Lilac's uniform sleeve. The smell of burned flesh mingled with the acrid smoke. She was catching fire. But she didn't feel it.

She really didn't feel pain. "Oh, God." My voice was hoarse. Speaking wracked me with coughs.

"I get to watch this time." Lilac laughed, but then she coughed, too.

The smoke hung thickly around my neck. It grew denser as my fat braid began to dry, began to burn. It stank.

Tears stung my eyes. From the smoke. From the stench of my burning hair.

Think, think, think. I refused to die here. I didn't survive my childhood, survive the island, for it to end like *this*.

I coughed again, and she was coughing, too. The cave felt airless. The smells noxious.

Then it hit me. I stood still, frozen in her grasp.

I knew why the steam reeked. It wasn't fresh water that'd soaked my hair. It was water from a hot spring. Springs contained sulfur. This one was rich with it. The walls dripped with it. I could still taste it on my lips.

Burning sulfur created sulfur dioxide. Sulfur dioxide was a toxic gas.

Craning my head away from the thickest smoke, I sucked in a last breath. My chest spasmed, protesting the poisonous air in my lungs. But still, I held my breath.

And then I held *her*.

I slid my legs behind Lilac. Snaking my free arm around her neck, I hugged her head to me, trapping her face at my shoulder.

She began to cough and didn't stop.

My lungs felt like they were going to explode, but still I didn't breathe.

Her body seized, hacking and hacking. She lost control.

I shoved her away, and her body thrashed backward. She fell to her knees.

I thought I might cough up a lung, but my body felt on fire. Hunched over, I ran to the water and dove in. I heard a split-second sizzle and it sickened me. The pool was black and impossibly deep. I kicked to the surface, fighting my instinctive alarm.

Pushing away panic, I focused on the warmth of the water. It soothed my charred back. I was burned badly, but the thick fabric of my uniform had offered some initial protection.

I swam to the edge. My stroke was more confident now. Pain sheared through me with every reach of my arms.

I am water that flows. I am Watcher.

Calm clarity settled over me. This was all a mind game. Strength, power, memory, fear—all can be controlled with the mind.

I pulled myself out. The smoke was clearing and I coughed shallowly, tucking my nose against my arm. "Time to finish this."

When I shook off the water, I realized that my braid had burned off. My hair hung unevenly at my shoulders, and my head was lighter. Large holes had burned through my top, and the cool cave air kissed my scorched back.

Lilac rose, wobbling on her feet. Her torch had gone out. The rage in her eyes told me she wasn't done yet. She ran for my switchblade and plucked it from the ground.

Hands out, I assumed a defensive posture. "You're like the creature in the horror movie who won't die."

"You're the one to die." Despite the chest-wracking cough

that shook her, Lilac braced in a wide stance. Arms outspread, she held the knife in a loose attack position.

"You know, as much as I'm enjoying our little chat, it's clear I'm not getting through to you." I squatted, pulling the four shuriken from my boots.

Imagining steadiness, I centered myself. Cool composure. *I am roots in the earth. I am grounded.*

I threw.

I'd aimed for an artery, but my star hit her shoulder. She glanced down, brushing it away like it was nothing. She strolled toward me, coughing only occasionally now. "They made me leave home, but I've got a new place now, and I'm not going anywhere."

I rejected the unsettling notion that Lilac might've wanted to find a new family as much as I did.

Edging away, I threw again, hitting her thigh. She didn't notice. Just kept coming at me.

"This *no-pain* thing is really quite disturbing." I threw again and it missed her neck, pinging off the cave wall. I had one star left.

Her face twitched. "You're so cute with your little stars. But I told you they'd do no good. You're no good."

I backed away, but she tracked me, slowly circling through the cavern. She was bizarrely calm, her arms down at her sides, my switchblade gripped in her hand.

I threw my last star and it hit her knife arm. She didn't seem to notice—it just stuck there, and she hadn't even flinched.

Swiping a hand across my eyes, I glanced around for another weapon, though I knew I'd find none.

"Having trouble seeing?" Lilac stalked toward me. As her

arms swung, the blood gushed from her wound, pooling in the cracks of her fingers. "Because I'm not. I'm used to the dark. My parents would shut me in the closet, you know. Because of Sunny's lies. I had to use Daddy's lighter to see. I heard her with them. I'd sit in the dark, listening to her lies, flicking that lighter until my thumb was numb. Until it burned."

My second star was still lodged in her thigh, and firelight twinkled off the steel. Her pants stuck to her leg, soaked with blood. But she just kept coming at me.

I wasn't done yet—I just needed to find a way.

My back hit the wall. I was cornered. Lilac was armed and she was stronger.

But this was a mind game, and I was smarter. She'd obviously had some serious issues with this foster sister of hers, and I'd mine that for all it was worth. "Daddy and Mummy never loved you, anyway."

She froze.

Bingo. I kept at it. "That's why your *mom* took her in. She was looking for a girl to replace you. Looking for a new daughter—*on the streets*. Because you weren't good enough."

Her lips peeled into a snarl. She lunged, but the switchblade slipped from her blood-slicked hand. Perplexed, she looked at her open palm. She finally saw the stars and plucked them free. She looked up. Torchlight danced on her face. She looked woozy, drunk.

Lilac was bleeding out.

She staggered. Stumbled toward me. Her feet thudded awkwardly, like she couldn't get her balance. "Can't be better than me," she said, her tongue slurred and thick, "when she's dead."

"But now here I am. Another girl from the gutter. *Better than you.*"

She was just a few paces from me when she fell, crumpling into a heap.

There was a moment of silence, and then I heard the distant gong. Watcher Priti's voice echoed through the cave. "Acari Drew is the winner."

I dropped to my knees. People surrounded me.

Yasuo and Emma appeared at the forefront. They each had peculiar expressions on their faces—relief, concern, and something else, too. Uneasiness, maybe, at the sight of watching their best friend go to some seriously messed-up depths to brutally murder a classmate.

Emma said something, but the audience was chattering loudly and her words sounded jumbled and a little distorted, like I'd suffered a bad clout on my ear. I probably had.

I looked away, realizing Lilac's body was already gone.

I trembled badly now, the adrenaline that'd flooded my veins leaving me shaking. Every injury, every bruise and break flared to life. My back was throbbing, pulsing agony.

I huddled on the ground, trying to figure out how I felt about things. I wasn't as elated as I thought I should've been, and imagined I was probably in shock.

I hunted for Ronan, but he was nowhere in sight. It made me feel a little bit alone.

But then I felt arms wrap around me. They were cool and comforting on my battered body. I glanced up, my neck stiff. It was Master Alcántara.

Up close, he was magnificent. Strong and steady, pure power emanating from him. Though his body was hard, it felt of flesh, not wood. He took my breath away.

I inhaled deeply. Distantly, I searched for some identifying scent. Maybe it was that I'd just thought of Ronan, whose fresh, seashore smell always struck me so viscerally. But Alcántara smelled like nothing—flat and dry, like a page from one of their library books.

He smoothed the wet hair from my brow, looking pleased and oddly self-satisfied. "My compliments, Acari Drew. That was a most thrilling exhibition."

And that's when it really struck me. I'd won. I'd go off-island. I'd go on a mission with him. We'd be alone. I'd have my chance at escape. "Thank you," I managed.

"Yes, congratulations, Acari Drew." It was Ronan, staring down at me, his face a studied blank. "I knew you could do it."

He nodded, and I watched as he turned and walked away. Sadness seized me by the throat. *The only paradise is paradise lost.*

Why did it seem like those would be his last words to me? It was impossible to swallow around the ache. I tried to breathe, but the pain was sharp.

I would go on a mission with Alcántara and I'd escape. Which meant I wouldn't see Ronan again. I knew this. I'd wanted this. So why did my heart feel like a sliver of glass lodged in my chest?

I looked back at the vampire holding me.

"*Cariño,*" he whispered. "I, too, knew you could do it."

His face broke into a smile. And not just any smile, but a smile worthy of sonnets. His mouth was just a little bit crooked, his expression wickedness and humor and hunger, all alight in eyes that were black like coals burning with an inner heat.

It was a smile just for me. I knew I'd never be the same.

"And now answer me, *querida*. Are you ready?" He stroked a slow finger down my cheek. "For it has begun."

Read on for an excerpt from the next
novel in the Watchers series by Veronica Wolff,

VAMPIRE'S KISS

Coming soon from
NEW AMERICAN LIBRARY

A s my friend Yasuo the vampire Trainee would say, *Headlines*. As
in, here they are:

1. Girl Genius Flees Crappy Home Life, Discovers Vampires over the Rainbow
2. Army of Females Vow to ~~Beat~~ Mold Girl into Vampire
   Operative
3. Girl Finds Success and Friendship and *blah blah blah*
4. Girl Pledges to Escape at All Costs
5. Girl ~~Accidentally~~ Kills Classmates to Survive
6. Girl Wins Massive Competition, Will Participate in
   Mission Off-Island (repeat #4)

I sat with Emma on the sand, contemplating my situation, but my
uncharacteristically optimistic outlook was squashed as I realized my
butt was getting wet. I shifted, peeling the cotton shorts away from
my skin. "Dammit. Are you *sure* he said the beach?"

304 EXCERPT FROM VAMPIRE'S KISS

Today's gym class was to be held outside, and my friend and I had shown up early—partly because we took every chance we could to hang out, and partly because the new gym teacher totally freaked us out. Ronan had been our instructor last term, but he'd gone away to God knew where, so some guy named Otto was his replacement for the summer semester. He was a Tracer like Ronan, meaning one of the guys responsible for tracking and bringing girls like us to this sorry island—only this particular guy didn't strike us as someone to mess around with.

"He said the beach." Emma gave me one of her signature flat stares, and I rolled my eyes. I knew the saying went "still waters run deep," but did she have to be so damned still *all* the time? Sometimes a little expression was called for.

Sadly, I often had expression enough for both of us. Like, just the thought of which bizarre oceanfront punishments might await us that morning was causing me to get surlier by the minute. Not to mention I was hyperaware of the damp sand now—it stank like dead sea creatures and was lumpy with pebbles and jagged bits of shells that were digging into my skin.

"I hate beach days," I grumbled, not ashamed that I probably sounded like a four-year-old. But Tracer Otto had a thing for doing sit-ups while being thrashed by the freezing surf, and I wasn't the biggest fan of swimming. I'd recently learned how, but I doubted I'd ever get used to the sensation of water whooshing into my nose and ears.

I thought of our new teacher's sharp, austere features and well-combed blond hair. "Or maybe it's just that I hate *Otto*. Him and that German accent. It's like he's auditioning for the role of Evil Nazi Number One in a remake of *The Sound of Music*."

Emma looked nervously over her shoulder. "You should hush."

"Yeah, yeah, Farm Girl. I'm hushing." I straightened my legs in the sand—even with the vampire blood to speed my healing, they were looking ugly, my knees mottled yellow and pale green with fading bruises. I scraped a shell from where it'd stuck to my calf and began snapping it into tiny shards.

Other girls began to drift in, wandering along the sand, waiting for class to start. Our numbers were fewer now—fighting your peers to the death had a way of trimming the student body—and I noted some were doing their best to conceal limps and other injuries, some fresh, some still lingering from the recent Directorate challenge. It may have been summer term, but the vampires weren't about to let up on our physical trials to give us a chance to heal. Only the strongest and the fiercest survived.

Emma sidled closer in the sand, reading my thoughts. She pitched her voice low, knowing as well as I that none of the other girls could be trusted. "Not many of us left."

"And we'll lose more this summer." My words were a harsh whisper, but they were true. Our numbers would dwindle each semester, until only a handful of our original group remained. I thought of the girls who'd died already and tried not to consider what it might mean that I'd forgotten so many of their names.

"I imagine more will arrive in the fall."

I gave Emma a sour look. "More of *these* people?"

"Well, now that Lilac's gone, they'll need to give you a new roommate."

I shuddered. "Is that your way of putting a bright spin on things?"

It chilled me, but Emma was right, and I studied the other Acari, which was the creepy name they had for us girls. It was clear the vampires had a penchant for good-looking teenagers—everyone here was pretty in some way, if not outright gorgeous. It was annoying and sexist and gross, though thinking about it, if you were training an army of Watchers—which, as far as I could guess, meant female agents/assassins/guardians—they might as well be easy on the eyes.

Other than that, we were a mixed bunch. Farm Girl Emma, accustomed to hard work and solitude, was fairly unique on the island. Lilac had also been a rare breed—of the rich-bitches-gone-bad variety. We all had our individual talents, too. Mine was being a girl genius who knew how to take a punch (thank you, drunken, no-good dad). And Lilac had been a pyro—witness, for example, my shaggy, burned-off hair.

But there was one distinctive characteristic each of us shared: We were all outcasts. Gang girls, runaways, you name it—we'd all fled our homes, and not one of us was missed.

Emma eyed the other Acari along with me. "I noticed some of the Tracers are gone. They must be out gathering new girls."

Her comment got me thinking. Was *that* where Ronan went? He was rounding up new candidates for the next incoming class?

Like all good Tracers, his job was to identify, track, and retrieve fresh batches of Acari, doing whatever it took to convince girls that leaving life as they knew it for some distant rock in the middle of the North Sea—where they were either good enough to become Watchers for a bunch of vampires or they *died*—was a good idea. I didn't know how other Tracers did it, but Ronan had special powers of persuasion at his disposal.

Emma guessed where my mind was. "*That's* probably why you haven't seen Ronan," she said in a gentle, understanding tone that annoyed me.

"I wasn't thinking of Ronan." I frowned, because I was *totally* thinking of Ronan. He was one of the few people on this island—hell, he was one of the few people in my *life*—who'd ever shown concern for me. He'd managed to weasel his way into my consciousness—the dream of having a guy to look out for me like a thorn in my heart that wouldn't leave me be.

And, of course, I was remembering how he'd duped me, too. When he'd approached me in a Florida parking lot, I'd thought he was just a hot college guy giving me some deeply soulful looks, but it turned out he'd been trying to hypnotize me. *Hypnotize*, for God's sake.

But my mind wasn't that easily swayed—being a kid genius had to be good for something, I guess—and he'd had to use both eyes and touch to persuade me to follow him onto the plane bound for *this* rock. *Eyja næturinnar*, they called it. The Isle of Night. Which at the moment was a laugh, because summertime, or the dimming, as the vampires so annoyingly referred to it, meant zero hours of dark per day. Just unending gray, gray, gray sky pressing down on us.

Once, I'd been afraid of the dark, but Ronan had warned me I'd miss the black of night. He'd *known*. As he seemed to know and understand so many other things about me. Really, if I'd thought about it, I could've said he was one of my first friends.

So I tried not to think about it.

Instead, I stared out across the roiling gray sea, pretending I didn't have any use for hot guys and soulful looks. And who was I kidding? I missed Ronan. Like, really missed him. Not just as a teacher, though

I'd have traded just about any other Tracer for Otto. But something was, I don't know, missing without him around.

Like Ronan's steady green eyes, always so focused on me.

"Okay, so you're *not* thinking about Ronan," Emma said, and I heard the skepticism in her voice. She shifted, considering. Long speeches weren't her way, and she spoke slowly, choosing her words with care. "It just seems like you've been . . . distracted since the Directorate challenge. I used to see you and Ronan talking a lot. But then there was the competition, and you won, and then I didn't see you two together anymore, and I thought maybe—"

Emotion stabbed me, so sharp and sudden that I had to scrunch my face against it.

She thought maybe I might miss him? She thought I'd taken him for granted? She'd be right on both counts.

I cut her off, saying, "I just have some questions for him is all."

Like, a *bunch* of questions. Questions I'd never ask, of course. After I'd won the competition, beating Lilac and winning a trip off-island and a shot at escape, I'd caught him watching me, and something about the look in his eyes—regret? grief? longing?—haunted me.

What had the look meant? Did he know I planned to escape?

"Do you think he's jealous of Alcántara?" Emma's voice was barely a whisper, which was the wisest course when discussing a vampire. Particularly Hugo de Rosas Alcántara, of the fourteenth-century Spanish royal court.

"Jealous?" It would imply there was something between me and Alcántara. Though I *did* suspect he'd had something to do with my winning. And then there was the way the vampire had scooped up my broken body to hold me close after my victory. But if Ronan was jealous, it'd mean he was interested in me. My belly churned. "No way. Ronan's not jealous."

He'd probably just been disturbed by the glimpse of my dark side, perceiving the secret, savage pleasure I'd taken in beating my rival. Because even I had trouble considering *that*. "Maybe the whole fight-to-the-death thing weirded him out more than he let on."

Emma solemnly shook her head. "He's more used to that than we are. You two are friends. He wanted you to win."

"Friends?" I inhaled sharply. *Friends* was a dangerous word.

Alcántara had warned me about *friends*. And besides, it wasn't very friendly how Ronan had gotten me here in the first place.

I scraped my sandy fingers through my hair, cursing the jumble of thoughts in my head. I finger-combed some more, this time cursing my hair—*such* a hassle since Lilac burned off my braid, leaving me with a shaggy, shoulder-length do. "Stupid hair."

What I really wanted to say was, *Stupid Ronan.*

Although he and I had forged a sort of alliance, the memory of his initial betrayal made me surly. When we first met, he'd touched me, and I still felt his fingers hot on my skin. And yet the reason he'd touched me wasn't because he'd wanted to—not because he was a guy and I was a girl—but because it'd been his *job* to touch me. It'd been his job to make me so warm and gullible and *dopey* that I'd find myself on an airplane bound for nowhere.

I thought of the new girls Ronan was out there gathering. And *touching.* Every one of them a total teen hottie, no doubt.

"Great," I snapped. "Either way, he's out there, finding new *friends* for us to spar with, snipe at, stab in the back, and eventually kill."

Emma stared at me. If it weren't for her blinking, I swear she could've been mistaken for a sphinx. Sometimes it really annoyed me, and this was one of those times.

"What?" I demanded.

"I still think it has to do with Master Alcántara."

This time I was the one glancing around nervously. "Would you *please* stop saying his name? I'm scared you might summon him or something, like Voldemort."

But I worried she was right. It did seem that Alcántara had taken a liking to me. Whenever I caught him looking at me—and I seemed to catch him a lot—it was like he was plumbing the depths of my soul, puzzling through some sort of master plan written there.

It was hard not to feel disturbed by the whole thing, and not in an entirely unpleasant way. I mean, Alcántara was young and he was hot . . . or at least he had been several hundred years ago. But he was a bit like a panther—darkly seductive, yet a predator nonetheless. To be feared and—according to Ronan, at least—avoided.

"Yes," Emma agreed. "Best not to call attention to yourself."

"Thanks, Sherlock. I'll take that under advisement. Though I don't know how I'll avoid him when the time comes for our mission."

"Do you know—"

"Nope. I don't know where we're going, I don't know what we'll be doing, and I don't know why we'll be doing it. All I know is that I have to wait till the end of summer term to do it. Alcántara insists I need more training."

What I didn't tell Emma was that, if all went according to plan, I wouldn't get too much of a chance to consider our mission anyway, since I'd be too busy *getting the hell off this rock.*

That's right: escape. It was all I thought about now. I'd begun considering it pretty much the moment I arrived, but then got lulled into a sense of security, of family. I had smart teachers, was learning cool things, and making a couple of the closest friends I'd ever had in my life. I'd begun to believe that being a part of something—being a Watcher—might give me a sense of belonging, like finding the family that I'd never had.

Until the challenge, when I'd seen what the Isle of Night was really about, which was to kill or be killed. I'd triumphed, and sure, partly it was because I was smart, but I wasn't as strong as some of the other girls, and I suspected it was only Alcántara's help that'd pushed me over the top. I'd triumphed over Lilac, and she'd disappeared, and now I'd started to worry that maybe I should cut my losses and find a way out of here before the vampires changed their minds and decided *I* should be dead, too.

I tried to think proactively about it all, but my mind kept wondering what might've happened to Lilac's body after I beat her and how mine might suffer the same fate if any escape attempt was to fail.

There was movement around us, and we followed everyone's eyes up the beach. Tracer Otto was approaching, carrying burlap bags.

My shoulders sagged. "*Crap.* Adolph brought the sandbags." Sandbags were part of a pleasant little pastime in which we scooped handfuls of sand into bags and proceeded to run around like a bunch of morons, carrying them over our heads. "Arduous *and* pointless."

A half smile quirked Emma's lips—the equivalent of a belly laugh from my redheaded friend. But then Otto turned our way, and she bristled. "*Shh.* Here he comes."

I tucked my head toward hers, quietly singing, *"The hills are aliiiiive . . ."*

She shot me a panicked glare. "You hush!"

I smiled placidly as the other Acari joined us to sit in a row on the sand. I leaned over again, lowering my voice to the barest whisper. *". . . viss ze sound of muuuuziiic. . . ."*

Tracer Otto stormed up the beach and proceeded to pace up and down the line, dropping the empty bags at our feet, instructing us in his best drill sergeant impression. "You will fill the bags," he said, with a decidedly German accent—all he was missing was a little whistle around his neck—"without delay."

He reached the end of the line, and as he turned, I couldn't resist murmuring, *"Vizout delayyy."*

"Acari Drew." A mellow voice spoke from behind me.

Oh, God. Too late, I noticed the shadow that had fallen on me. My skin rippled with goose bumps, as if it were a chill breeze at my back instead of a vampire.

I looked over my shoulder and had to force myself not to startle when I saw how close Alcántara had managed to come behind me. *Stupid.* Things like that could get a girl killed in my world.

He stood there, tall but not towering, with bottomless dark eyes and smooth black hair that brushed the collar of his black leather jacket. He looked like a beautiful indie rocker . . . carved out of marble.

I hopped to my feet as reverently as one could when one was wearing damp, sand-encrusted gym shorts. It struck me that all the other Acari had grown quiet around me, and even Tracer Otto was standing in respectful silence. They knew as well as I did how the sudden appearance of a vampire could mean somebody's imminent evisceration. I hoped only that it wouldn't be mine.

I cleared my throat, speaking slowly enough to ensure avoiding any tongue twisting. "Master Alcántara."

One side of his mouth crooked up in a wicked half smile, and I didn't understand how it was possible to feel cold on my skin but so hot in my belly all at the same time. "Acari Drew," he repeated, stretching my name out on his tongue. "You have no taste for sand-bags?"

Crap, crap, crap. I racked my brain. What, exactly, might the correct answer be? *No, sir,* and I'm a troublemaker; *Yes, sir,* and I'm an intellectual dullard.

"So silent all of a sudden?" Though Alcántara addressed his next words to Otto, he held my gaze, speaking slowly as though imparting his message with significance. "Tracer Otto, it appears young Miss Drew doesn't relish the gritty futility of your selected workout." His smile grew broader. "I think perhaps Acari Drew craves more of an intellectual challenge."

Alarms shrilled in my head. Had he read my thoughts? Or was it just a weird coincidence that he'd spoken my mind?

"I . . . Yes," I stammered, second-guessing myself. *What's the right answer?* "And no. The challenges I crave are of both the mental *and* physical variety."

Alcántara barked out a satisfied laugh, and I felt a hot blush creep from my chest to my hairline. How was it his laughter made my words echo in such a naughtily suggestive way?

Eager to change the subject, I glanced to the limp sandbag at my feet. "Is it time for the . . . for *these*?" At that moment, I'd have definitely traded running up and down the beach with a sandbag over my head for being the object of Alcántara's uncomfortable stare.

"Yes—"

"No," Alcántara said, speaking over a visibly shaken Tracer Otto. "I am finding this exercise too . . . *vulgar* for Acari Drew." The vampire's voice was as smooth as brandy, with a faint sultry Spanish accent, his murmured *vulgar* managing to make sandbags sound like the crassest trailer-trash endeavor ever conceived by man.

I snuck Alcántara a tentative look, uncertain whether to feel thankful or terrified at just what other endeavor might be headed my way. The glint in those black eyes decided it, telling me the appropriate emotion was definitely *terror*.

"There is a different assignment in store for Acari Drew. Today Acari Drew begins an . . . *independent* study."

Like her heroine, **Veronica Wolff** braved an all-girls school, traveled to faraway places, and studied lots of languages. She was not, however, ever trained as an assassin (or so she claims). In real life, she's most often found on a beach or in the mountains of northern California, but you can always find her online at veronicawolff.com.